CHILDREN OF SOLITUDE

MICHAEL G. WILLIAMS

DEDICATION

For my husband Michael,

and for anyone who has been surrounded by family and felt alone.

ACKNOWLEDGEMENTS

I'd like to take a moment to thank Jason Roach and Gold Dust Publishing. In autumn of 2023, I typed "the end" on the very first draft of this book and undertook a renewed effort to find an agent and/or a different publisher, one who would "get" this book, the type of story I wanted to tell, and the characters made to endure it, and I could not have found a better home than Gold Dust. They and I were on the same wavelength from the very beginning, and I have never felt more at home.

I'd also like to thank the NC chapter of the Horror Writers Association, especially Richard Dansky, who hosts our meetings; P. M. Raymond, our chapter organizer and co-chair; and Jon Carroll Thomas, who serves alongside me as co-secretary. I have never met a more active, welcoming, encouraging, and inspiring group of writers eager to show up for one another and cheer each other on. HWA NC has been life-changing for me as a writer, and I will never be able to give back as much as I have gotten.

In similar vein, I'd like to thank Sarah Adams, Samantha Bryant, and Emily Lavin Leverett for inviting me to the critique group they formed and the steadfast friendship, professional support, and boundless enthusiasm for one another's work I enjoy there. I have learned so much from each of them and look forward to more reading and opining over good coffee.

That project to find an agent and/or a new publisher took ten months, by the way. During that time, I queried 140 agents and 50 presses.

It was a slog, to say the least. A near-majority never bothered to respond at all. The rest almost always responded with a form letter. Despite some truly flattering, uplifting, and encouraging responses from some agents and some presses, at many points, I nearly gave up altogether. I have been told by others that speaking aloud about such efforts greatly reduces the chance of getting an agent in future, but I despise when useful information is hidden behind a veil of gatekeeping secrecy. If someone had told me how difficult it would be, I would have found it much easier to see the project through. I hope, if you are also a writer, that hearing my numbers makes it easier for *you* to stick with it because *you absolutely should stick with it!*

Even though you are holding what is my *13ᵗʰ* book, writing and publishing is never as easy as it looks. If you are a writer struggling to find people who "get" your stories, or you feel no one reads your work, or you wonder whether it's worth it to keep trying, let us clasp hands across time and distance in solidarity with one another. Keep writing new stories. Keep sending them out. The world is richer, and your life is better, for having told those stories despite how difficult every other part of the gig may be. Find fellow writers who sweat and struggle as you and I do, others with whom you can lament and celebrate face-to-face in real time, and you will find strength and camaraderie beyond your wildest imaginings.

Someone in the world has waited their entire life to encounter the story you write next. They will sing your praises forever when they find it, so get your tail in the chair and write.

--Michael

"Appalachian America may be useful as furnishing a fixed point which enables us to measure the progress of the moving world [...] As we need a fresh air fund for the little ones of the city, we need a fresh idea fund for these **sons and daughters of solitude**."

—William Goodell Frost, "Our Contemporary Ancestors in the Southern Mountains," *The Atlantic*, March 1899

CHAPTER ONE – THE VISION

October 2021

Reginald Voth's dead mother first appeared to him at the moment of her own demise: a quarter to four on a Tuesday morning as he sat in bed trying to read.

He knew he had not nodded off and dreamt it. Reginald, wide awake, held a cigarette in one hand and his book in the other, an old paperback novel he picked up at the thrift store. Reading always kept him awake rather than putting him to sleep.

As Reginald reached to tap ash into a big glass tray on the nightstand beside him he jumped halfway out of his skin at what sounded like a shotgun going off in the room. He might have screamed, might have awakened the man snoring softly next to him, perhaps have called 911 or reached for his old Louisville Slugger or *something* in response if Dorothea Voth, his long-suffering and long-inflicting-suffering-on-others mother, had not appeared standing at the foot of the bed in a bright purple bathrobe, its lapels embroidered with lilies. Under that she wore a too-loud orange and yellow nightgown patterned in stars and moons. Dorothea's chosen layers clashed horribly, and Reginald found himself embarrassed that was what he thought first.

Dorothea stood, arms upheld, her hands extended as though she reached to catch something tossed aside by the gods. She bore an ugly expression of agonized beseeching on her narrow, upturned face. Her eyes stood out wide and solid white, but Reginald saw no pupils, no irises. Her flesh had been torn open all over by countless tiny cuts and scrapes. Blood matted her white-black hair, ran down her neck, and stained those lilies on her lapels. Leaves and twigs clung to her bathrobe all over. Pine needles matted against innumerable wounds.

Dorothea Voth might have been standing up and shouting, but she also was clearly and unmistakably dead.

Light surrounded Dorothea like a spotlight on a stage, a light so bright and sharp it hurt Reginald's eyes to look at her. Dorothea's mouth gaped in a silent scream. Reginald realized time passed for him, but not for her. Smoke from his cigarette drifted through the room, but within the column of light all matter stood still as stone, fixed as a photograph.

My mother is dying, Reginald thought. He took a long drag from the cigarette, held the smoke, let it out. *My mother is dead.*

What surprised him most was how this didn't feel like some news item delivered from outside. Reginald felt the certainty of Dorothea's death from deep within, like a thing he'd already known and forgotten.

Reginald listened to the old grandfather clock in his single-wide trailer's front room as it ticked away, talking to itself. It was part of the background machinery of life one eventually forgets to hear until it's all one *can* hear. Five seconds passed while he counted, then ten. He took another drag off the Virginia Slim and stage whispered, wanting to speak but afraid of waking the sleeper beside him. "Mother," he hissed. "Mother, speak to me." When she neither said nor did anything, Reginald reflexively went for the insult. "Mother, you're facing the wrong direction. Pretty sure you're supposed to be on the elevator *down*."

Nothing.

Dorothea Voth spent 37 seconds standing at the foot of her son

Reginald's bed, 37 ticks of that grandfather clock standing in his trailer 37 miles from her home, and never took her not-eyes off whatever she saw in the place where she stood dying.

It would be three months before Reginald noticed that coincidence of time and distance.

The spotlight on Dorothea went out.

A silhouette of Dorothea lingered a moment longer, a shadow in the dark room, perhaps no more than a reverse-imprint on his retina. Then it, too, was gone.

Reginald stubbed out the Virginia Slim and took another from the pack.

The man next to him stirred in his sleep as Reginald lit the new cig. "Are you awake?"

Reginald didn't look down at him. "Couldn't sleep," he said.

"Everything okay?"

"Hard to say," Reginald answered. He picked up the little glass of whiskey next to the ashtray and drained the last from it. "It could be things are getting better, though." Now Reginald finally looked over in the direction of the man's voice. His eyes had started adjusting to the darkness again and he could make out the man's long, straight hair and the curve of a shoulder. "Tell me your name again?"

Three hours later, Reginald's phone rang to tell him what was no longer news.

Reginald's family had been full of stories like this, of course. His great-great-grandfather had spent the end of the 19th century convalescing in the upstairs bedroom of the family home. As the end neared, the story went, old Alexander Voth went blind by inches, watching the world he knew disappear from sight one small—and then large—detail at a time. "Just as well," he'd say, "I don't recognize what the world's come to anyway."

His daughter had held his hand and begged him to speak, to impart some blessing, to make his peace with the many he believed had wronged him. Instead, he spent it speaking to the ceiling, where he addressed a long series of his own departed siblings, then his mother, then his mother's father. One more little stain on the memories of him she would drag back downstairs when he finally died. He ran her ragged, night and day, right up to the very end. It had seemed to go like that down through each generation. The Voth family lore always carried with it that both the parent and the child had either given or needed too much or too little.

Reginald stared at the spot where an image of his mother had appeared and pondered that long line of parents and children disappointing one another. *Name a family where they don't.*

The man next to him, it turned out, was named Clark. Reginald said that rang a bell, and Clark said something both predictable and filthy about being happy to ring Reginald's bell any day. Reginald liked Clark's enthusiasm, and he very much liked his look: hair and skin that said Cherokee, height almost to match his own, and a dick that wouldn't quit under court order. Reginald gave Clark his phone number, somewhat to his own surprise. Reginald liked his privacy. He liked space. He liked to set his boundaries and have them respected.

Reginald also liked Clark. He just wasn't sure he *liked* liked him. It felt childish to phrase it that way, but he used it because it fit. He didn't want serious, deep, adult relationships any more than he wanted the language around them. He wanted reliable fun and to do what he wanted at night. "Reliable fun," however, carried with it a requirement for at least the possibility of repeat visits. Maybe Reginald's usual boundaries could be stretched. *And maybe you're turning into a lonely old queen.* Whatever. It was just a phone number, not the end of the world.

I'd like to see you again soon.

Clark had texted that from his car before driving away from Reginald's trailer, away from Reginald's life, away from the place where a specter of agony had appeared to Reginald while the dick that wouldn't quit snoozed beside him. Reginald tried to picture Clark walking back in the door and something about it didn't fit. That had been another thing in their family: they weren't psychic, they couldn't predict lottery numbers or anything like that, but they were good at predicting whether a given future might or might not come to pass. His mother had always told him she believed in "feelings" and "intuition" and that "sometimes Heaven shines a little light on what's going to happen if we close our eyes and look for it." To Reginald, this sounded like a lot of bullshit, but he found himself doing it anyway. He'd close his eyes and try to picture a given *something* happening, and either it would look real or it wouldn't. He didn't even know if he could describe the difference between them, but he knew it when he saw it. It wasn't *knowledge*, though. It was less prophecy and more statistics. He simply chalked it up to being very good at trusting his gut.

Still, Reginald couldn't picture Clark walking back in the front door, so he simply didn't respond. Instead, he packed two bags, his laptop backpack, and extra chargers and cables. He got his wallet, fished his stash out of the shoebox over the fridge where he kept it, and got everything into the back seats of the powder blue '91 Geo Tracker sitting in the drive. Thirty years old and two hundred thousand highly unlikely miles, but it was paid for, and Reginald could manage to keep it on the road, so it was good enough.

Reginald went back into the house, flipped on the front and back porch lights, turned on a lamp in the bedroom and the light over the stove to make the place look a little bit lived in, and locked up behind himself. His old jump boots crunched the gray gravel of his front walk all the way back to the car, where he folded his long, skinny self into the driver's seat.

Moriah Bald was a little less than an hour away, but it had been a long time since he'd made the drive. It felt like going on a *trip*.

At the last second he pulled out his phone, ran some searches, and

5

called the old motel on the edge of Hazel Branch, the place everyone meant when they said "in town" when he was a kid. Sure, they told him, they had a room to rent for the night. It cost a hell of a lot more than Reginald wanted to pay, but he didn't like the alternative at all: driving to his mother's house and trying to stay there.

She just had to die in the middle of peak leaf season, didn't she?

Reginald took out a Virginia Slim, cranked the handle to crack his driver-side window, and lit the cigarette.

Time to go "home."

CHAPTER TWO – THE BODY

Reginald eased into a space on the side of the long, low flank of the funeral home. A sign bolted into the brick read GUEST PARKING and another, under it, intended to look the same but not quite making the cut, announced OFFICE with an arrow pointing to the left. He shifted the Tracker into neutral, turned the key, and pulled the hand brake quickly so it gave that satisfying sound like a giant zipper breaking. The motor dieseled only briefly, shuddering to a cantankerous halt. Reginald pursed his lips and frowned at his dashboard. He didn't need fuel injector problems, not even in a car as old as his. He didn't need *any* problems, to be honest, but especially not the kind that cost money to fix.

He looked up at the two signs affixed to the otherwise blank brick wall just a few feet away.

And yet here I am. He'd blown the cash for two nights in that awful motel plus meals from the diner in town and pizza delivery, avoiding going to his mother's house, avoiding seeing his brother Bobby there, avoiding having to run into any of his various cousins who might be there to pick at the corpse of her estate. The money was starting to add up, and the funeral hadn't even happened yet. He wondered if mortuaries offered payment plans. Well, this one had better. It wasn't like they could repossess his mother's coffin in a month.

Reginald stuck a thin cigarette between his lips, brandished a disposable lighter with a knockoff comic book character on the side, and flicked the switch a couple of times. Sparks bright as a campfire danced out and nipped at the corners and crags of his thin hands as he took a long drag. He leaned back against the seat and headrest for a second, let the smoke start to escape him, and then puffed it all out in one go.

No point lollygagging. He scolded himself only lightly, though, opening the door and unfolding his grasshopper legs to the pavement before standing away from the car. The cigarette dangled at the corner of his mouth as he dusted himself off here and there with one free hand, purely a matter of habit. With the other, he dug in the pocket of his old leather coat for a gray knit hat he didn't need and his mask. The mask had a cartoon cat on it: black, its fur standing out straight, an angry expression on its face, one paw held up with claws extended. Reginald smoked two thirds of the cigarette in three long and businesslike drags, then dropped it on the pavement, crushed it with the toe of his secondhand boot, and slipped the elastic loops around his ears. He fiddled with the nosepiece a moment, slipped his glasses back on, and shut and locked the door on the Geo.

As he strode over to the sidewalk, the gently curving letters on the huge, wooden sign in front of the building slid into view: *McLaren Family Funeral Chapel & Crematory Service Since 1967.*

McLarens had been laid out like a three-way car crash between a church, a stately old family home, and a furniture store. It had three main entrances, one for each of those purposes. The larger of its two parking lots ran along the side of the funeral chapel, accommodating the crowds a real winner of a stiff might draw for services. The business office half-hid behind the part that looked like a house, a bit embarrassed about the world seeing its commerce on display. Paying customers parked in a small lot beside the house where, presumably, the original McLarens lived while running the place. Reginald had no idea who owned it now. It might or might not still be actual McLarens; either way, they certainly wouldn't change the name. Everyone in Hazel Branch knew what "he'll be at McLarens soon" or "you won't believe what she wore at McLarens last week" meant. You don't throw away brand recognition like that.

The "house" part had a broad, deep front porch with several rocking chairs and benches under its overhanging roof. Reginald had no difficulty picturing grieving family—close enough to be there and get a pat on the arm, but not so close they'd be expected to join the receiving line—sinking into wicker and plastic, fanning themselves, talking about how summer didn't used to feel so hot and that's how they knew they'd gotten older.

No, it's actually just getting hotter. Reginald caught himself pursing his lips again in annoyance at these imagined relations of some hypothetical dead and their demonstration of the persistent stupidity of humankind, but that was one of the reasons he loved this era of masks and social distancing: nobody could read his expression. Reginald had never felt particularly pressed to owe anyone a smile, but now at least his natural demeanor cost him a little less social currency. His eyes still gave him away, he was sure, but people had to get close for them to convey his misanthropy and Reginald learned a long time ago not to let anyone get too close for too long.

Reginald opened the front door and stepped in, warm air rushing out and welcoming him in. The *real* cold hadn't settled in yet over this part of the mountains, but they'd have flurries within a few weeks and snow on the ground for Christmas. He could feel it in his bones, even here, in mid-October. The winter would be a rough one, that was for sure.

But not yet: Not in here, anyway. Not in the lobby of the funeral home, with its warm bulbs in recessed fixtures giving the whole place a windowless, late-afternoon-forever glow. Fake plants—attractive, but Reginald knew what he saw when he saw it—in large, brass pots kept the corners of the lobby from feeling lonely. A loveseat and coffee table with tastefully fanned magazines huddled with two matching armchairs to one side. Reginald would have bet five dollars on the spot that no one had ever sat on that couch for more than a few moments. *Those magazines could be Highlights from 1977 for all anyone knows.*

No signs pointed the direction to anything in particular, but Reginald found himself carried forward—one part momentum, one part layout of the space pushing him ahead—into the big room full of display caskets. He wondered if they had exciting model names the way cars did: *Mustang* or *Corvette* or *Spyder.* The caskets were all set up in display mode, meaning they were tilted slightly towards the viewer with their lids open, some sort of long, silk garment draped over the edge and hanging off the side. They looked like fancy dinner napkins or maybe gym towels. With the lids gaping, the silk napkin *things* struck Reginald as looking like tongues hanging from the mouths of dead or very stupid people.

"Plenty of both around *here*," Reginald muttered.

"I'm sorry?"

Reginald spun on the slick soles of his cheap boots, his eyebrows up.

A shortish white man in a black suit (Reginald's brain ticked off boxes: wool, not cheap but also not tailored, made him look a little plumper than was probably the case) smiled gently and said, voice soft, "I'm sorry, I thought you spoke to me." He gestured at himself, touching the center of his tie clip with the side of his own hand. "I'm Jeremy McLaren." Jeremy took a few steps closer and extended a hand.

Reginald put up a hand to stop him. "Oh, uh, nice to meet you, Mr. McLaren. I realize your clients are already dead, but I'd prefer if you wore a mask. I'm not too interested in needing your services for *myself.*"

McLaren hesitated a beat, then slipped a little black number from the inside pocket of his coat and slid it around his ears. "Of course," he said. "My apologies, sometimes I forget. And please, call me Jeremy."

Like hell you do. Reginald looked down as Jeremy re-extended the hand and nearly laughed. "I don't shake hands, either, Mr. McLaren."

McLaren rubbed his fingers against his palm as he lowered the hand.

"Certainly. I apologize."

Reginald waved it off. "Don't bother. And I'm afraid I'm not shopping for a casket. We've already got one." Reginald nodded his head in the direction of the funeral chapel. "I'm Reginald Voth. I'm here to…" Reginald hesitated. Why was he here? Theoretically he stopped by to check on the arrangements for the next day. But really he came because he needed to see the body. He tried to recover. "I'm here to review the makeup."

McLaren seemed unsure whether to fold his hands in front of himself or behind, and for just a moment looked like he might try both at once. He cocked his head to one side and said, softly, "Mr. Voth, your mother… well, her wishes were quite clear."

Reginald arched an eyebrow at the man. "Go on."

"She didn't… want makeup." McLaren cleared his throat softly.

He's new at this. Reginald imagined someone finally inheriting the place after decades of parents and grandparents running it for themselves, only for the heir to realize he never learned the *art* of this trade: the creation, maintenance, and resolution of a human element to every interaction. The guy had no bedside manner, no antilock braking system designed to keep him from showing any feeling he might later wish to have not shared.

"I know," Reginald said. "I remembered that even as I said it." He tried to laugh and it came out just as strangled and awkward as anything McLaren himself might say. Instead he coughed and cleared his throat. "But I'd still like to see her."

"Her instructions…" McLaren seemed to debate something with himself and then resolved to see it through. "Well, sir, her instructions were that no one was to see her once she had been placed in her casket." The man gulped some air and looked pale. "She was very emphatic in the instructions. *No one.*"

Reginald stared at the man. "Mr. McLaren, my mother died in a fall. She didn't anticipate her own demise, much less write up instructions for what to do after it. Or does McLarens employ a medium?"

McLaren stiffened at that. "Mr. Voth, I—"

Reginald cut him off. "Look, I'm sorry." The apology caught McLaren by surprise and gave Reginald the opening he needed to keep jerking McLaren around until he got what he wanted. "I'm grieving, and I keep finding myself snapping at people. For no reason. And the thing is, of course, in times like these almost everyone a body meets is just trying to help as best they can. So I *extra* apologize. Really, though, I do need to see my mother and you're the only person who can make that happen. So either show me to her or to wherever I can find her myself and leave me at the door." Reginald gave the order a moment to simmer, then said, much more kindly, "Please. Out of the kindness of your heart, your desire for a good online review, or your recognition of the fact that ultimately I'm the one signing the check for this." Reginald tried not to smirk. "Do any of those work for you?"

McLaren nodded once and gestured as he turned. "Right this way, Mr. Voth."

"Thank you." Reginald hesitated. "Jeremy."

The chapel smelled like a deodorant truck had turned over on the highway: flowers in wreaths, flowers in vases, blooms woven into green and white Styrofoam in the shape of an elaborate cross. Reginald found he had to stop at the back and collect himself, and he wasn't sure whether from the sensory onslaught or from the fact the silver-gray rounded-off rectangle at the front of the not-church of a funeral chapel held the body of his dead mother.

McLaren, his voice low, said, "I'll need to open the lid for you. I'm afraid I can't allow you to operate the casket alone."

Reginald didn't look at him, and the reflexive sarcasm—*don't worry I'm wearing steel-toed boots*—died before he even started to speak it. Instead he drew a shallow breath and said something much more sincere. "That's fine. I just need a minute first."

He spent that minute letting his eyes roam all around the room: the high ceiling, the gentle blue-gray walls, the pale gray carpet. The front of the room included a small choir loft and a baby grand piano. As far as Reginald knew, the services would feature neither. It would probably be easy enough to find a dozen people willing to sing at his mother's funeral, but it'd be hard to make them sing anything sad.

Finally Reginald stepped forward and strode directly to the front, stopping beside the casket.

McLaren had to half-jog to keep up and then get ahead, reaching the coffin no more than a step or two before Reginald did. The man did some stuff with the edges that looked like turning screws, then placed a hand around the flange of the lid. "Are you ready to see her?" He asked it plainly, no embellished sympathy, no pretense of deep concern.

Reginald waited one moment, then another, then nodded. "I am. Do it."

McLaren cracked the lid and raised it slowly to reveal Dorothea Voth lying in state. Her hands were clasped and she wore a simple black gown with a high neckline and long sleeves. A triple string of pearls had been clasped around her neck. He recognized it from her collection of artificial jewelry, kept in a separate box from the few items she had of what she always referred to as "the genuine articles." Reginald's brother Bobby had probably made sure they wouldn't put any of Dorothea's real valuables in the ground with her. It might well be the first time he'd agreed with Bobby about anything in twenty years.

Dorothea's lined skin was pale beyond white, into the shade of sheets of typing paper and about as thin. The funeral home had, in the end, put makeup on her anyway: some thick foundation and a little powder. Nothing fancy, but whoever did it must have been frightened by her wounds. The hospital had told Reginald over the phone, after she died, that the fall had left scratches and bruises all over her body. The gown covered that up, but whoever got her into it had to see it all, and stare at her empty, pallid face, the many small wounds tearing tiny new mouths all over her, scrubbed of blood but not of bruises. McLaren was all fired up about last wishes, but his staff were the ones who had to go home and dream the faces of the dead, so of course they put some makeup on her. It would be a good way to paper over having the torn skin underneath be the last thing anyone had seen.

"The woman who dressed her was from her church," McLaren spoke as though explaining how he'd dented the fender on the family car. "She doesn't work for us. I told her your mother's request had been for no makeup and no hair styling, but she insisted. She said she owed your mother too much. I apologize. I told her to stop, and she did, but it didn't occur to me to have her remove what she'd already done."

Tight curls of white and gray with black underneath, like yesterday's newspaper left out in the rain, pressed to her head in uncombed bunches. Her lips formed a flat, gray slash. *Even in death she isn't one for smiles.*

Reginald held his breath, studying her for a long moment, then nodded again without taking his eyes from her. As McLaren lowered the lid back into place, Reginald spoke directly to him. "Thank you." Reginald hesitated and then waved a hand vaguely in the direction of the back of the funeral home. "And it's fine. I get it. She thought she was doing something kind. And she was." Reginald sucked his cheeks and pursed his lips. He wasn't accustomed to being nice to people he'd decided to despise. "And so did you. So, thank you again. I appreciate you indulging my need to see her one last time."

"It's not unusual to need closure." McLaren was very diplomatic.

"Oh, I don't need closure." Reginald smirked behind his mask. "I needed to make sure."

McLaren considered Reginald a moment. "Of what?"

Reginald lifted one shoulder at him in a half-shrug. "That she's dead. I just needed to be totally certain she's really, truly dead. And she is." He began slowly letting out his breath, trying to hold back a sigh. "I can finally relax." The rest of that breath left him in a long gust. "Oh thank *God.*"

CHAPTER THREE – "HOME"

It had been twelve years since Reginald Voth had stepped foot on his mother's property, but the drive up to it was as easy and familiar as if he'd done it twice a day the entire time. He knew every turn: Left off the main highway, around a series of curves rolling up and down the nearly abandoned length of two-lane Botterman Road, then right at the old building with the signage of a defunct enterprise: *MOUNTAIN ACRES REAL ESTATE*. It had been built, opened, and shut down over the course of, what, his fourth-grade year? Someone had tried to cash in by getting ahead of a land boom they correctly foresaw. They were simply thirty years too early to catch the train. The little building where someone's dream died had faded long ago: on a road like this, one that didn't go much of anywhere, who did they think would see it and decide *here* was the place to buy?

Reginald found himself wondering if it would still be standing, and to his surprise it was not: it had been replaced altogether. Now, instead of an old wooden-framed building with fewer and fewer intact panes of glass, the signs peeling away from their plywood backing, he found a paved parking lot and one of those miniature travel trailers, the little round ones that looked like a teardrop made of aluminum. A canopy extended over an open window at each end, and painted along the side in block letters were the words *YE OLDE CAMPER CAFE* over a line-art mug with cartoon steam coming from the top. As he slowed to turn, Reginald saw three picnic tables spread out behind it. A man in a suit and a woman in a long, black dress sat at one of the picnic tables and watched him drive by.

Wonders never cease. He thought about stopping and asking how long they'd been open, privately betting with himself this dream, too, would die, and in less time than the real estate business. Slowing for the turn, but enough that he could think about stopping in, Reginald jumped when the car behind him blew their horn for him to hurry up. He'd driven this road countless times over nearly four decades and he'd never once seen it have traffic. *At least someone around here finally has someplace to be.*

He skipped stopping at Camper Cafe. He needed to get ho—he stopped himself: he needed to get to his mother's house. He could make coffee there. She certainly wouldn't be. *Probably find Bobby making himself two cups just to vex me.* Reginald took the turn onto Summit Church Road, downshifted with his right hand while holding the wheel and another Virginia Slim in his left, and began the ascent up the side of Moriah Bald.

The road immediately began its slow slithering climb, and Reginald turned up the radio to try to cover the whine of the Tracker's tiny engine as it strained against gravity. By the time the road leveled out, Reginald knew, the road would climb over 800 feet in the span of three and a half miles—and that it would take ten minutes. The posted speed limit was 45 but he knew he'd be lucky to be doing 30 by the time he got there. As a teen he'd had two cars die on this hill and he did not relish the possibility the Geo would get dumped in the same grave.

The reason why there had been cars around presented itself for the hundredth time as Reginald left the valley floor behind and scaled the steep road: October in Appalachia meant hillsides painted in every possible shade of autumn. Gold, red, orange, some damn near purple, and they blanketed the hillsides around him as far as the eye could see. The mountains in fall were a sight to behold, to be sure. The trees were about the only thing Reginald missed, when he let himself miss anything at all.

Reginald took one more long drag, flicked his cigarette butt out the driver's window, and let the smoke in his lungs chase it. He left the window cracked, though. He liked the brace of autumn air up in the mountains, where you could feel the *real* cold, the ice-knife memory of when Appalachia's ancient peaks reached higher. He tried the radio, tuning in WASU, the student radio station from App State. Something in the realm of modern rock blatted out of the Tracker's somewhat tinny speakers. The one in the driver's door buzzed whenever the band played a certain chord. Reginald had no idea what the song was or who had sung it—he was long past paying attention to such things—but it beat the hell out of an onslaught of country and western he feared would be all he could find.

Three largely interchangeable songs later, the road leveled off and he started to pick up a little speed again. The old X-ray film factory had been turned into a state park, and to his surprise there was a gravel lot brimming with SUVs, their hatches adorned with bike racks. Reginald chuckled to himself over that, not even sure why he found it funny. It was just so *strange* to think of Moriah Bald as a place to go, a destination. Everyone he'd ever known in this place thought of it only as somewhere to leave, and the ones who never did tended to lacquer over the grain of bitterness inevitably stuck between their gums and cheek with a kind of twisted pride: *at least I never abandoned this place* and other such nonsense.

Reginald reached into the pack in the right cupholder, fished out another Virginia Slim, and lit it without thinking.

I will never manage to quit.

Two hundred yards later, he turned the last curve, the one just past Summit Union Chapel—an old, one-room, white clapboard structure built at least two centuries before, now used only to celebrate very specific kinds of nostalgia such as its annual homecoming and a couple of family get-togethers—and very nearly drove past his own dead mother's house.

In place of her old white mailbox stood a sign proclaiming *Moriah Bald Estates*. Past that, he recognized the curve that vanished around the mountain to wend its way to the other side and the King place at the end of the road.

Under *Moriah Bald Estates*, in smaller block print, the sign practically whispered, *A Montford Homes Community.*

Where her gravel driveway had wended through a long front yard and up to the house her great-to-the-nth-degree-grandparents had built, with ruts so deep people who came to visit had to drive with one tire on the curb and one tire on the raised middle, there was now a wide, paved street. It wasn't a long one, just enough to get someone off the road and onto the oval loop of asphalt where her long front yard had once been. Along its outer edge sat eight brand new, high-quality, two-story homes. Every one of them was a little too big for the lot, covered up in that light gray vinyl siding that says to a prospective buyer *don't worry, absolutely no one will think you're special or weird.* At the center of the cul-de-sac stood an open, airy, slightly slanted lawn area with an enormous jungle gym and four picnic tables. Reginald found himself thinking of Ye Olde Camper Cafe back down the mountain. *Must be a lot of picnics in this neck of the woods.*

It amused Reginald to see one kid of twelve years, maybe thirteen, sitting on one of the swing sets of the jungle gym. He had a phone in his hand and a look of sullen intensity on his face. *Good, kid. Look up somewhere more interesting to go when you grow up.*

Reginald had always dreaded that driveway, and driving up it. Every time he turned off the road and into the yard he felt like he'd left civilization. Every car he heard pass in the middle of the night as a child had sounded like someone making their escape.

At the back of the cul-de-sac, like a patriarch at the head of the table for some awkwardly formal Thanksgiving feast, stood Reginald's mother's house: two stories, with the roof angled so steeply it almost looked like some ancient pyramid. It was an old, wood-sided farmhouse, but over the years and generations the rustic, Appalachian cottage had been replaced, piece by piece, with something more like a patchwork quilt of impulsive architectural whims. As a child, Reginald had spent long hours sorting and ordering old photos he'd found in a suitcase, assembling a chronology of each modification as it unfolded. Taken together and ruffled with his thumb, it almost looked like the original house had broken out in architecture like a bad case of chicken pox.

The end result had been nice enough, though: the wood-sided house with a steep overhang above stone steps into the main floor had, over time, morphed into something more like what the word "farmhouse" might suggest: white paneling, a front porch running the width of the front of the house and around one side, with the roof held up by pillars of brick and beam. The front door, also white, had three diamond-shaped windows set into it at different heights from one another, and three tall chimneys jutted from the ancient metal roof. An Old Man's Beard tree marked the yard's boundary at one corner, a massive elderberry marked the other, and mountain laurel lined the street between the mailbox and the Old Man's Beard.

The last thirty feet of what had been his mother's driveway jutted from the paved street like a badly broken bone: a few yards of inexplicable gravel in an otherwise modern and thoroughly unremarkable development. Her ancient mailbox on its equally ancient post stood there now rather than out by the main road. The house where Reginald grew up remained, brooding in the shadow of Moriah Bald, draped in autumn's finest shades, but the *farm*, the place he pictured in his head when he remembered his childhood, the image still attached to the word "home" despite his best efforts and a few failed starts at talk therapy, was gone.

Someone had planted two rows of houses down the heart of it.

The Tracker's suspension creaked as Reginald turned off the street and into the driveway of his mother's house.

He stopped, pulled the handbrake, and turned the key.

He took a long drag from the cigarette, started to flick it into the yard, and caught himself as though his mother might see him—his mother, dead now, finally dead, no longer the vulture circling over the life he'd made for himself, waiting for him or it to die. *I guess this is what winning feels like.*

He'd always thought he'd relish it more.

Reginald climbed out of the Tracker, shut the door, and crunched down the gravel drive to the mailbox. In it he found a keyring and three days of untouched mail. Bobby had emailed him to say he'd leave their mother's keys in the mailbox. Reginald hadn't exactly expected a surprise party to welcome him "home"—the word had a bitter edge in his mind—but this was surprisingly frosty, even for *him*. He folded the mail up around itself, shifted the keys into his other palm, and walked back up the drive to the front porch. A sticky note in spidery handwriting on the storm door read: *Welcome back.*

"Three cheers for me," Reginald said aloud to himself. He felt the occasion needed something with a little more flair, so he added, "Ding dong, the bitch is dead." It felt hollow, though: not because he missed his mother, not by a long shot, but he'd expected to feel *something* and now he mostly just felt… blank.

A subtle feeling of being *just about* to encounter someone—an unknown figure on the other side of the door, the sound of a footstep on a stair, but without actually seeing or hearing anything, just a *knowing* they were nearby—reached into his guts and curled its cold fingers around them. Reginald stopped, the keys halfway to the deadbolt lock on the door, and he felt his heart flutter for a moment. He could have sworn he saw something move beyond the door. He peered in on nothing, the house beyond a dark well showing only shadow. How could he have seen something move when he couldn't even see the room where it would have been moving? And yet…

A voice from the yard—young, higher than it wanted to be and trying to pitch itself downward—broke the spell and startled Reginald so much he nearly dropped the keys in his hand. "Hey, you can't go in there! We're supposed to stay out of there."

Reginald turned and glared down his long, thin nose at the kid from the swings in the circle. "What are you, the security guard?"

"Oh," the kid said, "you must be Reggie."

Reginald narrowed his eyes. "*Reginald*," he replied, "and I'm guessing that means you know my brother Bobby."

The kid turned and pointed at the nearest of the houses on the cul-de-sac, one of its yard's professionally manicured corners touching a corner of Dorothea's own. "He lives there."

Reginald raised both eyebrows in surprise. He knew his mother had sold his brother part of her land to build a home. Neither she nor his brother had ever mentioned they parceled out the farm's front yard to build half a dozen others while they were at it. Reginald smacked his lips and said, "Exactly how much of this plot did my mother even own anymore?"

The kid—average height, deep brown skin, hair clipped short, with a too-big hoodie someone expected he'd grow into some day—shrugged at Reginald like that was the dumbest question in the world. "I don't know. This house? This yard? Maybe the woods behind it?"

Reginald sighed softly. "Well, so much for *that* dream."

"What dream?"

Reginald fluttered a few fingers at the boy. "Oh, selling the place myself and finally seeing some compensation. What's your name, kid?"

"I'm Ham."

"As in 'Hamilton?'"

"No, Abraham. But nobody calls me that."

Reginald used the bundle of mail in his hand to touch his forehead in a little salute. "A pleasure to meet you, Ham." He started looking through the dozen or so keys on the keyring to find the house key again but stopped to add, looking back up at Ham, "And remember: *Reginald.* Just like you're 'Ham' and not 'Abraham.'"

Ham shrugged again, the way kids do, like they're little machines designed to generate performative indifference on demand. "Okay." A long moment of silence passed while they sized each other up, then Ham added, "Sorry about your mom." He said it with sincerity but without depth of emotion.

He knew her well enough to not particularly miss her. Reginald sighed before he spoke. "So am I, but for different reasons." Then he twisted and stuck the key in the lock. When Reginald looked back to speak further to Ham, something in the boy's expression made him draw up short. "What?"

Ham just watched him for a long moment, then waved it off. "Nothin'."

"No." Reginald shook his head, very firmly. "If you want to say something, say it. I've heard worse, trust me."

Ham had the good manners to look embarrassed, and finally asked, "Your brother says… No, forget it."

Reginald allowed himself a sour little smirk. "Oh, Ham, I can *only imagine* what my brother says about me. I assure you all the worst parts of it are true."

Ham ignored that and nodded at a different part of the front yard. "Who'd you bring with you?"

The corners of Reginald's mouth didn't slip, but his brow furrowed a little. "No one. Me, myself, and I. Why, was Bobby scared I'd bring a boyfriend and embarrass him in front of all the other high-functioning Southern Baptist drunks? Well, I imagine he'll be *tryingly* relieved to find out I'm flying solo."

Ham, his mouth open a little, looked at that part of the front yard again—the corner of the house, the one the porch did not include, out of sight where Reginald stood—and then back at Reginald. "Oh." He waited a moment. "Okay." He waited another beat, then, "Are you sure?"

Reginald frowned now, deeply annoyed. "Yes. Why? Has somebody else been here? Maybe some other kids in this…" He looked down the street at the houses on either side, a head-on collision between suburban and rural life. "Neighborhood, I guess I have to say?" He looked back down at Ham. "They been poking around my mother's house a lot the last couple of days?"

Ham's expression turned to uncertainty, then he shook his head. "I'm it, mister."

"Reginald."

Ham corrected himself. "Mister Reginald. I'm the only kid around here."

Reginald cocked his head. "*Just Reginald.* Jesus Christ, Ham."

"I ask, 'cause I saw someone get out of your car and go around the corner of the house when you parked."

Reginald crinkled his lips like used tin foil and glared. "Very funny, ha ha."

Now a flash of irritation, even anger, shot across Ham's eyes as he said, "Hey, screw you. You want to sneak somebody in, I don't care. You don't have to be a dick about it."

Reginald startled at Ham's response, grinning despite himself. "Well, *my!*" Reginald blinked a couple of times and tried to wrestle the grin into a mere smile. "Cussed by the first child to cross my path. That *is* a good omen, frankly. Okay, sure, I believe you think you saw someone, but it must have been a reflection in my car mirror or something, 'cause I didn't bring anyone with me, Ham. Whatever you saw…" He nodded at the phone in Ham's hand. "Don't stare at that thing too long or you'll *keep* seeing stuff."

Ham rolled his eyes and moved to go, but they both paused as a massive vehicle—a late model domestic pickup, the kind that cost twice what Reginald made in a year but was marketed as perfectly embodying the simple, acid-washed life of everyday people—grumbled and growled its way around the right side of the big oval in the middle of the neighborhood and wheeled into Bobby's driveway.

The driver's door opened and a slim, fair-skinned woman with long, straight hair cut with sharp definition climbed down. She reached into the extended cab and pulled out two bags of groceries. She closed the door, turned away from her own home, looked directly at Reginald just once for precisely two seconds, then went inside. The truck's horn barked once when it locked.

"That's Bobby's wife," Ham said.

"Oh, I know. She's ignored me over enough Thanksgiving dinners for me to remember." Reginald clucked his tongue. "Thanks for stopping by, Ham."

Ham shrugged. "I really saw it." He turned and started walking away.

Reginald saluted his back a final time. "See ya. Come by anytime."

After Ham crossed the boundary from yard to sidewalk, Reginald unlocked the door, cracked it open, and listened for the sound of footsteps or creaking boards from inside.

He counted to ten.

Nothing.

Reginald frowned again and went inside.

GENERATION ONE – ALEXANDER

Alexander Voth stood in the middle of a ruined stand of corn and beans. He'd planted the latter to climb the sturdy stalks of the former, the way the Cherokee did it before him, and he had liked how efficient and clever that had been. Getting them to grow had taken monumental work, however. He'd had good luck at his old place, which had been bottomland along a creek that fed into the French Broad River. But one of the new railroad companies and the lumber operation they co-owned had come along and told him he had to sell. He knew he wasn't actually required to comply, not by the law, but he also knew he didn't stand a chance if he tried to stay. Alexander's choice had been clear: take a little money and move on, or get pushed out with nothing. Forty dollars in cash today, or the cabin catches fire tomorrow. Nobody'd needed to say that part aloud. Alexander had seen it in the railroad man's smile.

By then, though, the bottomlands around him were either all bought up or headed that way, so he'd had to go up on a ridge. That meant the soil wasn't as good, and the water ran faster, the well had to be dug deeper, but it also meant fewer people around. He went farther into the woods than he might have done, hoping it would take longer for the loggers and the trains to get to him this time, and in the end he counted himself lucky: he'd found ten acres of relatively gently sloped woods on the side of a mountain topped with a bald, a natural clearing atop the mountain where nothing larger than grasses, clover, or wildflowers seemed able to grow. Appalachia was dotted with balds here and there, a curious detail of the Almighty's design. Dense forest ran all the way up to the very rim of the peak and abruptly give way to a bare clearing under endless sky.

The balds were lucky, everybody knew that. The Cherokee had stories about a giant bird that stole children and ate them, so the Great Spirit had cleared off a bunch of mountain tops so their warriors could stand guard, watching for the bird's attacks. The balds were a gift from Heaven. Alexander had even found a stone table up there, atop the mountain where he'd bought land. It stood almost in the very center, as though someone had cleared a path through the blackberry brambles and tended the timothy and bluegrass to make it a special place in some formal garden. A Bible story sprang to Alexander's mind the moment he first laid eyes on that rock, and the mountain had been Moriah Bald ever since.

Now, though, he felt a hundred days' walk from that moment of simple beauty. He stood in a patch of broken corn stalks and trampled beans ground to splintered mush in soil he'd had to scratch and scrape and fortify by hand with one bucket after another of shit from the very pigs who'd unraveled his endless work. Mad with hunger, they had breached the fence after running out of forage. It was going to be a light winter, or so he hoped, but that meant whenever Alexander turned the hogs loose in the woods to feed themselves, they came back having eaten something less than enough. In desperation—or perhaps in misplaced revenge—they'd broken out of the sty where they spent their nights and destroyed two-thirds of what Alexander, his wife, and his child were to eat over the winter. No corn for meal or boiling, no beans to make a stew.

Anger welled in Alexander, and for a moment he considered killing the hogs in rage—but even as his fingers twitched the corn knife in his hand, something stayed his fury.

A voice spoke to him.

Things can be set right.

CHAPTER FOUR – LET IT GO

The home of a dead person is a corpse in its own right, and the body of Dorothea Voth's home was still warm to the touch. The TV remote sat on the coffee table atop a copy of the Entertainment section of the newspaper from three days before. A half-finished scarf and a couple of knitting needles stuck out of the top of a wicker basket in the middle of the couch. A wedge pillow with a cord was crammed into the corner by Dorothea's having sat against it. *Back problems*, Reginald thought. *Always had to have her special heated pillow.*

The walls of the living room bore exactly the same decorations as they had in Reginald's childhood: collages of family photos, at least four framed cross stitches of Bible quotes bordered by flowers, and the old painting of Moriah Bald behind the house. Reginald had always liked to go up there as a child. It felt like another world, like something out of one of those tales where a kid gets sucked through a mirror and rides a dragon. It was a little slice of storybook waiting for him at the end of a long, rough trail up the side of the mountain. Once he was old enough to be out of her sight, and especially when his mother would tell him in open annoyance that he should "get out of the house and do something," that was where he went. It felt far enough away to be safe.

Reginald stepped closer to the old photos, his eyes gliding over them without taking in any specific one. He realized with some surprise he was actually just checking for two things: to see if any had been replaced and, if so, if any of those missing had been of him. They had, and some were. He'd gone all of thirty-seven miles away and stopped attending family functions and inch by inch, 4x6 print by 4x6 print from the Eckerd's drugstore in town, he'd been erased in punishment for it. It wasn't that his mother had replaced photos including him with new ones that didn't. She'd replaced the ones including him with *old* ones that didn't. He realized an old photo from Thanksgiving one year—he must have been twelve? eleven?—had been removed and replaced with a different photo from the same holiday the same year. His grandmother had been in the old one, and she was in this one, too, wearing the same clothes, the same glasses frames, the same blue rinse in her hair. But, importantly, Reginald had been beside her in the old photo. This was one of her on her own. *So that's how it is, then.* Reginald let out a huff of breath and then corrected himself. *Was.*

Reginald turned from the photos to go look at the painting of Moriah Bald. When he asked his mother about it as a child she said it had been painted by "somebody way back, I don't recall." His grandmother said she had no idea who painted it. It had been in their family "forever," and so it had always fascinated him to see such a familiar place as an object of mystery. Reginald felt wonder when he walked up the mountain to Moriah Bald, but this painting was like something out of Indiana Jones: an artifact of mysterious origin, heavy with unspoken meaning waiting to be divined. Who painted it? Did they paint anything else? Were they an aspiring artist frustrated by living in this nowhere place in their no-when time?

Reginald must have stared at this painting for a thousand hours as a child: the open bald atop the mountain, blue hills vanishing into the distant horizon, and the emerald and yellowish greens and browns of the meadow it described. The big rock slightly off-center in the middle of the bald painted in grays and blacks and navy blue was surprisingly well rendered. A couple of birds flew away from the bald in an upper corner. It occurred to Reginald that as a child he had appreciated it for what it represented but he hadn't had the education or experience or perspective to appreciate it as an example of craft. As a kid it had been a weird old painting with an interesting story. As an adult he was impressed with its making in addition to everything else about it.

Reginald blinked at it twice.

This wasn't the same painting his mother had on the wall in his childhood.

It was a painting of Moriah Bald, sure, but it was from a slightly different angle, as though the painter's perspective hovered slightly higher in the sky and off to one side. The brush work was more visible. The details were sharper. It wasn't exactly a forgery. It was like someone had seen the original and said, "I could paint that," and then done so in their own way. They had copied it, yes, but not precisely. Either they'd done a lousy job or they hadn't set out to duplicate it. They wanted to paint the same scene, not the same *painting*.

Reginald surprised himself by speaking aloud. "I wonder which of my shitty relatives ruined the first one? Dumbasses." He shook his head to himself, then startled at a faint burst of static elsewhere in the house. Tinny, fast-paced violin music and a high male tenor voice sounded from somewhere very far away, distorted by airwaves and the lousy speaker on some ancient mono radio receiver. It sounded to Reginald like one of the radios they used to have when he was a kid. He'd carry it out in the yard at night, at the far end of the property from the house itself, against the tree line, and with the volume turned low he would turn the dial with the molasses-slow patience of a safe cracker with his ear to a vault door. If he was very lucky, Reginald would catch a staticky, raspy few minutes of a talk show from somewhere far away, New York or Texas or Ontario, their AM signals bouncing off the vault of stars overhead.

At the moment, though, it offered no talk shows from distant parts. Instead, it spat out bits and pieces, a few seconds here and there of what sounded like old-school country music: not a violin, Reginald realized, but a fiddle, and behind it a guitar or something like it holding up the voice of a singer whose heart was breaking.

Dorothea must have had the radio going when she died, he realized. Its batteries must also be about to die. Distracted now from the question of the painting, Reginald turned to explore the house and put that radio out of its—and his—misery.

In the kitchen he found clean plates in the dish dryer, dirty ones in the sink. The trash had started to smell rancid, and the whole place reeked from it, but mostly it stank of *her*: that rose water lotion she used all the time, and mothballs tucked in all the coat pockets in the front closet, old coffee, fried chicken. Reginald knew when he opened the cabinet to take out the trash he'd find an old Crisco can half-filled with used fry oil. No radio, but the erratic sound seemed a little stronger. Reginald wondered if perhaps the radio had been left outside.

The back door out of the kitchen opened onto a small concrete stoop with cinder block stairs running down to the ground. Reginald moved the old, thin curtain out of the way to look at the back yard. A couple of folding beach chairs sat on the grass, turned to face the house. He wondered why his mother would want to sit back there under a warm evening sky, or maybe a hot summer morning, and look at the house instead of the woods beyond the yard. *Probably counting shingles to make sure nobody stole one.* The thought left a sour taste in his mind, and he tried to steer himself back to the center like one of those failed therapists had suggested, using something she'd said. *At this point, what I do with thoughts about her is on me, not on her. Let it go.*

Reginald turned his gaze to the old oversized shed in one corner of the yard. His parents had always called it "the barn," but it was more like a ramshackle workshop: century-old walls held up by the tools leaned against them, a couple of worktables in the corners, an old riding tractor parked beside the plow and harrow attachments they had for it. A long, narrow garden, terraced flat by digging out part of the slanted yard around it, ran the rest of the length of the back yard. She'd been growing tomatoes, now done for the season. A few potato plants remained, needing to be dug out. Onions going to seed, a few carrots, a row of corn with string beans growing up their stalks. As a child, Reginald had hated working in that garden, stringing beans, shucking corn. He remembered the time some kind of woolly worm crawled out of an ear of corn and stung the back of his hand while he tried to shake it off. It had hurt like fire and electricity all at once, hot and buzzing, deep-stabbing pain that got even worse when he crushed the goddamned thing as he tried to get it off.

He'd been nine years old, and he'd been so mad at the worm, so embarrassed at having been stung, and so certain his mother or his brother would mock him for it that he'd cried from anxiety, not from pain, as he ran his hand under ice cold water from the spigot by the back steps. Blood had oozed up out of what looked like dozens of tiny bites as he squeezed it, hoping there was some poison or venom or something he could get out of his flesh to make the blinding pain stop, and he'd watched the water wash it away with a relief he now realized came from concealment of imperfection or failure. The pain didn't stop when the cold water turned his hand numb, but it stopped bleeding. He'd finished shucking the rest of the corn his mother needed, taken it inside to set it on the kitchen counter, and sprayed Bactine on his hand in the bathroom. By the time his mother saw it, his hand was splotchy red and covered in tiny scabs. He told her he fell down in the driveway and scraped it. Clumsiness was somehow preferable to the worm, and as a child Reginald had not consciously known why. It had been a lie told from instinct.

As an adult, he understood: Falling down was normal for kids growing up out in the country on the side of a mountain. At worst it meant he'd been playing rough, a display of enthusiastic physicality. Getting stung by a corn worm, on the other hand, would somehow be seen as failing one of the nonstop tests of mountain living, a sign of weakness. What kind of a man could he grow into if he couldn't shuck corn?

Reginald shook his head at the memory, at the kid he'd been then, totally unaware of a wider world just beyond the reach of his day-to-day life, hinted at on special trips to malls in the towns and cities an hour or two away.

He walked over to the sink, opened the cabinet, took out the reeking Styrofoam and plastic packaging of chicken his mother had opened and cooked some days ago, and carried it out the back door. After he dumped it in the trash can—the new rubber kind, not the old metal ones he expected— he walked over to the garden, unzipped his fly, and pissed on the first corn stalk in his dead mother's garden.

Fuck letting it go.

As he did so, he noticed the gap in the woods at the back of the yard and the path worn into the trees, the one leading up to Moriah Bald. The mouth of the trail up the mountain wasn't a worked thing, nothing intentional. It was a cavity in the line of trees and old prickle bushes and a row of wild blackberries sheltering beneath the canopy, not quite in the sun and not quite out of it. The trail itself was just old, worn dirt, packed hard by boots and the bare feet of children, the hooves of deer, and countless rainstorms. Parts of it were so steep the rocks more or less had to be climbed as a staircase. His parents had always warned him away from trying to reach the top on his own as a small child.

And now that path stood there, a tongue hanging from an open mouth in the forest, and Reginald felt the slightest tingling of an urge to climb inside and be swallowed whole.

The wind shifted, and for just a moment he'd have sworn he heard the music again, not the radio this time, but being played by people at some great distance. Like the radio, though, this music was old-fashioned, harsh and tinny and in a minor key. The very first thing that crossed his mind to use as a comparison was the sound of someone passing by, windows down, radio blasting country music, in the middle of the night when he was a child. But it didn't come from the road on the other side of the house, down the street, at the end of the neighborhood where he once played and dug in the dirt and stared at the stars. It came from the woods—no, perhaps even from *beyond* the woods—as though music from some next-door universe had leaked across a place where the boundaries between worlds had worn a little thin.

Come to think of it, maybe it *was* the same song he'd heard coming from a radio.

The wind shifted, and he could almost make out words. He found himself turning his head this way and that, trying to cast a net in which to capture the faint tones and shouted whispers just beyond his perception, and for a moment he thought perhaps he'd heard a shred of proper lyrics sung in a high and haunting tenor:

The woods did part and the

The wind shifted again and that tiny thread of sound went with it.

Three or four silent heartbeats later, Reginald realized he was standing in the yard with his dick in his hand. He shook off the last drop, zipped up, and groaned aloud when the doorbell rang inside the house.

Reginald walked back through the kitchen, back out into the living room, and reached the front door just as the bell rang a second time. He glanced out the middle of the diamond-shaped windows in the door and saw a white, 30-ish redhead with her hair in a ponytail and pronounced freckles peeking around the jade green mask she wore to match her cardigan. Beside her stood a 30-ish Asian man in a grey tee shirt and a bright blue hoodie and a black mask with a sports equipment logo on it. Reginald did a double take. The man looked *so* familiar, even with half his face concealed. Reginald just knew he'd seen those eyes before.

Reginald pulled the mask from his own coat pocket. He hadn't even managed to take his jacket off yet, and here came the welcome wagon. *Best to get it over with.* He opened the front door and realized the man and woman stood a little way apart from each other: only a few inches but farther than he'd have expected from a couple.

They all stood looking at one another through the glass in the storm door. Finally the woman spoke. "Hi, I'm Kate Spangler." She held one hand flat against her own chest as she introduced herself, then gestured over her right shoulder with her thumb. It had the overdone, too-animated air of stage acting. She added, pointing, "Number 14, just down the street. Middle of the right side." She looked back, then turned to face Reginald again. "Well, your left, I guess." Then she laughed, a start-high-and-descend chuckle completely incongruous to the moment and to what she said.

Reginald tried to make his eyes smile a little. "A pleasure. I'm Reginald Voth."

The man nodded, started to offer his hand to shake, realized the door was still closed, then slid it into his hip pocket. "Good to meet you, Reg." He pronounced it like *edge*. "I'm Lewis Gwan. Number 11, across from Kate."

Reginald looked past them at the row of houses on each side, then back to Lewis. "Reginald," he corrected. Then, "Good to meet you, Lewis. How can I help y'all?"

Kate had a ready answer with no hesitation. "We wanted to come by and express our condolences on the death of your mother." She ducked her head in polite sympathy. "I can't imagine how difficult this is for you, and if there's anything I can do to help, please don't hesitate to ask."

Lewis was less confident. "Yeah. What Kate said. Same here. If you need anything, just let me know."

"I'll look you up and send a friend request," Kate went on. "No pressure, it's just so you've got a ready way to message us any time. I'll get a chat going with Lewis and you and me in case you need anything right away. And I'll send you links to the neighborhood on OneDoorDown so you can get added there and start seeing announcements."

Reginald batted his lashes at her. "We have a neighborhood? On OneDoorDown? With announcements?"

Kate gestured at him as if to say *you'll catch up*. "Yeah. I mean, it's pretty low-traffic, but it's good to be plugged in. Like, if one of us wants to have lunch out in the greenspace and wants company, or if they want it to themselves. You know, different ones of us have, um, different comfort levels right now, which is very understandable. Anyway, we'll get you all hooked up."

Reginald shook his head at her. "Sorry, Kate, but I'm not planning to live here forever. I'm just planning to take care of getting this house sold and then I'm going right back home."

The sound of a plate shattering in the kitchen made all three of them jump, and Reginald let out a reflexive, "What the *FUCK!*" He turned away from the still-closed storm door, walking to the doorway into the kitchen. When the storm door opened and Kate stepped in, Reginald looked back over his shoulder.

"Are you alright?" Her eyes were narrowed in wary concern and yet, in the dim light, they glowed emerald green.

"Oh, well, sure," Reginald sighed. "I'm fine, but the plate probably won't make it."

Lewis lingered in the doorway behind her, holding the door open but not quite stepping in.

Reginald waved at both of them. "We're all wearing masks, so fine, come in. Or maybe, I don't know, stop by later. I need to clean this up."

Kate waved a hand at him. "Oh, of course, of course. Here, let us help, and then we can connect online." Kate looked over Reginald's shoulder at the kitchen. "More than just a plate," she said, voice low.

She was right, of course. All five plates in the dryer and two coffee cups on the mat beside it had exploded. The biggest chunks were no larger than a pea. Mostly they'd been turned to dust. It looked like someone had sprayed them—and only them—with machine gun fire and managed to leave the rest of the kitchen untouched.

Reginald opened a pantry and pulled out the broom and dustpan, right where his mother had kept them for fifty years. "Jesus Christ," he said under his breath, and didn't know himself whether it was at the destruction or at the muscle memory of knowing where to reach for the cleaning supplies. "What in the *actual* fuck, you know?"

Lewis produced a chuckle at Reginald's outcry, and though Kate seemed a little more prim she seemed to stifle something as well. As Reginald started sweeping, she reached into the still-open pantry and pulled out a handheld vacuum. "You get the big pieces and I'll clean up the dust and we'll be done in no time." She tried to sound upbeat. "And after that we can talk about online. You'll want to be able to get in touch if you need anything. And OneDoorDown *is* really useful."

Reginald sighed a little. "Well, I certainly appreciate the sentiment. But I'm really not staying."

The two of them cleaned in silence for a couple of minutes, Lewis standing awkwardly at the edge of the kitchen entrance. "How did it happen?" He vaguely gestured at the rest of the kitchen with his elbow, hands in his pockets.

Kate waved it off. "Old china is very sensitive to temperature changes. If you turned the heat on when you came in, and the vent was pointed just the right way, and…" She shrugged and started vacuuming.

Bullshit. But Reginald said nothing, too rattled to speak for once in his life. As they got up the last of it, he turned to Kate. "Thanks."

She smiled at him, and Reginald realized her eyes smiled effortlessly, an understated note of sincerity with a little sadness behind it. He appreciated her help, and the boy in him who'd cowered at the tiniest accidents, the most minuscule chip in an old cup, a single ripped seam, tried to hide under the blankets in the back of his brain while he held it together out front. "Oh, it's nothing," she said. "I'm sorry that happened." She gave another of those chuckles. "Maybe the dishes don't like doorbells." Again, it made no sense; again, she laughed just once: *ha.*

Reginald produced a muted noise of polite amusement. "Maybe not. And as for OneDoorDown…I'll see. In the meantime, maybe I could just give y'all my number and you could text?"

Lewis and Kate both produced phones. With stops and starts they each texted Reginald and Reginald texted each of them. A few seconds later they were both in his contacts, and he in theirs. Lewis's and Reginald's phones dinged with a text from Kate: *Welcome to the neighborhood—it'll feel like home in no time.*

Reginald's and Kate's phones dinged a second time with a response from Lewis: *sorry the welcome wagon smashed up the place lol*

Reginald noted with some surprise they both seemed to be smiling genuinely at each other after reading. "You two must be pretty good friends, I take it?" He lifted his eyebrows at them.

Kate looked at Reginald, took a second, and then laughed again. This time it was higher and more natural. "Oh, Lewis and I are BFFs," Kate said. "He's my bestie with the testes."

Lewis flushed pink. "Oh, Jesus. That kid."

Reginald found himself smiling with genuine amusement. "Is that one you picked up from Ham?"

"You've met him?" Lewis tried to grimace and smile at the same time, his cheeks doing complex gymnastics behind his mask. "I like him, but he's got a catchphrase for everything. I don't like *that* one."

"Well…" Reginald started to say *you know how kids are*, or something like it, and then stopped. He was tired, and he wanted a cigarette, and he hated platitudes and small talk. "Thanks for stopping by."

Kate looked away from her phone. "Don't forget that friend request. And I just messaged you the link to join the neighborhood on OneDoorDown. And remember, anything you need, you just ask." She started to walk to the front door but stopped and turned back to Reginald. "By the way, what do you do for a living?"

Reginald didn't miss a beat. "I run coke for the Colombian cartel. You?"

Kate blinked in surprise, but now Lewis laughed, an easy, low chuckle, much more genuine and relaxed than before. He had a deep voice and it went deeper when he liked something.

The penny dropped, and Reginald realized from where he knew Lewis. In his head, he said the name again, but with quotes around it: *Oh, "Lewis." Of course I didn't recognize him. He's wearing clothes.* Then he grinned like the cat that ate the caged canary.

"OK, you got me for just a second. Nice. No, I was wondering if by chance you're a Maker or anything. Johnny's always looking for chances to cross-promote."

Reginald shook his head slightly. "I'm afraid I have no idea—oh. Like, selling stuff online? No, sorry, I only sell myself." He very carefully did not let himself look at Lewis. "I slice myself up into one-hour chunks spent doing medical transcription and trade them to my employer in return for the short end of the stick." Reginald paused a moment. "Well, I muddled my metaphors. But anyway, no, I don't. And thanks."

Kate leaned an inch closer as though dredging a confession from deep within the well of her most secret self. "Sure thing. I work in tech-- Assistant VP of Acquisitions for CloudHome Telecom. I'm why you see the little signs in half the yards around here." She grinned and bent her head forward slightly as if accepting applause. "But my husband is an *influencer.*" Reginald couldn't help hearing a touch of something in the neighborhood of sarcasm escaping her attempt to squelch it. "He goes by Johnny Spangles. Mostly, you know, wood art and landscaping content, but sometimes he gets into baking when the mood strikes." She added the next part in the tones of a car salesman from a TV ad. "New content every Tuesday, Wednesday, Thursday, and Saturday! Look him up!"

Reginald managed not to snort at her, but it took effort. "I'll do that. I guess y'all must have pretty good Internet?" He looked around at the interior of his mother's house. Its most recent technological innovation was probably a slow cooker from the 1980's. "One reason to get back home. I'm sure my mother has whatever is the cheapest and worst Internet service possible, if she has any at all."

Kate winked at him as she replied. "Oh, we can get you fixed for that. I had the whole neighborhood wired for fiber. I can get you two gigs for fifty bucks a month."

Reginald was sure that was supposed to impress him, but honestly he didn't know what it meant. "Good to know," he said. Then, walking towards the door himself, he nodded at them. "Thanks again. But I really need to get unpacked and find out the details on the funeral."

"Sure," Lewis replied, "we'll leave you to it." This time he offered his hand and Reginald, much to his own surprise, took it.

"It's a pleasure to meet you, Lewis." Reginald turned and saw Kate offering her elbow for a tap instead. He returned the gesture. "And you, Kate."

She nodded at him as they tapped. "The pleasure is all ours, Reginald." For just a second, her earlier sincerity flickered like a light when someone brushes the switch by accident. Kate nodded in the direction of the kitchen. "If any of your mother's china is valuable, I'm sure Johnny knows the right people to flip it online. He could do a whole series of videos on reselling vintage. I could make you a very attractive offer. I've always assumed your mother had a lot of stuff like that: she's been here forever and she never has a yard sale. I could come back tomorrow, take a look around the place, we could negotiate a package deal on anything that catches my eye. It would make your life a lot easier."

The shift from helpful neighbor to corporate shark had been so quick, it left Reginald too jarred to reply. The three of them stood in silence for a moment, then she put the helpful neighbor mask back on and spoke with what registered as genuine kindness. "And really, no matter how long or short you're here, welcome to the neighborhood."

Lewis and Kate said their goodbyes once more and shuffled out. Reginald closed the door behind them, very softly, with a slight click. *Maybe it would be good to have friends in the neighborhood.* Reginald glanced over at Bobby's house catty-corner to his mother's. *Or at least allies.* Reginald favored the world outside his mother's home with a small and bitter smirk. *And if I sold everything to the grabby neighbor down the street, it would sure get Bobby's goat.*

Reginald pulled his phone back out, flipped on its flashlight, and began taking slow, quiet steps around the house. *But first, I will goddamned find whatever broke those plates, and I will find that fucking radio.*

Forty minutes later, he gave up. The house was empty. The staticky music from earlier was gone. The batteries in the radio must finally have died. The worst things he'd found were his mother's unmade bed, the dirty laundry in a hamper beside it, and thirty years of *Southern Living* magazines inexplicably shoved between the mattress and box springs.

CHAPTER FIVE – THIS PLACE IS FUCKING HAUNTED

Reginald couldn't bring himself to sleep in his mother's bed—not when her pillow would still smell of her hairspray, her Oil of Olay, her gray and weathered skin. Every time he looked at it he saw his dead mother in her casket, then he saw her frozen in the light at the foot of his bed—the one back home, in his trailer, a mere 37 miles and a lifetime from here. Standing in the bedroom had nearly made him whimper aloud and he wasn't even sure why.

He had stripped her bed that afternoon after searching the place to try to find what had shattered the plates. He imagined himself opening a closet door and being scared silly by a jumping cat, some sort of beloved Hammer Horror slapstick like that, but his mother had never been one for indoor animals. *They carry filth*, she'd always said. In her house—*this* house—they had been forbidden to pet the dogs or the barn cats without immediately washing their hands the moment they went inside. His mother never called it "petting the dog," for that matter. She always called it "handling the animals." He'd walk in the back door and there she'd be, facing away from him, not even willing to turn around and look at him. *Have you been handling the animals?* She'd be standing at the sink so of course she could see out into the backyard where he'd been playing with whichever dog they had at the time. She knew the answer, she just wanted to have a question to ask in a hostile tone.

They'd had a lot of dogs in his childhood. At the time, up here, they were the only house for a half mile in either direction. The Voths had a reputation, though, as a house where an animal could end up and it wouldn't starve. Maybe a dozen times throughout his childhood and teen years a dog had shown up out of nowhere in their yard. They knew it had been dumped there by someone who didn't want it or couldn't care for it. The industrial base had dried up two or more decades before, even then, and a lot of people were eking out a living by the skin of their teeth, nothing more than subsistence farmers eating what they could grow and doing odd jobs here and there for a little cash under the table. Reginald hadn't realized it at the time, but there were a small but non-zero number of people there, as late as the 1980's, who'd essentially been living the same lives as their ancestors a century before. The main difference was they had an electric refrigerator and an electric stove, and the ancestral shack had an aerial television antenna bolted onto the end of the roof.

For families in such dire straits, hunting was a major source of survival nutrition, and hunting meant dogs. Dogs meant puppies, and sometimes there were too many puppies for the mother to nurse, or sometimes the puppies grew up into dogs who wouldn't hunt. There were a lot of ends to that circumstance, and one was to dump the animal in a stranger's yard and hope for the best. It was a way for people to tell themselves, as they did about so many things, that they'd left matters "in the hands of the Lord," as Reginald's father—who was not a Voth—used to say before he exited the stage. From this, the family had gained six or seven dogs over the years and as many cats. The cats would form semi-feral colonies in the barn and the woods beyond it. Reginald's mother hadn't needed a mousetrap so much as once in his youth. They kept the garden and the crawlspace free of vermin and seemed to live contented lives free of the need for any human to take routine care of them. They were as happy as any other feline to get the occasional scritch behind the ear, however.

Dogs, on the other hand, needed to be fed and played with, and that always fell to Bobby and then to Reginald. Bobby imagined he'd teach these dogs to hunt, trying to coax them into the woods with him from time to time. Sometimes they went with him, more often not.

Reginald had no such expectations, laid no such obligations on them. He just wanted a dog to play with and to lick his face, and he got that every time. Inside his parents'—and then his mother's—home, Reginald felt oppressed, like he was trying to breathe smoke he couldn't see. Outside, in the yard, playing catch with dogs named after one TV character or another— Kitt and Rockford and Gilligan—Reginald felt a little taste of freedom. At the very least he'd see blue sky above him, and that was better than the ceilings of his mother's home.

Other than her, his brother, and the dogs, there had been precious few people around. There were the Kings around the other side of Moriah Bald, either a thirty-minute walk through the woods or a three-mile drive around the other side of the ridge on an old, single-lane road the state had never bothered to pave. There were Blandings and Thomases a half mile or more in either direction, but they were kin to each other and engaged in a long-running feud. He remembered having to come inside once, when he was six, because they were shooting at each other from woods at opposite ends of the straight-away out front. He'd cried because his mother wouldn't let the dog come inside with him. The dog was fine, but it broke Reginald's heart to watch Rockford hunker down under the front of his mother's old station wagon and hear rifles in the distance.

Reginald emerged from a long, winding jaunt into that stream-of-consciousness of remembrance to find he was still standing in his mother's bedroom maybe fifteen minutes after he'd walked into it.

No, no cats leaping from closets or knocking over plates.

Still, he never found anything, so he decided to unpack and start taking pictures.

He stripped his mother's bed and started laundering the linens from it, then managed to get the door to the "spare" bedroom open—in practice, from as early as Reginald could remember the "guest" room had been his father's. He and Reginald's mother had slept apart. Old shopping bags stuffed full of discarded clothing and boxes filled with magazines had been shoved, tossed, and piled so haphazardly in the room they at first had held it shut. Reginald found the closet was still bulging with his father's three suits and half the shirts in creation. Reginald was not surprised his mother had never gotten rid of them. Personally, he would have held a giant yard sale or given them away, anything other than leaving his absent father's closets exactly as he'd left them. Instead, she'd gone to court to give his name away, and to have Reginald's changed as well. "We're back to being Voths," she'd said, and though it took a lot of time and some money she was able to have that reflected in the eyes of the law. He had to admit he admired that.

Reginald made a little bet with himself, opened one of the small drawers at the corner of the enormous old oak dresser against the wall, and won the bet: the sock drawer was still crammed full of his father's socks. *Welcome to hoarder's paradise.* He shuddered. He liked keepsakes, to be sure, but he'd made an effort to keep his little trailer free of clutter. He told himself he was doing it to avoid his mother's hoarding, which, to be honest, wasn't bad enough to rise to the level of that term but had always been one of those *things* kids watch for as their parents age: one of the many slippery slopes she trod up and down on her way to senescence. Still, he wondered from time to time how much of his own unfettered lifestyle was a conscious choice not to collect *things* but *people*, which is what he told himself explained his long string of toxic relationships and countless fuckbuddies, and how much of it was an attempt to make sure he could cut his losses and run without leaving too much behind. His father had traveled light when he left, and now a part of

Reginald nodded in recognition of some previously unrealized family resemblance.

At first he thought sleeping in his own father's bed might be a little less weird and quickly found he'd been wrong.

Reginald backed out of the room, stepped two feet down the gallery encircling the staircase from the ground floor, and put his hand on the doorknob of his own bedroom, the one where he slept as a child, the one in which he'd grown from a little boy into the tall, spider-thin man who stood here, now, wondering why the fuck he hadn't just stayed at the trailer for all this. *So it's an hour each way? Who fucking cares? And the neighbors are already trying to hook me up to their Internet plan and get me on their fucking social media.*

Reginald turned the knob, opened the door, and looked in on his teenaged bedroom. It remained exactly as he'd left it the last time he moved out—the start of his third year of college, the time he'd told himself all the way down the long drive, and all the way down the mountain after it, that he'd never spend another night in this house.

In the mirror on the nightstand, Reginald saw an old man standing where he should be.

It took him a moment to realize it was *himself*, nothing special, just *him* as he was *now*.

For half a second he'd have sworn he saw the swirl of a neon-bright pastel housecoat as though someone behind him in the hallway had spun to run away.

He thought of the housecoat his mother wore in his vision of her, took two deep breaths, and closed the door to his childhood bedroom. "I said I'd never spend another night here and I am keeping that promise, mama." He spoke it aloud, and if his voice shook then he told himself it was better than screaming.

Reginald turned, walked to the other end of the gallery, and half-jogged down the stairs with his suitcase in his hand. He put on his jacket by the front door, opened it, went out, pulled it shut behind him, and didn't even bother to lock it. *If any of these misplaced suburbanites want her shit badly enough to walk in and steal it, they can have it.* He could drive home and be in his own bed by shortly after midnight. Those linens in the wash could take care of themselves until the morning. He wasn't even letting himself think about what he'd just seen upstairs, ready explanations trying to push their way onto the stage of his mind: a trick of the light, the way things look in an unfamiliar mirror, the carpet, the wallpaper, who even knows. Reginald told himself he was leaving because he wanted the *continuity* of going back to his own home for the night rather than shacking up in his mother's house. Reginald hated the way people assumed he would now move into his mother's home and take up life there. *My life is not a holding pattern, some eccentric orbit guiding me to return.* Yeah, that was the ticket. He just needed to get pissed off about something mundane and then he could forget all the things that were not.

He got into the driver's seat of the Tracker, hesitated before cranking it, and instead pulled his phone from his other pocket. Clark's was still the last text he'd received, and he popped off a quick reply. *Any chance you're game to come over?*

Having sent it, he gave the dim and ancient house one last look, barely illuminated by the light over the stairs, and promptly fumbled the keys in his hand as he tried to start the car. They clattered to the floorboards.

When he sat back up from fishing them out from under his own feet, every light in the house blazed at full brightness.

A figure looked down at the driveway from upstairs.

The silhouette of his mother stood, clear as day, on the other side of the sheer curtains in her bedroom.

Reginald stared at the figure up there, waiting for it to move, for the curtain to shift and reveal it as some optical illusion, anything. Hell, he waited for it to come screaming through the wall and swoop down on him like some specter out of an old movie.

Instead, it just stared back at him. Even in silhouette, even with the sheers between them and the angle tight, Reginald *knew* she was staring at him just as intently as he at her.

And he knew who she was, too: *her.*

Mother.

Reginald slowly, as though afraid to startle his dead mother's ghost, lifted the keyring and slid the car key into the Tracker's ignition.

He turned it.

Nothing.

He hadn't left the lights on. His battery had just been replaced two months before. But now it was dead as a doornail, so dead he couldn't even get a *click* when he tried to crank it.

Be that way, he thought. He swallowed with a dry mouth, disengaged the parking brake, pushed in the clutch, and pumped the brakes as hard as he possibly could while he rolled the car backwards out of his mother's driveway and into the little street, cranking the wheel so that he got the car's ass to swing around so its nose pointed down the slope. He let off the brake, threw the shifter into first, and prayed to whatever might be listening—up there, down there, around here, *anywhere*—that the Tracker would start rolling under its own weight. *I'd give anything for someone to push. I need a boyfriend for emergencies.*

A long second went by as the Tracker shuddered, debating whether to roll forward.

Reginald glanced up at the house. If anything, the lights inside had gotten brighter.

The figure in the window still stared at him.

The Tracker creaked, long and low, and moved a couple of inches.

Reginald watched over his shoulder as the window of what had been his mother's bedroom slid into view. The grim silhouette of shadow beyond the sheers, standing impossibly in what he knew to be an empty room in what he knew to be an empty house, took a step back and dashed to the side.

Oh fuck she is coming after me, and with that thought he clapped his right hand over his own mouth to stifle whatever sound he almost made.

The car lurched forward.

The axle squealed, slow and high, a shriek of agonized metal as the car began to roll.

Reginald saw the silhouette return, this time in the house's living room.

The front door of his dead and damned mother's house began to open, light erupting out from around its edges, a hellish glow slicing open the night as though every lamp and bulb in the place blazed brighter than they ever had.

Gravity took hold.

The car rolled two feet, then five, then began to coast downhill.

Reginald popped the clutch out.

The silhouette stood framed in the open front doorway, the light behind it brighter like a spotlight, iron-smelting white, the light of the sun through a magnifying glass as the ant beneath it starts to sizzle.

The engine coughed, sputtered, coughed again, and screamed into life—then immediately backfired, loud as a rifle blast, and Reginald finally let out the combination of roar and moan he'd been trying to hold in. The radio lit up and for two seconds a fiddle blasted out of the car's speakers at him.

The car shook, coughed again, and stalled.

His mother's storm door began to open as the silhouette pushed.

Lights went on in a house down the street. Reginald cranked the engine, cranked and cranked and cranked, but nothing, the motor just wouldn't catch, *couldn't* turn over, and as that form of shadow—ridiculous, the shape of an elderly woman in a housecoat grown too big for her as she shrank away inside it, and as menacing as any elder demon from an old Italian horror film—stepped down onto his mother's front porch. It lifted a hand and it *beckoned* him. Reginald could practically hear his mother's voice as it did so: *come home, son, come back forever, it's time.*

Reginald stared at it in his side mirror, gaped at the spirit he *knew* looked directly at him in return though it had no face, no eyes, no features other than its outline. He sat there, mouth open, face twisted, as tears welled up and mercifully blurred his vision.

The malevolent spirit of Dorothea Voth—Reginald had no doubt, could not have fathomed another explanation had he taken time to try— descended from the porch onto the top of the little stone staircase leading to her quaint front walk.

Reginald, eyes squeezed shut, clapped both hands over his mouth to hold in a wail of desperation and terror. A feeling—an emotional assault he felt as a physical sensation he could not have named and did not ever want to feel again—pushed up from somewhere deep inside, squeezing his heart like a giant, cold, electrical hand. He had to go, he had to *leave,* he had to *get away.* He swiped at his eyes and opened them again, ready to run from the car, to leave his beloved 1993 Geo Tracker sitting in a street that should never have existed and flee this place on foot if he had to, and when he looked in the mirror one final time it hit him like a slap across the face that the spirit— *his mother*—had vanished.

The house sat as it had before: brooding on its haunches in the shadow of Moriah Bald.

Reginald could see a single light, the one hanging in the gallery on the second floor, its dim glow illuminating the stairs and a little of the front hall.

The front door was closed.

Lewis knocked on the glass on the passenger window of the Tracker and Reginald screamed at the top of his goddamned lungs, startling them both.

"Are you okay?" Lewis's voice sounded muffled on the other side of the glass. "I thought I heard a—"

Reginald climbed out of the Tracker and leaned against the driver's side. Lewis came around the car to talk to him, sandals slapping against his feet as he walked.

"Uh… Reginald, what's going on?"

Reginald lifted his head and rubbed his eyes, then actually looked at Lewis for the first time. Lewis wore a pair of flannel pajama bottoms, thick socks, and sandals with a running shoe logo on the wide band across the tops of his feet. He had no shirt on, and even this flustered Reginald couldn't help but catalogue Lewis's slim, articulated musculature there by the light of the moon, the stars, and a circle of halogen streetlamps. Thick veins stood out where they ran up and across his biceps, and his collarbones formed a perfect V.

Lewis looked at Reginald's expression, then down at himself, and made a little sound of embarrassment. "Sorry, I, just, I heard screaming and then I thought I heard a gunshot."

Reginald looked up from Lewis's crotch to meet his eyes and said, "I need to tell you something, and I realize you're going to think differently of me after, probably negatively, and so I'd like to preface it by saying you're really sweet and I genuinely appreciate you and Katie stopping by today even if I was, I don't know, a little snide."

Lewis didn't grin at him, nor smile, nor laugh. He nodded once. "Alright. You're welcome. Now tell me what you need to say."

Reginald liked that: straight to business. "My mother's house is haunted. Specifically by my mother. And I think she wants to trap me there. Or, at least, I think she's angry that I don't want to *stay*. Earlier when I said I wasn't going to live there, that's when her plates shattered for no reason. And just now I decided to drive back home and spend the night there instead of here, and… oh, never mind. I sound like a total basket case." Reginald took half a dozen steps away from the car, towards the picnic tables in the greenspace at the center of the neighborhood. He stopped and turned back to face Lewis.

Lewis took that in, turned his gaze from Reginald's face to the house at the end of the street, up and around and all over it, then back to Reginald. "Alright."

Reginald held his breath a moment and then pushed it out in a gust. "Okay, see? You think I'm crazy." He stood up straighter, patting his pockets for his keys and then making a little *oh fuck* as he realized they were still in the ignition of the Tracker. "I'll just… well, I'm…" He paused, cleared his throat, and tried again. "I'm just going to see if my car will start now, and if it will, I'm going to drive back to my home, back to my little life, and never come back here again because that—*that*—"and here he pointed at his car, then at his mother's house— "is the *only* reasonable reaction to what I just experienced. Sorry to say hello and goodbye in the same day, Lewis. For the record," he cleared his throat again, "I know who you are, and what you do for a living, and I *love* your work." Reginald blushed hard as he said the last part of it, his cheeks flushing like they hadn't in many years.

Lewis ducked his head. "Ah. So, you know…"

Reginald waved a hand. "Oh, Lewis, don't kid. I'm doing it enough for both of us. Anyway, I'm a premium subscriber. There was a period of time when LewsTube was my homepage on my computer at the house. Before you moved over to InterFans."

Lewis grinned a little despite himself and looked up at Reginald. "Really?"

Reginald shrugged. "*Fuck* yes. Let me tell you, you may not technically have been there for it but we've gotten off together more times than I can count. Anyway, have a nice life. Don't let my mother's ghost take over the neighborhood, she probably pushed people around enough when she was in the world of the living. And if by chance you ever have the burning urge to fuck a slightly older man who knows you're out of his league, and you can't hunt down that text from earlier with Kate, you can find my number next to the nearest truck stop glory hole. It was lovely meeting you, Lewis. I hope my mother's ghost doesn't eat you alive." Reginald started walking toward the Tracker where it sat, door open, dome light on, warning chime ringing to tell him the keys remained in it. He fished out a Virginia Slim from his jacket pocket as he went, stopping at the door to his car to light the cigarette behind his hands.

Lewis walked to within a few feet of him as he did so and said, "Look, Reginald… well, first, thank you for your support." He didn't stop when Reginald produced something between a laugh and a snort. "I mean that. I don't… well, I hear a lot of feedback, but I…"

Reginald turned, taking a long drag, then grasped the cigarette between his first two fingers and exhaled upwards at an angle. "But it's mostly horny old goats like me wondering how much it would cost if next time you'd say their name before you unload or something like that?"

"Oh, those are the nice ones." Lewis smiled, but there was anger in it. "The rest of them are racists."

Reginald felt real sympathy, and it showed in the sudden sag of his shoulders and the way his features unwound. "I'm sorry that happens. I guess that's a part of the long tradition of how queer people get handled rough: a lot of times people want to tell us they hate us after they fuck us so they can pretend it wasn't their idea." Reginald took another drag and gestured at Lewis's crotch as he talked around the smoke on its way out. "I'm guessing a lot of those guys are jealous."

Lewis grinned. "Look, I'd like to hear what happened. And you seem pretty shaken up. You should calm down before you drive."

Reginald shook his head. "No, I've already imposed on you. And probably woke up half this neighborhood." He looked around: no other lights had come on, but that backfire had been *loud*.

Lewis waved a hand to dismiss him. "I won't take no for an answer. Come in and let's have a cup of coffee. It'll wake you up for your drive home."

Reginald gave Lewis a look of open longing mixed with some sort of regret. "You are very kind. Too kind, probably. Kinder than I deserve, anyway." He folded himself into the driver's seat. "I'm just going to go home, sleep in my own bed, and come back in the daylight. This is all a lot. I need to get home and let you get some rest."

Lewis stepped back from the car, and Reginald thought perhaps he saw real compassion on Lewis' face. It looked a lot like sorrow. "You're sweet, Lewis. Don't sit up all night waiting for my mother to come out and play, though."

Lewis smiled faintly at Reginald and lifted a hand for an awkward wave. "It was nice meeting you, Reginald."

Reginald quirked up the corners of his mouth. "You're too kind. God*damn* you have the most beautiful eyes. Oh," he added, "And you might have to push my car."

Reginald cranked it and the engine started right up. He laid his arms atop the wheel and rested his forehead against them, suddenly exhausted by all of this. Thirty seconds of weird—no, *terrifying*—shit in his mother's house and he felt completely drained of all energy.

Now Lewis chuckled and spoke over the sputter-purr of the engine. "You *sure* you're okay to drive?"

Reginald looked up again and shook his head. "Never. How'd a guy as pretty as you wind up so nice, anyway? Seems monumentally unfair." He put the car in first and eased off the clutch to pull away before he stopped himself.

Trying for more, trying for *anything*, that would be stupid. The road to hell is just as often paved in romantic fantasies as it is good intentions.

The road back down the mountain was utterly dark and silent. Reginald turned off the radio and rolled down the window and listened to the air as the Tracker sliced it. He downshifted for the long final descent back to the main road and was surprised to see lights on at Ye Olde Camper Cafe at this hour. When he reached the stop sign beside it, he realized the cafe wasn't open, it just had lights on to keep the place illuminated. *Probably all the security*

system a place needs in the middle of nowhere like this. The thought the place needed any security at all, but only this much, was a tiny slice of comforting naiveté.

The lights were string lights crisscrossing the umbrellas over the picnic tables to form a whimsical zigzag pattern in the air. It was lovely. Reginald found himself surprised at the straightforward appreciation he felt, no cynical edge whatsoever digging into his enjoyment as he savored it. He thought it would be a nice place to catch his breath, so he turned from the road into the parking lot of the cafe, parked the Tracker, killed the motor, and climbed out.

He sat down atop one of the picnic tables, his boots on the bench, his ass on the tabletop, with his back to the strings of fairy lights. Looking up, with the lights behind him, he had almost as good a view of the stars as he would have had from the top of Moriah Bald. The autumn sky was perfectly black, studded with gold and silver sequins of stars. He wished he had binoculars or a telescope. The moon loomed above him, a ring around it. In colder weather he'd have counted the stars inside it to see how many days before it snowed, but it was too early in the season for that just yet. The sky was peaceful, a few thousand benevolent spectators watching the world slumber beneath it. Reginald smiled at the thought. He usually found the idea of guardian angels or of ancestors keeping tabs from on high, that sort of thing, to be horrible. He hated the idea of being unable to leave those people behind, live one's life in private, not constantly look over one's shoulder, but in this one moment it felt good to imagine the stars standing watch while everyone else took a breather. It felt *right* somehow.

Reginald's phone vibrated in his pocket and he ignored it. *Clark can find somebody else to fuck tonight*, he thought. He was flattered, mind you, but he just didn't need that right now.

The phone buzzed again to tell him he had a voicemail.

Ten seconds later it rang again.

He pressed a button without even taking it out of his pocket, sending it to voicemail.

Ten seconds later, it rang a third time.

Frowning, Reginald yanked the phone out of his pocket and looked at the face of it.

It wasn't Clark. It was Lewis. Reginald raised one eyebrow and decided to have some fun with this.

"If you're calling about my car's extended warranty, I'd like to know what time you think it is," he said as he answered.

"Oh, uh…" Lewis hesitated on the other end. "Oh, man, I am so sorry. I didn't mean to bother you. I just thought, uh, maybe you'd want to talk while you drove, you know, to help you stay awake? Um, sorry. I'll, yeah, sorry, I'll let you get back to driving."

Reginald felt himself blush so hard his face heated like a furnace. "Oh, Jesus, sorry. I'm just fucking with you. I knew it was you. I just, I don't know, I wanted to seem clever."

They both sat there in silence for a moment, and then Lewis laughed aloud. "Okay. You got me. A point to the visiting team."

Reginald waited a moment and then faced the worst thing he could immediately imagine. "You called three times. Is my mother back?"

"No, no, fuck no." Lewis hesitated. "This will sound really anxiety riddled, I admit, but when you didn't answer the first time I thought, shit, what if he's had an accident? Or something? That's stupid of me, I know. I just got worried."

Reginald drew a slow, shallow breath, then said, much more calmly, much more gently, "I appreciate you thinking of me. I actually stopped down at the cafe at the bottom of the mountain to just, I don't know, clear my head for a minute."

Lewis was quiet for a beat or two. "I love to go down there at night sometimes and just look at the sky. I mean, the coffee's great when they're open, too, but it's one of my favorite places to just be by myself but out in the world."

Reginald found himself smiling and he didn't even know why.

"That's exactly why I stopped."

"Look, Reginald, that offer still stands for you to come to my place, have some coffee, get ready for the drive."

"And tell you what happened?" Reginald heard himself grin as he said it, though.

"Mostly just the coffee." Lewis sounded like he was grinning, too. "Well, the coffee is a real and significant part of it, anyway.

Reginald thought about it for one drag, then a second, then dropped the cigarette on the gravel of the cafe lot, stepped down from the table, and crushed the butt under his boot. "Okay," he said. "Fine. If you're *making* me. But if this is a sex thing, you can just *ask*."

Lewis laughed good-naturedly, and Reginald felt a little pang of disappointment at the absence of a yes.

"Go ahead and park in my driveway when you get here. I'll meet you down there."

"Thanks."

Reginald hung up the call, put the phone in his pocket, stretched so that his shoulders and elbows popped, and climbed back into the Tracker. He nearly drove off right then. He wanted to, he knew that. And he *should* want to. *Just do it, just leave. You've done it before.* And so had his dad. It ran in the family.

To his own surprise, he pulled into Lewis's driveway and parked in front of the garage door.

Just a cup of coffee. I'll always wonder, if I don't.

CHAPTER SIX – LEWSTUBE

"Have you ever…" Lewis hesitated. "You know, seen stuff like that before?"

Reginald waved a hand as he sipped coffee. "No." One sip later he shrugged. "I mean, my family is chock full of stories of stuff like that happening. But it's always the dying who see the already-dead, come to think of it. I don't think I've ever heard one about someone who's died already coming back to visit folks who're supposed to stay alive for a while."

Reginald let out a little breath, a tiny huff of surprise. He hadn't intended to tell Lewis every detail of seeing his mother's dying form while he lay in bed the other night, but he had, just as soon as Lewis said to tell him everything. "Sorry," Reginald added. "But you did say to start at the beginning." He offered Lewis a wan little smile. "At any rate, I figured it was just, you know," and here Reginald fluttered a few fingers at the world beyond Lewis's slightly cold, pale grey kitchen, "acid flashbacks or something." Reginald shrugged at Lewis's surprised chuckle. "What? We all had our fun in the '90s, didn't we?"

Lewis grinned at him. "Sure, I had a hell of a time watching *Teletubbies*. Very trippy."

Reginald scowled at Lewis, but only half-sincerely. "You don't have to remind me that you're practically still a child and I'm a withered old prune.

I thought you asked me in to make me feel better."

Lewis laughed now, and Reginald watched the corners of his eyes crinkle, and the sparkle of amusement in his eyes, and said to himself *oh no you don't this whole place might as well be a very expensive cradle and this exceptionally hot young man does not need you creeping all over him, trying to rob it, but Jesus fucking a watermelon he is gorgeous those shoulders I would give anything to watch him strain while he*

Reginald cleared his throat and looked around. "You have a lovely home," he said, and in his mind's eye he clutched at the string of pearls he wore over an imagined housecoat, as prim as a church lady in front of company on Saturday night.

In truth, Reginald thought the house needed a little less magazine-spread and a little more, you know, mismatched tchotchkes from trips to Gatlinburg. The interiors of these new houses were all beiges and light gray, white accents here and there, smooth surfaces, generic artwork conveying no more objective meaning than a Rorschach test, empty vases, plastic fruit. They reminded Reginald of the houses he saw on those TV shows about people who let the hosts redesign their house and then decide whether to stay in it or sell it off. This one had an open floor plan, with a bar-height counter between the square kitchen and the six-top dining table where they sat. The open living room, dominated by an enormous television and tasteful black entertainment center beneath it, with a plush sectional sofa pointed at them, lay just behind Lewis's side of the table.

Reginald had grown up around people whose houses were packed willy-nilly with the detritus of long, small lives: the unskilled art of children, intricate woodworking by dead ancestors, snapshots, family bibles, half-finished crochet projects, mail left unopened until it didn't matter anymore. It had never occurred to Reginald, but many of the people in his family had grown up in a time when people had precious little, and few prospects of getting more, so they kept everything just in case it was useful later. They'd wrapped gifts in Sunday funnies from prior decades, lined garden beds with the same newspapers that provided their wrapping paper, stored onions in legs cut from old pantyhose, kept crows out of the corn by tying used pie tins to tall stakes so they'd flap and bang and sparkle in the wind on sunny spring and summer days.

Reginald suddenly snapped back to the here and now.

Lewis watched him, his eyes full of sympathy. "Thanks," he said, "but what happened *tonight?*"

"I was trying to decide where to sleep." Reginald fluttered his lips and then puckered them, annoyed with himself. "I'm sorry. It isn't that what happened didn't happen, or anything like that. Like, I have always been someone to listen to my instinct and to believe the evidence of my senses, so my reticence, if you'll forgive me, is not because I'm unsure what happened. It's just, I feel so silly whenever I try to figure out how to say it aloud."

Lewis flexed his arm as he lifted his coffee cup and Reginald found his eyes resting on the perfect curve of a well-maintained bicep.

"So just say it," Lewis said, and then he parted his lips and the coffee cup…

Reginald almost squeaked when he spoke. "I had decided to go back to my place rather than sleep here." He pointed, taking his eyes off of Lewis's face, Lewis's lips, Lewis's arm, to glance in the direction of Dorothea's house at the end of the block. "I mean, it's only an hour, big deal." Reginald recapped the car not starting, trying to get it to roll so he could pop the clutch, and his mother—he stumbled when he said it—emerging from the house in agonizingly slow pursuit. "And when it backfired, she was gone." Reginald shrugged lightly, deflating at how mundane it sounded when he said it aloud. "The end."

Lewis frowned a little as he asked, "How did she appear? What did she wear?"

"Her housecoat, I think. Or a nightgown? She was mostly, you know, backlit. I didn't exactly see details." He waited a moment before adding, "I know you think I'm crazy, but I saw it, and that's that."

Lewis shook his head at that and took another sip of coffee. "No, not at all. You saw a *gwisin*." He smiled a little at Reginald's blank expression. "Korean ghost." His expression grew more serious as he asked, very tentatively, "Were you and your mother very close?"

Reginald laughed so suddenly he startled both of them. "Oh, *fuck* no. I haven't been back here in twelve years. No exaggeration. We email every now and then." He caught himself. "Email*ed*."

Lewis frowned a little. "I'm sorry for your loss."

Reginald waved that off, too. "Don't be. I'm not." He could see Lewis didn't know exactly what to say to that, so he tried to let him off the hook. "I'm sorry. Our relationship was not good, and I don't really know yet what I'm going to feel now that she's gone. So far I seem to be doing a great job of fending off the dead by being a prick to the living." Reginald thought for a moment, coffee held halfway between the table and his mouth. "No, fuck that. I'm *not* sorry. I mean, it was not my intention to make you uncomfortable, but also don't feel obligated to fall back on platitudes or to handle me like the good china. I appreciate you saying that, I mean it, because it shows you're compassionate. Thank you. But also, don't worry about my feelings. They're too jumbled up at the moment for me to sort myself, much less anybody else have to deal with them."

Lewis smiled softly at him, his eyes crinkling again. "You're certainly an open book."

"Only by the light of the full moon," Reginald replied. "The other 28 days of the month I'm all briars and stink-eye." He smiled back as he said it, though. "So, what's a *gwisin*?"

Lewis gestured in a *you asked* sort of way. "Well, since you said not to give you any special treatment, they're revenge ghosts." He lifted a shoulder at Reginald. "Did your mother have anything to get revenge for?"

Reginald snorted. "Oh, only every single thing anybody else ever did. At least, that's how she acted most of the time."

Lewis nodded back at him, one corner of his mouth turning down.

"Sorry to hear that. So why did Bobby stick around? They seem close." He corrected himself. "Seemed?"

Reginald shook his head. "Bobby didn't turn out a terrible disappointment, so they got along just fine. Look, not that I'm ungrateful for the company and the conversation—believe me, this is a little slice of real-world pie I very much needed after… that." He cleared his throat. "But I don't mean to keep you up all night and I really should go home."

Lewis looked at him over the rim of the coffee mug. "You sure you don't want to go back up there and see if she's still around instead?" He raised both eyebrows. "Or are you chicken?"

Reginald flipped him off good-naturedly. "Fuck off, handsome. Goddamned right I'm chicken. Sorry, but that kind of stuff doesn't work on me." He smiled more broadly, the easiest and most relaxed moment he'd felt since he walked into Lewis's lovely and yet psychically *absent* home. "I'll head on home and come back tomorrow morning to keep working a little before the service."

Lewis gave Reginald a sly smile. "You *sure* you won't go back, just to lock up?" He pressed his lips together and curled up the corners just like the Grinch admiring his own wicked ways. "It's just, I've always wanted to see a haunted house. And also, Kate would *die*."

Reginald blinked at that. "Kate? Oh lord. Is her husband some paranormal PhotoGram bullshit guy?"

Lewis grinned at that. "Don't let her hear you say that. She says PhotoGram is on the way out."

"Is it?" Reginald smiled a little.

"I sure as hell hope not. It's one of my best on-ramps."

Reginald quirked his brows up for a second. "Guess I need to start spending more time on PhotoGram."

Lewis met his gaze, and for about a tenth of a second, Reginald would have sworn twenty thousand volts of electricity passed between them. Lewis smirked at him. "I'm @lewstubegram. I'd hate for you to have to hunt for it." He paused, and as he said the next part, he made small movements—adjusting his stance here, putting his hand on the back of an empty chair there—so that by the end he stood on Reginald's side, right beside him. "I can't help but notice you keep saying you want to go home but you haven't stood up. So come on, let me go put on a shirt and some real pants, and let's go check out your mom's house for, like, *one minute*." Just as Reginald was about to speak, Lewis added, his eyes lidded and his low voice breathy, "Or do I have to beg?"

Reginald opened his mouth, licked his lower lip to pass a second while he worked up his nerve—he very badly wanted to say something sassy about pants being optional—and then nearly bit his tongue when someone knocked at Lewis's front door.

"Kate sent me over to make sure everything's okay. She thought she heard a gunshot, and your house was the only one with lights on." Reginald couldn't see much of the person speaking, but he was a thirty-something white guy with curly red hair, and he stood nearly a foot taller than Lewis. That put him around 6'5", maybe a little more.

Lewis waved it off. "Oh, Reginald's car backfired." He turned halfway, his arms crossed over his bare chest, and nodded at Reginald where he sat at Lewis's table. Reginald could just see Lewis through the cut-out between the kitchen and the living room.

"Oh, hi, Reginald." Johnny walked in without waiting to be invited—Reginald found himself sourly wondering whether he picked it up from Kate or Kate had picked it up from him—and walked over to offer a hand. He wore a pair of paint-stained jeans, brown slip-ons, and a rumpled tee shirt for a band Reginald had never heard of. Something about that made him feel old—or like Johnny was very, *very* straight. "Kate told me about meeting you earlier today."

"Stay back, Mr. No-Mask," Reginald said before Johnny could make it all the way to the kitchen. "You can say hi from right there."

Lewis blushed hard, and Reginald immediately hated himself. He meant it, but also he'd said it just to be a dick to the guy who'd cockblocked him in the moment he intended to make a move. *Well, whatever, I don't want to be any of these people's best friend anyway.* But Reginald had been rude to a guest in Lewis's home, and that made *him* a bad guest, and the little machine in the back of his head put there to steer him through the impossible labyrinth of politenesses old and new whenever he was in this place—his mother's land, his childhood home—whirred and hummed its disapproval of everything he did and every thought to cross his mind.

"Oh!" Johnny stopped short of entering the kitchen and cleared his throat, looking around as though surprised to find himself in Lewis's home. "Sorry. I… sorry. We thought there might be, you know, an emergency."

Lewis smiled gently and walked closer. "I appreciate you wanting to look out for me," he said. "Tell Kate I said thanks, but we're fine here."

"You sure?" He looked meaningfully at Lewis, some set of concerns transmitted in a glance, a shift of the eyes, a shoulder.

"Oh, yeah." Lewis grinned. "Reginald had a… well, he got spooked and I invited him in for a cup of coffee so he could catch his breath."

Johnny's eyes widened just a hair. "Spooked? Why, somebody come around? You know, that happens a lot: people coming around after a homeowner dies. They probably saw the obituary and decided to try to rob the place while the pickings were good. I'll check our doorbell camera and see if it caught them."

Reginald sat back, away from the table, and sighed audibly.

"No, Johnny," Lewis chuckled as he answered. "Nobody came around. Nothing like that."

Johnny gave off the vibe that he always hit the ground running like that, some sort of innate puppy energy, and Reginald hated him a little for it—and liked him a little for it, too. He turned to Reginald and said, "What scared you then?"

Reginald felt his face flush hot as a kettle about to boil. "A bad dream. It was nice meeting you, Johnny."

Lewis's gentle smile took on an edge and he said, "Reginald, you can tell him if you want. Johnny's a good guy. I promise."

Reginald went stone-faced with irritation and glared at Lewis. "Oh great."

Johnny glanced back and forth between them. "C'mon, not fair keeping secrets, fellas. I mean, unless you two were…" He waggled his eyebrows, subtle as a blow to the forehead, and Lewis laughed as Reginald groaned.

"I have to go home," Reginald announced, standing up. He pointed at Johnny. "And *you people* like to barge into other people's houses when you haven't been invited." Then he turned to Lewis and, mouth open to say something sharp he hadn't even formed yet, he faltered. "And… and I really appreciate you listening to me when I needed it."

Lewis's face fell a little and he seemed unsure what to do or say. "Reginald, look, I'm sorry." He turned to Johnny. "Just forget what I said. I was just teasing Reginald at your expense. Really. Nothing happened. His car backfired, I went out to see what it was, he seemed a little shaken up by it, too, and… here we are." He gestured at the table. "But seriously, thanks."

Johnny took the hint, finally, and put up both hands. "Okay, okay, I'll go. Reginald, I… apologize for whatever I did to piss you off." He laughed when he said it, and Reginald found himself struck by what a sincere laugh it was while still being a little kind, a little self-deprecating even, when paired with his body language and what he said next. "I do tend to come on strong. I'm just one of those guys. But it was good to meet you in any circumstance, and I hope you believe in second chances." Then he turned to Lewis. "Game night on Friday?"

Lewis smiled at him. "Of course. I'll bring the daiquiris."

Johnny chucked Lewis on his bare shoulder and laughed. "See you then." He turned and pointed at Reginald. "Maybe you could join us? Practice a little self-”

Reginald, without looking at Johnny, his gaze instead turned up to the ceiling, said loudly, “I swear on the Bible, if you say ‘self-care’ I will scream until one of us is bleeding.”

Johnny startled, Lewis laughed, and Johnny startled again at the laugh. Then Johnny forced a chuckle as he backed towards the door. “Okay, okay. See ya, *Reg.*” He grinned as he pulled the door shut behind himself, and left Lewis and Reginald standing alone inside.

“Uh, sorry.” Lewis sounded like he meant it, which somehow annoyed Reginald even more.

“Oh, don’t be. I’m a prickly old bitch.” Reginald drew a long, steady breath, then let it out through his lips. “I just…”

Lewis shook his head as he walked into the kitchen. “You don’t need to apologize for not wanting other people to tell your stories before you’re ready to tell them yourself.” He lifted his shoulders—*gorgeously rounded he probably does special exercises just for that it’s like he’s wearing shoulder pads Christ his body is even more amazing up close*—and then looked up at Reginald through the curtain of his hair spilling over his forehead. It was an angle Reginald had seen more than once, but only in recorded video. Reginald felt his own guts clench at seeing it in the flesh. “But… if you’re game, I’d still like to go just check things out. Even if it’s just to lock up before you drive back to your place.” Lewis’ eyes sparkled as he produced an impish little twist at the corners of his lips.

Reginald wanted to say no, to storm out, to call his brother in the morning—his brother, who *still* hadn’t said so much as one fucking word to him, knocked on the door, called him, *nothing*—and say he wanted his half of whatever the property sells for, preferably as a check in the mail and a have a nice life. He wanted to forget all about this, never look at his dead mother’s house again, much less his dead mother. He wanted to drive away from Moriah Bald and never come back again.

Reginald also wanted to spend a little longer basking in the reflected heat given off by this gorgeous man he'd watched fuck and get fucked in every possible position by every kind of guy.

"Okay," Reginald said. "Just… you know, let's look around, make sure everything's in order, then we can lock up and I'll go."

Lewis grinned at him. "Let me get that shirt I mentioned."

"Well don't hurry on my account," Reginald said before he could stop himself.

"No distracting me when there's a ghost around," Lewis teased with a wicked wink. "You'll have to save that for *after*."

GENERATION TWO - VICTORIA

Victoria Voth had spent most of her adult life with three men too many, but she was about to be down to one. *Eber isn't yet a man,* she corrected herself, *but he will be soon enough.*

She'd tried her hand at raising burley tobacco this year, growing it from some seeds she'd bartered off the Kings around the other side of the mountain. They'd been growing an acre on their patch and built a drying barn for curing it. In exchange for eggs and half a hog, they'd given her enough seeds to plant a decent number and a promise she could use their barn when it came time to cure the leaves.

But then her husband had gone, and her work had doubled. Now the tobacco plants she'd tended for a season were starting to flower. The huge, pink blossoms, trumpet shaped and smelling so sweet, were beautiful to look at but they meant she had little time left to harvest. She'd counted on selling bales of cured and pressed tobacco for cash this year, and she needed that money more than ever now that the father of her child had cleaned out the few bills they kept pressed between pages of a Bible.

At least I know how to read it. More than he could ever say.

Sometimes husbands just went, of course. It rarely left the women better off, but Victoria knew she would only miss him in the field or come time to kill that hog she still half-owed the Kings. Otherwise, he was little more than a place to dispose of whiskey. He'd always hated her father, hated the name she still used despite them having gotten a traveling minister to read the banns in front of the Kings. Having a child didn't make him hate any less. It just gave him a third ready target. It had been a mercy when she'd awakened one morning to find him, his few clothes, and seventeen dollars gone.

And now even those worries had to be set aside, because she saw young Eber lead Alexander from the back of the house. Her father could barely walk with a cane in each hand and the boy's hands on his waist. He looked too old by thirty years.

Victoria drew a deep breath. A moment before she'd dwelt on broken promises, but not all faith was lost. They'd had good years here on Moriah Bald, and she couldn't allow this one bad year to erase them. She'd grown enough of one thing or another each year to keep them fed, sold enough excess to expand the cabin. She'd put glass in the windows and gotten a second horse. If things went well, maybe next year they'd be able to sell a pony. Maybe Eber would learn to ride. Maybe next year the seeds from this tobacco would grow another crop.

But first, she had to keep some promises.

CHAPTER SEVEN – HOUSE OF MIRRORS

Lewis tried to take it slow walking up the narrow, cheaply-paved street. Reginald, on the other hand, nearly left him behind in his haste. When he realized he'd started to pull ahead, Reginald looked back over his shoulder and tried to smile. "Look, I'd like to get this over with."

Lewis nodded and picked up his pace, and the two of them went most of the rest of the way in silence.

Reginald noted the lights go off upstairs in the house across the street and figured that was Johnny getting back into bed. Deep in the pit of his stomach he hoped he hadn't disturbed anybody else's sleep with the engine backfiring. It wasn't that he gave such a shit about them, whoever these people were, living in these tacky houses in his dead mother's front yard. He just didn't like to think of eyes in the dark windows, peeking out at him through the blinds. Reginald wanted to lock up the house, leave it behind, and not have anyone remember he'd even been here for—

Reginald glanced down at his watch—old-fashioned as ever, in his way—and did the math. He'd been back on Moriah Bald for barely fourteen hours, and he'd already gotten scared off. A part of him, an old part he hardly ever heard from anymore and even less frequently indulged—told him to stick around, fight back, slay the dragon whatever it might be. He'd been that way as a kid, been that way in college. Now he just wanted to live his life, emphasis on *his* life. There was no such thing as that on Moriah Bald. There was no such thing as that in his mother's house. He'd had a lot of years to realize that, not just as an intellectual abstraction but as a thing he felt deep in his bones and had since he was a very small boy. He'd gone to therapy about it. He'd done drugs in his twenties, pushed people away, held his family at a distance, made a few friends. None of them lived in these bland constructions littering his mother's lawn. None of them were any of these barnacles on the great, silent, unmoving ship looming out of fog and darkness that was Moriah Bald.

"Penny for your thoughts," Lewis murmured from beside Reginald, and it startled him out of the shadowed valley of his own thoughts so that he jumped and gave a little yelp. Lewis didn't let himself chuckle, but he did grin and reach out to put his hand on Reginald's elbow. "I'm sorry. I didn't mean to scare you. You just looked like you were pretty far down a rabbit hole there."

Reginald smiled and huffed a breath or two before he shrugged with his other shoulder—he didn't want Lewis to take his hand away. "Just thinking. There's a lot to unpack with…" Reginald looked up to indicate the house only to realize they stood in the street in front of it. "Fuck."

The old house rose from its stone foundation like some ancient shrine. Not quite a cube, not quite a pyramid, parts of it stood at perfect 90-degree angles and other parts sloped at unexpected heights, too high up to be at the break of a first story and too low to be the ceiling of the second, like seeing a person whose arm has its elbow in the wrong place. Reginald knew the white clapboard exterior—probably vinyl siding by now, he had no idea—was itself a facade over what he thought of as the *real* house: the original cabin some ancestor had built and then expanded into a farmhouse. Ancient planks still sat behind some of the drywall sections inside, a skeleton with a sheet of modern materials draped over it.

All the lights, save the one over the staircase, were still off. Exactly as they had been the moment before he saw his mother.

No, *felt* his mother before he'd even seen her.

"Well, I don't see anyone in any of the windows." Reginald tried not to sound disappointed. He wasn't, but also, he worried it made everything he'd said sound false.

"C'mon, let's take that look around and lock it up." Lewis still had his hand on Reginald's arm and gave it a little squeeze before letting go. "And no splitting up. I've seen too many movies."

Reginald smiled at that and it felt good. "Okay. But youth before beauty."

Lewis laughed, a sharp tenor that rang pleasantly like a bell. "Oh, you mean bitch."

"I warned you not five minutes ago, didn't I?" Reginald walked up onto the porch and pulled open the screen door. He gestured at the front door itself. "After you."

Lewis shook his head. "No way. It's *your* mother in there."

Reginald waited a heartbeat, processing that. "You really do believe me, don't you?"

Lewis ducked his head in a way Reginald found ridiculously attractive. "I mean, why wouldn't I? You've got no reason to lie."

"Oh, you sweet young man." Reginald sighed slightly. "The world is going to beat the shit out of your heart someday if you keep saying things like that."

Lewis allowed the first truly sour expression Reginald ever saw on him, and it practically dashed across the stage, departing as quickly as it appeared. "You don't say?"

Always such a fucking smart mouth. Why the fuck do I talk down to people all the fucking time, I'm a fucking idiot. But Reginald didn't let himself say any of those things aloud. He'd learned a long time ago the internal monologue had to stay that way or people got put off by what he honestly thought. What he said aloud was altogether clumsier but had the advantage of being inoffensive. "Well, anyway."

Lewis took one step closer, ready for whatever angry spirit might come screaming out when Reginald opened the door to his mother's house.

Reginald drew a breath, turned the doorknob, and stepped into hell.

The light in the house was far too bright, for one thing. It washed over Reginald and through him, so that he felt for a moment like he might have become partially translucent or perhaps had started to dissolve. The light burned cold, blanked out his vision, muffled sound, pressed against his skin as if binding him in a straitjacket. The sensation lasted only a moment, perhaps not even two seconds, and then, even as the back of his mind registered the words "radiation exposure," it faded out, and he stood in his mother's house again.

His mother's house was full of his dead relatives.

Hands took hold of his own, and he realized it was his mother. She looked younger by decades, and another part of his mind crossed out "mother" and scribbled "mommy" in its place.

Oh good, she said to him, *you're just in time for cake.*

Happy birthday, Reginald. His Aunt Myrtle, who died in that car accident when he was in high school, stood beside the other end of the couch. She had no face, but Reginald knew it was her when she spoke without sound. *Are you ready to blow out the candles?*

Oh who's getting to be so big? Ancient Granny Stutt clapped her frail hands together twice where she sat on the piano bench. *Come give Granny a kiss Reggie.*

Reginald looked up-down at his hand as his mother led him along by it. He was a tiny child again and a grown man at the same time, seeing his mother's hand both above and below his own line of sight, but somehow it wasn't confusing. It made perfect sense.

"I guess we're all always ourselves and the children we used to be," he said to his Granny Stutt as his mother picked him up and half-set him in

Granny Stutt's lap. She couldn't really hold him anymore, as Reginald remembered his great-grandmother turning 100 to great fanfare when he was a tiny child. Three weeks later she didn't wake up one morning and everyone spent her funeral talking about how much fun the party had been. Reginald's mother let maybe a quarter of his weight rest on Granny Stutt's knee while she gave him a kiss like sandpaper dipped in rosewater hand lotion, the same his own mother would use when her hands got as old as the rest of her.

*Yes, it **is** your birthday, show Granny how old you are.* Granny Stutt laughed and laughed as Reginald held up three fingers spread across two hands. *That's right, you're three! You know when I was three there were only thirty-eight states.*

Then Reginald was back on his feet as his mother ushered him past dead cousins, two who died in Aunt Myrtle's back seat when the train hit them because she'd stopped atop a rail line while waiting for the car ahead of her to make a left turn, and another who had a stroke at 43 years of age (he'd never seen his mother cry until that funeral), and then his mother's brother to whom she didn't speak for the last twelve years of her life. "Uncle Blake," Reginald tried to say as he was dragged past, "Don't sell that stock, my mother thinks half of it should be hers," but Uncle Blake grinned and tousled his hair and said *Yes, Reggie, I'm Uncle Blake alright. Ha, look at this handsome little lady-killer!*

Then Reginald found himself at the head of the dining room table, the one his family only used for special occasions like birthdays and games of Pinochle. A chocolate cake—skillfully baked and frosted, but still obviously homemade and all the more beloved for it—sat on a raised cake server with a glass dome over it.

Reginald's faceless father stood nearby and even though he bore literally no expression Reginald knew he was smiling. "I guess I'm not old enough to have started disappointing you yet," Reginald said, and he heard his father laugh. *Of course you'll be as big as me some day, son. Now blow out your candles.*

The dome over the cake was gone. Three blue and white spiral-striped candles burned atop it. *Make a wish*, his mother said.

"You're all dead," Reginald explained to them.

Then he blew out the candles.

The faceless army of his family, the figures who crowded out the world beyond the yard in his childhood, the people who would one by one vanish into death or disappearance, exiled by time or by hating each other and themselves too much, people who would each either get Reginald flat wrong or skip out entirely, lined the table at which only he sat.

The table seemed longer than it had been.

He now only saw things from below: only small now, not both at once.

They stood in silence and stared at him as he stared back.

Now run his mother said in the flat, cheerless, uncharitable voice of the dead who don't give one flying fuck about the living, never have, and certainly never will. *It'll be a game. It'll be just like hide and seek.*

And then we'll eat.

Reginald squirmed down out of the chair, his heart pounding in his tiny chest, and he shot through a forest of legs as he twisted past them and ran into a hallway that did not really exist in his mother's house, one where the added-on garage would have been in the geography of material things, and the squeals and screams and panicked, frantic grunts of a child in terror escaped him with every bouncing, clumsy step.

Behind him, he heard something like the stomping footfalls of running people and the thunder of hoofbeats on packed earth.

Around him, the walls, painted eggshell in his adulthood but a pale powder blue in his childhood, grew dark, were swallowed up in shadows, and disappeared altogether.

Still the faceless relations of his long-forgotten childhood gave silent chase.

Reginald found himself emerging from the darkness into the eggshell of his dead mother's living room. He was an adult again, fully and completely, and he was moving at a dead run.

He also still heard pounding footsteps behind him.

He dove right at the first door he saw, slamming into his dead mother's kitchen table and crying out in pain. Something in the darkness snarled and howled, and Reginald knew it as a sound of hunger in anticipation of an imminent meal.

Reginald bounced off the table, then off the counter beside it, his leg absolutely killing him where he banged the middle of his thigh against the corner of the wood. He threw himself at the back door, yanked it open, and ran-limped-ran-limped across the old porch and down the two steps. He didn't look back when he heard the table again clatter and bang, his dead mother's dead breakfast from three days prior—or was it four?—shoved aside as the monstrous starvation chasing him ran right past what had once been perfectly good food with a sound suggesting it had about it the quality of a *crowd*. Instead, Reginald limped-ran-limped-ran around the left end of the skinny strip of garden, past the barn, propelled forward by the sound of the corn and beans and too-leggy tomato vines behind him being *shredded* like someone had backed a bush hog over them running at full speed.

The gap in the trees and the muddy old path into it yawned before him, spreading its arms as if to welcome him in, and Reginald did, oddly, find it welcoming. The sky swirled above him, too much open space, too many eyes looking down from the darkness, too many spies ready to tell the living hunger behind him what they saw. He ran-limped through the portal into the forest and started to climb, panicked, panting, the earth under his feet smelling like clay and shit even though it hadn't rained in days, the leaves bright and beautiful like a swan singing its one and only aria as it dies.

The trees around him had never been tended and their branches crowded the path before him just enough to scrape and bother. He put his arms up to shield his face, pressing forward, continuing to climb on one-and-a-half good legs, stumbling over roots here and there. To his surprise he also sometimes found stone steps he'd entirely forgotten, set into the earth here and there where the slope was too steep. His old boots slipped once or twice in inexplicable mud and the smell of wet, decaying vegetation and the night air of autumn pressed on him as though gravity were getting stronger the higher up he went. Reginald had no idea exactly how far it was from his dead mother's house to the peak of Moriah Bald, but it took too long to get there, and yet he seemed to arrive far sooner than he might have predicted in some calmer frame of mind.

He climbed seven stone steps up, lowering his arms as the unkempt limbs and briars finally receded, and then Reginald emerged, running now, his leg either numbed or no longer hurting, his breath ragged, his oft-abused lungs screaming at him to *fucking stop already*, into the open, almost manicured natural clearing which gave the mountain its name. Low, surprisingly tidy grass and earth draped the rounded peak like a fortune teller's silk handkerchief over a crystal ball. These treeless patches were what that word—*bald*—referred to in the name of a mountain, and no one knew why they existed or why they were so common in Appalachia.

At the center of the bald stood a stone with a more or less smooth, flat top.

Beside that natural rock table stood Reginald's dead mother as she appeared to him on Tuesday morning: standing, her hands held up as though begging the sky for something.

Light shone down upon her.

On the other side of the bald, at the far end of the clearing, perhaps a hundred yards away, stood a group of people holding musical instruments. He could not hear them, though. They were drowned out by what he heard pressing in all around him.

Reginald could hear the hunger roaring up the side of the mountain behind him.

He could hear it roaring down at his mother from above.

CHAPTER EIGHT – AND DOWN THE MOUNTAIN AGAIN

Dorothea Voth stood stock still, bathed in a harsh blue-white light. She wore an orange and pink floral patterned sleep bonnet over her hair and the enormous pink curlers he had seen almost every night of his childhood. The light surrounding her was pale and sparkling and cerulean, like the twinkle of a star on a winter night but cranked so high it struck with palpable physicality. That light *pressed* on Dorothea Voth, trying to push her to the ground, to her knees, as if every star in that cold, clear sky had focused their emanations into a weapon of subjugation. Dorothea's raised arms, Reginald realized, were not lifted in supplication. She was trying to push back against the weight of light strong enough to cross light-years of hard vacuum solely to command that she kneel.

Reginald's eyes climbed that pillar of cold and deadly light only to find that it grew dark and hollow as his vision climbed past the horizon of the far side of Moriah Bald and ascended into the rafters of the heavens. To be clear, the light did not *stop*. It simply faded from view. It still had bulk, a presence some inner or invisible sense could use to detect it even if it existed beyond the borders of human sight. The column of light around Dorothea

Voth was not some implement stabbing through the night from beyond it. It was the weapon the night itself had drawn with which to attack her.

Roaring and stamping echoed distantly across the vast cavern of the heavens, as though great and angry beasts behind some unseeable barrier neared and then withdrew, the stars nothing more than the holes they kicked in that prison's walls as they tested its strength to contain them. As they beat their fists and hooves against the other side of the sky they shrieked incomprehensibly, a mix of words and names and what Reginald knew were curses—by which Reginald knew, in some calmer, more analytical corner of his mind, even in that moment, that he meant both the cuss words for which his grandmother once told him he'd go straight to hell and the curses laid down across generations in the same Bible she picked up and waved around as she did so.

Behind him, coming up the same mountain path he'd walked, he still heard the chatter and churn of whatever force chased him from some twisted remembrance of his dead mother's house, but it no longer approached. Instead it taunted him from just below the edge of the bald, skulking and waiting among the trees, daring him to try to get back down the mountain again.

Two words leapt out at Reginald from that clamor beyond the stars above him, though they were roared in whispers by voices larger than planets and smaller than the stars they hid behind:

Promises

Reginald

Reginald's eyes snapped back down to fix on his mother as she screamed in protest at those words emanating from the chorus of hell in the sky above them, alone in her spotlight, *just the way she always liked it.* He saw tiny wounds open on the skin of her face and forehead, and on the backs of her forearms where she shielded herself from the light, as though that brilliance itself sliced into her flesh.

If blood ran out, Reginald didn't see. His dead mother broke free from the grip of that light beyond the sky and began to run, stumbling and pathetic in her slippers and in the darkness again, directly towards him.

"Mama! *Mama run!*" Reginald's voice came out strangled and hoarse, as though he hadn't uttered a word in years, the way it sometimes did when he took a long weekend from work and didn't hook up with anybody and spent three days never saying a word to another soul, just puttering around inside his trailer and being at peace with himself. Dorothea ignored his encouragement, though, and when Reginald held out a hand to take hers—to lead her back down the path, he realized, and to face whatever awaited them beyond the trees first rather than let her face them alone—it passed right through her, cold and insubstantial. She was a specter—or maybe he was.

The voices from the sky grew angrier, and a sound like snapping bones and twigs together came down out of the sky where she'd been standing. Reginald turned and ran after the ghost of his mother, running and stumbling just as badly as she did across the uneven ground and unmown grasses, the voices chasing behind him.

Reginald gave in to temptation and glanced back once and screamed, not because some monstrosity was chasing him but because he saw, behind and off to the side, his grandfather running as well. And beyond him, a woman he knew from photographs as his grandfather's mother. Reginald tripped once or twice as he checked his other side and saw, all around him, half-spectral images of men and women, most old, some not, as they ran as best their varying bodies could carry them. They ran away from the stone slab of the great rock in the center of Moriah Bald, towards the trail down the mountain and back to Dorothea's home.

Reginald knew them instantly and without question: these were his ancestors, back to whoever had been the first one to climb the hill behind that property and find a sky full of hell waiting for them there.

Reginald dove headlong down the path at the lip of Moriah Bald. The screaming and chittering voices of whatever had chased him up it were nothing compared to the hostile universe that waited to gobble him up if he stayed. Whatever that force had been did not stop him, however, or even try to harm him. Instead, as he tripped and stumbled and half-slid, half-tumbled down the path, his boots sliding around on old leaves and bounding down root systems sticking out of the dirt like spiral staircases, the cacophony that forced him from the house and propelled him to climb for his life simply *laughed* as he ran away again in the other direction. It laughed with the insincere and all-consuming enthusiasm of a laugh track on an old sitcom, recognizably false and yet effective all the same. The sky wanted to eat Reginald up, to swallow him whole or squash him flat or otherwise erase him from existence, he felt that deep in his bones the way he felt it when he was about to cum, or the way he felt it when he really needed a cigarette.

And whatever lived in his dead mother's house still, whatever remained after her departure, found that funny as all hell.

Reginald burst from the tree line, through the gaping mouth in the forest where the path emerged into his dead mother's backyard. The laughing from among the trees on the slope of the mountain had receded as he went, not even bothering to chase him this time, but he kept running anyway. He ran right through a couple of corn stalks wrapped in beans and knocked them over, then ran up to the back door of Dorothea's house—

—and stopped with his hand on the knob.

"Oh, *fuck no*," he said aloud, staring at the dark kitchen through the small window in the door. "The *fuck I am, no going back inside*, you *assholes*." And with that he stepped back down off the back porch and took two steps towards the side of the house.

Eyes in the darkness stared back at him: golden and shining, too big to be a human's, too tall to be any animal's. They stared at him, unblinking, from an impenetrable fog of night. Reginald knew to run to those eyes was to run to his own damnation. He stumbled backwards, then sideways climbed the steps onto the stoop, and staggered back through the door into the kitchen.

Inside, the house was restored to what it had been when he arrived: just the dead, musty house of his very dead mother.

Reginald flew across the house and flung open the front door.

Lewis bounded up the steps towards him—*his body so light and so athletic, movement so effortless and supple and smooth*—to put a hand on his arm again. "Oh, thank *fuck*. Jesus, lock up and let's go. I'm sorry I ever recommended this. Your mother's house isn't safe…" Lewis searched Reginald's eyes and nodded. "But, you know that by now, it looks like."

"Did you go in?" Reginald sounded scared *because he was*, and he realized both at the same time. "Did you go in behind me? What did you see?" His voice caught for a second, his eyes burning with sudden tears. Reginald whispered the next question. "Did you see my birthday?"

Lewis's posture shifted from the coiled spring of someone ready to drag Reginald away from this place by force if necessary. He didn't smile, he didn't laugh, he didn't frown in judgment. He met Reginald's gaze and shook his head. "No," he said softly. "I'll tell you what I saw—and you *don't* have to tell me what *you* saw if you don't want to. But I'd like it if we left this place. You were right to want to leave it earlier, but I don't think it would be good for you to be alone at *your* house, either."

Reginald's chest and shoulders spasmed once. "*Lewis, they were running from it.*" He drew air in a backwards moan. "*Lewis, they were running from it with me, and I think it killed my mama.*"

Lewis eased Reginald into a hug and held him while Reginald sobbed for two solid minutes.

When Reginald's tears slowed and then seemed to cease, Lewis gave him another squeeze around the chest. "Come on. I'll tell you what I saw. I'll make another pot of coffee."

"Fuck coffee," Reginald choked out. "I want bourbon."

"Let's split the difference: red wine." Lewis smiled a little.

Reginald waved it off. "Fine, whatever. As long as it's something to turn off my brain."

"You have everything?" Lewis moved to put one hand on Reginald's back in equal parts comfort and propulsion down the steps, away from the house. "Keys? Wallet? A necklace or a ring, anything like that? If you leave anything behind it can use that to try to draw you back next time."

Reginald's red-lined eyes bulged from his too-pale face as he blinked at Lewis. "What the fuck? You run a ghost hunting thing on the side or something?"

Lewis smiled softly again. "I watch a lot of movies."

"Pretty fucked up movies, from the sound of things."

"You'll be grateful when those movies save your ass, you know." Reginald could hear the sincerity in Lewis's flirty little smirk. "But actually, Korean ghosts are their own thing anyway. Totally different from, like, Jacob Marley or whatever white people get, so I might have nothing but bad advice." Lewis offered one little chuckle as a balm, and Reginald accepted it by returning it in triplicate.

"Oh, great, so now you're an additional danger instead of a help." They both smirked at that, and Reginald recognized in Lewis the sort of toughness that only comes from being hurt a great many times—and that Lewis saw the same in Reginald.

They walked back into Lewis's sprawling, bland McMansion. Reginald couldn't really bring himself to call it a *home* even in his own mind. Lewis lived there, sure. But he wondered where in that house Lewis *lived*. The rest of it looked like it was waiting for a realtor to show up with whoever might give it some personality. Lewis went into the kitchen and Reginald followed, quietly scolding himself for brimming over with opinions about how other people lived. *Nobody fucking asked you*, he told himself, and felt the familiar twist of something old and bitter in his chest when he realized he had "heard"

it in his mother's voice. *Not that she'd ever drop an f-bomb like that*, he quickly told himself. *That one was all me.*

Lewis pulled two juice glasses from a cabinet and opened a pantry door. Reginald stifled a laugh when Lewis filled the first juice glass almost to the brim with red wine from a spigot on the side of a cardboard box. *"Box wine?"* He quickly put one hand out to take the glass before Lewis had even offered it. "Not that I'm judging. I'm just admiring the convenient setup."

"Hey, boxed wine is pretty good these days," Lewis said as he handed Reginald the glass. He smirked a little as he did so. "But to offset that, if it offends your class sensibilities, we're *also* going to have espresso straight from the maker, because I contain multitudes."

Reginald waited for Lewis to fill his own juice glass, then they clinked a silent toast and drank deep. More accurately, Reginald *chugged* his wine, finishing it in one long pull. He smacked his lips and sighed with satisfaction as he set the glass on the table. "Well, if we're going to stay up all night—and I can't imagine any other reason to drink espresso at…" He checked the face of his phone. "Jesus, it's fucking late. Maybe I should—"

Lewis shook his head. "None of that shit. We're going to talk about whatever just happened before you can convince yourself it didn't happen."

Reginald sighed, looked around, then nodded at the back of the house. "Then, if you'll forgive me, I'm going to go take another seven minutes off my earthly sentence on your back porch while you make espresso." He stood and felt exhaustion all over his body, as though the chair itself were a hand trying to grip him. "Which I love, by the way. Espresso, I mean. I bought myself a little machine for it once. It was cheap. Broke right away. But I love espresso." He felt sadness wash over him and it annoyed him, so he frowned a little when he said, "Anyway, thank you for all your kindness. I don't really deserve it."

Lewis didn't reply, busying himself with the intricate process of making the coffees as Reginald strode over to the French doors onto the back deck. His joints popped and his body creaked, and he swore he felt like he'd run ten miles rather than down a little trail from Moriah Bald to the backyard of his dead mother's house. The night air was chilly, and Reginald realized he'd worked up a sweat—and kept sweating ever since he got back. He mopped his forehead with the hem of his tee shirt, pulling it up and stretching it out to reach, then patted in his pockets and produced a pack of cigarettes. His mother had never let him smoke at her house. She hated smoking and she hated smokers. His father had smoked, and maybe that was why. One of Reginald's aunts had, in the '70s, always gone into the kitchen to smoke cigarettes during family functions, as though no one else would smell it from there. She'd stand in front of the back window and tap ash into the kitchen sink, then run cold water over the cigarette butt, rinse the ashes down the drain, and throw the soggy filter in the kitchen trash. As a three-year-old, Reginald had marched into the kitchen and announced casually, *my mother hates it when you do that*. His aunt had gone out to the back porch ever since. Reginald's mother could hate the woman enough to rant about it for twenty minutes when she was gone, but his mother would never just come out and say something about it. She'd needed a toddler to do that for her.

Reginald shivered as he realized he'd gotten lost in thought again. That kept happening. He knew it was normal—stress, grief, anger—but he still hated it. He hated not feeling in control of himself. And that, of course, had been the root of everything.

He flicked the lighter beside the tip of the cigarette and the sunflower flame sprang to life, hurting his eyes, so he closed them. Reginald took a couple of quick puffs to get it going, then let the lighter go and held it in his hand to let the head cool down before putting it back in his pocket. He drew in a longish drag, held it a moment, breathed it out through his nose—*like a dragon*, he'd once said to someone about that—and opened his eyes.

The old woods on the west side of what had been his mother's expansive property stretched away at the back of Lewis's yard. Reginald could detect the corners of other houses' oversized back decks to either side. A sectional fence defined the border down the side of each little plot, creating the *sense* of privacy in the absence of the real thing. You could all still see what each other was doing. All you had to do was take three stairs up to the deck itself to see over. Lewis's deck had a walled off privacy area, though, with open air above it, for the hot tub. It had its cover on, but it was positioned so that neighbors could not see in while someone in the hot tub could still see *up* and *out*. Reginald had a fleeting moment of imagining himself in that hot tub, looking out on the woods, or up at the stars, and drinking a glass of wine. He imagined it would have been very nice.

The yard itself was uniformly tidy, cut short, and weed eaten to within an inch of its life. A long string of golden-glowing fairy lights zig-zagged between tall poles to either side of the open space. They illuminated a half-built flower bed off to one side, a pile of paving stones toppled over next to the partial arc around a bit of turned earth. The little garden looked lonely rather than lively given how much *nothing* sat back here.

Reginald took another drag and let his eyes finally go to the thing he'd already seen.

At the back of the yard, where there was no fence between the neatly mown and very boring grass of Lewis's lawn, shapes in shadow, undefined, dark gray and navy blue and night-sky obsidian, stood just inside the edge of the trees. He could swear he saw their eyes shine back at him. He would never have been able to draw them, could not possibly have described their shape in any detail. He saw them, though, and they saw him *seeing* them, and they stood stock still and watched undeterred. He wondered why they didn't shrink back into the cover of the trees or fly forward like specters from one of Lewis's movies. Reginald took another drag, still staring at them, the thin, twinkling dots of their eyes studying him in the sort of unnerving silence reserved for absolute confidence.

Reginald heard the back door open, and Lewis padded out in bare feet. He handed Reginald a tiny, steaming cup and spoke with no other preamble. "When you opened the door, what I saw beyond you was darkness. I don't mean that it was dimly lit in there, I mean it was without light. But I felt the wind—a *howling* wind that made no sound. I remember thinking it *should* make a sound."

Reginald knit his brows together. "I didn't feel that at all."

Lewis went on without reaction. "It hit me like the kind of wind that moans and whistles at the same time, the sort of wind you get standing on the beach at night or when a summer storm blows in with no warning. So much force it pushed me back. I staggered, nearly got knocked down. I tried to take a step forward, to keep up with you? But the door slammed shut before I could even push my way forward to try. And when it did, I smelled something. A lot of things. I smelled blood, and fertilizer, and old perfume. Thick and heavy. It was like the wind had barfed all over me. I know that sounds weird to say. But again, I got the sense it wanted to keep me out, to try to drive me away. And when I touched the front door it felt so cold it burned me. I literally was worried I might have gotten frostbite from it. It felt like touching the face of, I don't know, a glacier maybe." He smirked for a moment and looked down. "I had a gig in Iceland one time."

"I know," Reginald murmured. "I watched that video, like, forty times." He blushed deeply when he said it, and he did not let himself look at the trees, at the woods beyond them, at the spot where figures made of shadow and of cold nothing had stared back at him seconds before.

"Well, I'm flattered." Lewis said it very softly and smiled, then lifted his eyebrows. "But, back to your mother's haunted-ass house. I tried the door again, because… This will sound ridiculous, but the thought I had when the door shut was, *that house is going to eat him.*" Lewis's neck tightened for a moment. "I tried the door again and it wouldn't budge. I don't mean it was merely locked. I couldn't even rattle the knob. I couldn't push on the door and have it feel like it gave. It was as though the door, I don't know, *sealed itself* as soon as you got inside. So then… I didn't know what to do. I thought about throwing myself at the door, trying to break it down, but that seemed like it would just, I don't know, get me hurt. Or it might wake up your brother and he'd call the cops, and fuck *that.*"

Lewis looked away from Reginald now, his eyes roaming over the back yard, taking in nothing as he recalled the story in the course of relating it. "Then I thought, maybe I *should* wake up Bobby, maybe go knock on his door. Maybe he would have a key. He'd have a key, right? Then I thought, what if *I* called 911. But, what would I say? 'Hi, I need you to break into my dead neighbor's house because her son is trapped inside?' They'd show up and tase me, say I was high or something." Lewis' gaze settled on the woods beyond his yard now and he hesitated for a moment.

Reginald nearly looked at the woods, too, but a part of him whispered that if he didn't look at the figures peering out from behind the trees then he could pretend they hadn't *both* seen it. Instead, he urged Lewis to keep speaking. "How long were you out there before I opened the door?"

Lewis looked back at Reginald and showed no sign of having seen anything. "That was it. Maybe, I don't know, twenty seconds? You went in, the door slammed, I realized I couldn't open it, and I stepped back four or five feet. I'd just started considering my options when you showed back up. At first I thought, did he just run in, turn around, and come back out? But you were out of breath, and you looked…" Lewis lifted a hand as though to touch Reginald's face, but stopped short. "You looked so scared. So pale. And I was so relieved to see you."

Lewis started to put his hand back down but Reginald reached up and caught it. "Do you see anything in the tree line?" Reginald asked it very softly, his voice very quiet. "Golden eyes staring back at you from the shapes of what might be people?"

Lewis stared into Reginald's eyes, then reached down with his free hand, picked up the espresso, and took a long sip while looking out at the trees. "No." He licked his lips quickly. "Do you? I mean, it would be natural for you to be on edge. It would be understandable if maybe your brain is leaping at stuff to be frightened of, given what you've experienced tonight."

Reginald huffed out a half-laugh and relaxed. "Oh, thank *Satan*. I'm simply going mad. That's actually a relief."

The corner of Lewis' mouth twitched up and he said, "You don't actually mean that."

"The hell I don't."

"I mean, you actually did see something, and you trust yourself about that."

Reginald took one slow, shallow breath, shaking the whole time, then shot his eyes toward the trees.

Nothing. Just trees. Whatever had been there had gone.

Or they simply closed their eyes, a part of him thought, but that part? He knew that part, and it *was* a kind of madness. It was the long and possibly deadly—perhaps literally, perhaps only spiritually—spiral of anxiety and depression waiting around the corner for the right-wrong thing to get it started. Reginald had been in and out of therapy, on and off medication, for the better part of thirty years. He'd only ever had one *truly* bad spell, a few days when he lay in bed until he got tired of smelling his own stink and had used up all of the meager stream of sick leave an old job allowed, but he knew the feeling. Sometimes, when enough of the right kinds of stresses and worries approached the necessary critical mass, he had the sensation of standing in a glass-floored elevator, staring down into the lightless abyss, and wondering when the elevator would fall. Reginald drew a sharp breath, brought his gaze back to Lewis, and shivered in the chill night air.

Lewis leaned in and gave Reginald a soft, tentative kiss that, in the absence of rejection, grew bolder and more confident. They stood like that, pressed together, for five seconds, then ten, then pulled slowly apart. "Now drink your coffee," Lewis murmured, "So I can take you upstairs and fuck you."

CHAPTER NINE – DEAD & BURIED

Later that same night, across the street from Lewis' house, Kate's husband Johnny heard music.

Johnny woke from a light sleep to the sound of… was that violin? Viola? He could never tell the difference when just listening. He'd tried to get into symphonies, orchestras, *classical*, all that stuff, really tried to dig in and *understand*, but it never quite clicked for him.

Whatever, it was a stringed instrument. It sounded like it came from out in the street.

Jeez, Ham's moms are going to kill him if that's him practicing for orchestra class. He crept out of bed and over to the window, peeking out around the edge of one of the slate gray floor-to-ceiling drapes he'd had installed, what, three years ago? *Need to remember to add those to the refresh list.* Drapes and blinds were always good content. The deco-heads liked how technical they could get, and people window shopping liked the strong visuals. Slate was all the rage back then, but now, new phones—*new phone who dis* came from some corner of his brain where quotes and jokes and asides babbled to each other nonstop—with new cameras, he could look into something with a pattern, maybe some texture, something to look good in the feed.

Kate shifted in her sleep in their California King, and Johnny froze to make sure he did not wake her. The sound of the instrument faded as though the person playing had stepped around a corner or gotten more distant, some shift in the acoustics carrying the sound away from him, and he waited until her breathing returned to the slow, steady sound he knew made it safe to walk around.

Johnny looked up the street. The matching lamps at the end of every driveway glowed softly. Each identical off-white mailbox (*Oberlin Paint Co. #954, "Quarried Quartz"*) stood on an identical black polymer and steel post with an elaborately baroque y-bracket support brace between the post and the newspaper box integrated into the beam. Johnny was proud of those mailbox posts. He'd chosen them when the neighborhood was being planned.

He turned up the street, then down it. Nothing looked amiss, and not a phantom string player in sight.

The only yard without the one acceptable shade and size of mailbox on the one permitted style of post was *hers*. Dorothea Voth's. Johnny didn't take death lightly, and he would never have said this aloud, but he didn't mind knowing she was gone. She'd run hot and cold the whole two years they'd all lived there. She snubbed all eight of their welcome wagon parties in *the square* (how Johnny insisted on referring to the greenspace in the center of the cul-de-sac, despite it technically being an oblong) as each house sold, but the first time anyone did anything she didn't like (which took practically no time at all) she met them quickly enough.

She'd shown up yelling at him from the sidewalk as he filmed *Easy Raised Beds on a Budget*, shouting in anger at the mere possibility her house might be visible in the background of his footage, ruining the audio. That was why he had to build *two* raised beds, introducing the sort of symmetry he found tolerable only in the general, not as a personal statement. Eight essentially identical houses, four on each side of the square, all facing each other? That's a symmetry of *organization*. It made sense. Symmetry of *presentation* was boring. He'd wanted an asymmetric design with a curved front walk to challenge the eyes, wake up an observer. He wanted anyone watching any of his content to know exactly where he stood in his yard based on what they could see behind him. The neighborhood as a whole *should* be a backdrop: to the lives of the people in it, to his content, to whatever. But the yard itself was each resident's canvas, and Johnny wanted to make *art*. You didn't get likes and follows for a featureless green plane. You got likes and follows by making people feel like they could watch every video you posted for a year and still not see everything.

Dorothea Voth's yard stood empty, dead, *accidental* more than anything. It was a mess someone mowed. And that *house*. Christ. He'd heard from Bobby that the original cabin walls were hidden underneath that white vinyl siding. He'd give anything to renovate that place. There'd be a year of steady content there, maybe two. That would be, like, *TV deal* level content. Every time Johnny looked at Dorothea's house he *hungered* for the kind of engagement he would get out of revealing a two-hundred, maybe two-hundred-fifty year old *historic homestead*'s original timbers hidden under tacked-on vinyl siding from the era of the Carter administration.

Every window in Dorothea Voth's house blazed with brilliant, golden light.

Violin music came from inside.

He wondered who was playing.

Johnny pulled on the painting pants and his tee shirt for *Ethel M & The Humpback Wails* he'd left crumpled by the bed, tiptoed downstairs, and slid his feet into slip-resistant safety-toed work shoes. He patted his pockets for keys, then went out the door and closed it quickly behind him so the hinges wouldn't squeal. *I should do a TikTok about hinge lubrication. That would go over well.*

The *hated* garden beds glared at him. At least he'd put the second one off-kilter from the first. An enormous pile of dirt and mulch, almost as big as a compact car, hunched on the ground. He needed to get some guys in to turn that into a vegetable plot. He had *Preparing a Bed in Autumn* on his list, and planned to do a three-parter: build the bed, transplant in stages in the spring, then do a canning video in summer. That meant at least two more trips to Pisgah Forest to find day laborers, some creative filming to make sure he was the only one in any shots, and he'd probably have to edit "last time" intros for each or people would forget what he'd been making. Long-term content generation could pay off if a topic hit, but otherwise it was a lot of effort for nothing but comments from people asking where to find the first entry in the series.

But as soon as he stepped out onto the sidewalk and looked up the street at the old Voth house, all that fell away.

He saw only the warm, inviting light.

He heard only the music of the instrument that had eluded him.

Reginald peeled Lewis' snoring form from around himself in the morning, crept outside to the Tracker still parked in Lewis' driveway, fetched his overnight bag, and tiptoed back upstairs to the bathroom to shower. He needed to get ready for this *fucking funeral* and he was already running late if he wanted to get there *first*. For some reason that had become an important goal for himself: get there first, leave last. He wasn't quite sure why the urge to be in total control of the process by which the world said its piece to— and about—his dead mother had suddenly become important to him, but it had.

No, that was a lie. He knew: Because as long as he was there, they would have to whisper whenever they talked about him.

Reginald was honest with himself, also about not wanting to give his brother the chance to bitch about having to do everything himself. *Get there early enough*, Reginald thought to himself as he scrubbed his gloriously sore ass under scalding hot water, *and I'll probably catch Bobby cutting down a tree so he can build himself a cross*. Bobby always liked to have it both ways in all things, and it was no different with them and with their mother.

Bobby took great pride in having stuck close by their mother *and* resented never having gone anywhere or done anything with himself. Well, Reginald had always figured if Bobby wanted their mother so damned bad he could *have* her. And now, if everything worked out, Bobby could have exactly half of Dorothea's land, too, however much remained. As far as Reginald knew, the Voths had always owned their whole side of the mountain. Maybe that was still true. Maybe they'd only sold off the acre in front to build a bunch of houses. Maybe she'd still owned everything up to and including the bald. That would probably fetch a pretty price in the current real estate market. Hell, with the money he'd get from selling it Reginald could put a real deck on the back of the trailer. If he screened it in he could get a hot tub just like Lewis'.

Lewis' shower was bigger than Reginald's entire bathroom, with glass walls up to the ceiling and four shower heads. He recognized it, of course. He must have watched a dozen videos Lewis made in here, and he'd watched each video at least fifty times. Reginald laughed aloud, suddenly, at how ridiculous it was to find himself standing in it.

How'd the old song go? *But God's a dour prankster, done heard of every joke*, something like that? His grandmother used to sing it on the back porch sometimes when she strung beans. That was in the days when the "garden" was many times bigger, of course, multiples of the little patch in his dead mother's backyard. At any rate, that song had stuck with him in some way, much to Reginald's own surprise, and the point of it was that you never get to put one over on God. The implication, Reginald had realized at an early age, was that God would always instead be pranking *us*.

The star and sole proprietor of one of InterFans' top twenty gay porn feeds living in Reginald's gay-bashing evangelical mother's front yard had to be one of God's better gags.

"Great minds think alike," Lewis said from beyond the steam fogging the glass wall. The door to the shower opened and he stepped in.

"Oh, good morning." Reginald found himself suddenly shy, utterly ridiculous considering their itinerary from 1:00 AM to 1:45 AM the night before. "I hope you don't mind me showering before I leave for the visitation."

Lewis laughed. "I'm sure I'll think of some way you can repay the favor." He walked over and grabbed the right cheek of Reginald's ass in his left hand. "Then we can get some breakfast before the funeral."

Reginald flushed deep. "Believe me, I'd love nothing more than to show up to my mother's send-off freshly fucked by a gorgeous man, but I'm in a rush."

"Well, you're always welcome to say no, and I will absolutely respect that. But, uh, from the look of things you're as interested as I am." There was a meaningful pause, a shameless, confirming glance. "And if you say yes then I promise this won't take long. For either of us. I always find a little Eros helps the Thanatos go down." Lewis emphasized the last two words with a squeeze.

He was right, it turned out. They barely took two minutes.

Reginald reflected later, as he tied the plain black tie he'd brought to wear with a white dress shirt and the unfashionably bulky charcoal suit he'd bought at a thrift store several years before, that he did, in fact, feel a lot better for it. But he still wanted to get to the funeral before anyone else.

Reginald downed the cup of coffee Lewis offered him when he got downstairs in one go. "We'll have to skip breakfast. I need to get there early."

"Sure, you probably have to, I don't know, do last minute stuff with the funeral home. What *is* a visitation, anyway? I'd never heard that before I moved here."

Reginald waved a hand as though shaking water from it. "Oh, it's a chance for people to get a good look, up close, before the funeral. Sometimes people do it the night before, sometimes as a kind of opening act for the funeral itself: a little less formal, a little more nosy. Bobby, his wife, and I will have to stand up front, beside the casket, to let people come up and tell us how sorry they are for our blah blah blah, how mama one time did this or that and saved their bacon, all the usual funerary flattery. Mostly it gives everybody a chance to talk about how good or bad the hair and makeup job was. Not today, though. My mother wanted none of that."

"Hair and makeup—of the dead person?"

Reginald nodded and gave a little shrug. "Yeah. Any chance to talk shit in these parts, Lewis. Always remember that. But no, everything's already set and done and decided. I just really need to get there first."

Lewis didn't question him, but a look crossed his face.

Reginald tried to put on a smile but it wouldn't stick. "I can't stand the thought of walking in and thinking people have been talking about me or wondering about me. I can't stand the thought of Bobby getting there first and people soaking him in a lot of bullshit sorrow. I need *them* to walk into *my* space, not the other way around. I need to own the… what do they call the church inside a funeral home? I mean, it isn't actually a church."

Lewis' eyes turned softer and he threatened to chuckle. "The chapel."

"Then I need to own the *chapel*. I don't know how else to say it. So, I need to go right now, even though I'll be two hours early." Reginald started for the door. When Lewis stood from the kitchen table, Reginald stopped and turned around. He didn't know what to do or say. He didn't really feel like a kiss on the cheek would cut it. He didn't know what *would*. Reginald didn't let guys stick around for breakfast, and he sure as hell didn't very often spend the night as a guest. He didn't really understand why Lewis had allowed it of him. *Of course he did. He's probably bored as shit when he isn't getting off on camera. Look around, he's surrounded by identical gray McMansions with matching mailboxes at the end of every drive. And he's so gorgeous. And those eyes are looking right at me.* "Unless you're, like, almost ready. And you want to ride with me. I mean, the Tracker isn't exactly comfortable, it's not much in the way of a glass carriage, but it's paid for."

Now Lewis gave in to temptation and allowed his cheeks to lift a little as his eyes sparkled. "You sure you want someone with you? I mean, I get the whole thing about owning the space and what people say about you, and when. I *really* get it." He gestured around, overhead, everywhere, in one tidy arc of his shapely arm. "There's a reason why I don't simply live in San Diego and work for a studio like the rest of the industry. So, if you'd rather go alone, I get that. I could be ready in maybe ten minutes, sure, but I'd understand. Or I could be just ten minutes behind you. Or I can drop it altogether and stay out of the way. Whatever you need for wherever you're at right now."

Reginald had a very *present* sensation of something in his chest balling up and twisting. "Not to turn you into my emotional support top, what with you having to serve me coffee *and* booze *and* fuck me twice just because I saw my mother's ghost and then—" He faltered. *Not ready to talk about the inside of the house. Or the top of Moriah Bald. Not yet. Not until I know she's in the ground and she can't hurt me.*

Lewis snorted at that. "Uh-huh."

Reginald said it just as casually as he could and only let his eyes meet Lewis' again on the last word. "But I'd like it if you went with me."

Lewis got halfway into a grin. "Are you asking me on a *first date*, and it's to your mother's funeral?"

Reginald tried very hard not to blush. "Maybe. And maybe I just want to soak up all the scandal when everybody sees me at my racist mother's funeral with you on my arm."

Now Lewis laughed. "She *was* pretty fucking racist."

"Yeah." Reginald drew a sharp breath and his smoke-crusted lungs felt pinched. "Look, I hated my mother. OK? All cards on the table. I hated my mother from childhood, and I loved her, too. The thing was, I loved the mother she wanted people to see her being, and I hated the mother she was. I hope that doesn't sound too melodramatic. But she was always caressing with one hand and crushing with the other, day and night. She'd tell us how special we were, how much better we were than everyone else, set impossible standards so we'd never feel good enough *and* train us to look down on everyone *else* for never being as good as *we* supposedly were. She'd tell us she was trying to 'build confidence' in us. She was a racist, fundamentalist, self-loathing misogynist. She hated other women, got jealous if a man ever gave anyone else a lick of attention. She manipulated us, pitted us against each other, worked every angle she could to control us, all for the love of yanking us back and forth like we were on a little leash she held in her hand."

Reginald felt his eyes sting as he drew another breath and plunged ahead. "I don't mourn my mother. Not any more. I stopped mourning the mother I *wished* I had, years ago, maybe even while I still was a child. I'm *relieved* that woman is dead. You don't know how relieved. When I—when she *appeared* to me the night she died, I felt like somebody had taken off a choke collar I didn't even realize I still wore. Lewis, I am a bitter, mean old queen. I push people away, and criticize, and make fun, and hunt for reasons to decide I'm better off without other people because I do not trust other people. If you can't trust your own mother, who can you trust? Absolutely fucking nobody, right?

"But you, Lewis, you are absolutely gorgeous, and you fuck like a tank, and you have been exceptionally kind to me at a time when I needed it, and I honestly can't think of the last time someone was *kind to me* on this land, in sight of *that house.* At least, not since I was a kid. This morning I need both to own that fucking chapel when everybody else arrives *and* I am *fucking terrified* of standing around it by myself. So, I hope it's not weird that *I'm* weird about asking you to go with me, and that I kind of hope you'll say no, so I'm sharing too much, and also that I might *scream* if you say no." Reginald drew another breath, and it shook a little. "*That's* where I'm at right now."

Lewis spoke softly. "I'll make it five minutes, not ten. I'll drive. No way are you getting behind the wheel right now. And we're going to absolutely *kill it* at your mother's funeral."

Reginald sniffled once, long and high, and it was the most vulnerable expression of emotion he'd allowed himself in front of another person in two decades. "I don't suppose you've got any black masks, do you?" He held up his own, a deep, dark blue but a blue nonetheless. "I'd hate to think I'll clash." He cleared his throat, uncharacteristically unsure of himself. "And thank you."

Despite his dead mother's funeral not starting until 11:00 AM, despite a night full of terror, adrenaline, more terror, and getting fucked, and despite following that with a morning of getting fucked again and telling himself his meltdown was *not* simply stress, it was not madness, that he *had seen and experienced those things*, Reginald and Lewis arrived at McLarens at 9:05 AM.

Lewis' sensible little hatchback was the only car in the lot once they parked.

The doors to the chapel were locked still, but Reginald knocked—first politely, then not—until an employee answered it. At first she seemed exasperated and ready to tell them to go away, but when Reginald explained it was his mother's funeral she turned kind, told them he could of course come inside, and escorted them to the back of the chapel before disappearing to continue with preparations for the service.

Reginald excused himself to Lewis and spent five minutes puking out coffee in the men's room.

GENERATION THREE – EBER

October, 1891

Eber Voth came back down the mountain as the storm raged overhead. The long descent in gushing rain had not cleared the blood from him: from his clothes, from his skin, from the gash across his own chest, from the deep wounds in jagged rows around the outside of each of his upper arms. The homespun fabric of his crudely sewn shirt hung from his thin frame in long tatters, and his hat failed to protect him from the downpour. Branches bare as bones offered no more shelter than his hat, and cold water ran in icy rivulets from every bony corner of his small frame.

His wife Charlotte stood on the small back porch of the Voth homestead they'd spent the preceding summer re-siding while a crop of corn and potatoes mostly failed around them. Two of the little ones she'd borne him huddled behind her, trying to stay out of the wind and the rain, as the sky beat thundering fists against the ground in undisguised anger at Creation and what had been wrought in it.

Charlotte drew a breath to cry out to Eber through the storm. He approached, visible to her more as an outline than anything else in the near-total darkness, but her breath caught and wouldn't let words emerge. In the dim glow of the lantern she held she could see him only as splotches of color—dingy, sooty gray and white and red—and then the flash of yellow reflected in the long blade of the corn knife in his right hand. Charlotte put one fist to her mouth and waited for him to approach, but he stood back, rain be damned, at least twenty paces from her and from what meager shelter the overhanging roof might offer.

"Is it done, Eber?" Her voice got strangled as she spoke, so she had to try again. This time she screamed the words, howled them with what she hoped was enough force to keep the storm from tearing them away. *"IS IT DONE?"*

Eber Voth didn't respond. Stock still, utterly silent, he held the corn knife aloft for a moment. Lightning crashed nearby, and thunder shook the ground around them right after it—shook the house, even, so that Charlotte could hear its timbers and planks rattle.

"IT IS DONE," he shouted back at her, and then with one swift drop of his arm, he plunged the razor-sharp corn knife into the wet muck at his feet with such force it sank in at least three inches.

A gust of wind blew the rain sideways for a moment, and Charlotte heard the two children behind her whimper and yelp as they crowded into the back of her gingham dress. A heartbeat later the rain stopped as fast as it had started some quarter-hour before. The clouds above them began to part, and the light of a full moon dazzled them in its sudden brightness.

Eber's voice shook as he repeated himself, his voice softer this time, even wounded, "Yes, Charlotte. It is done." He reached down and withdrew the corn knife from the gash it cut in the thin, sour earth they'd been cursed to farm. Eber glanced skyward a moment, his eyes clear and youthful in a face turned old by too much struggle for too little reward. "They'll provide. You'll see. As they have promised, they will provide."

Charlotte did not shriek, did not curse him, but she did turn her back, huddling over her children as they wept and babbled at her. "The storm's over now," she said, scolding even as she put hands on their shoulders to comfort them. "Go inside and sleep. We'll need you up early in the morning. Work won't do itself."

CHAPTER TEN – GONE BUT NOT FORGOTTEN

"I hate everything about southern funerary traditions, but more than anything I absolutely loathe the whole visitation-receiving-line part." Reginald wore a sour expression as he said it, his lips pursed and a mean glint in his eye.

Aunt Myrtle let go of the pistol grip of her quad cane—a daring shade of lavender Reginald very sincerely admired—and clasped his right hand between both of hers. "Yes, dear, your mother was very kind. But she's joined that choir now. No more pain, no more fears." Her voice warbled as she babbled in utter ignorance of what Reginald had said. She then turned to Lewis and took his offered hand as well. "It's good to see you, Bobby. So sorry about your mother."

Lewis blushed a little and gave her hands a gentle, friendly squeeze. He didn't say a word, just let the woman shake his hand one more time before she took hold of her cane again and tottered slowly past the closed casket and the enormous framed photograph of Dorothea Voth on an easel in front of it.

"She's really that out of it?" Lewis whispered it, his voice full of wonder.

"Yes. Very kind, though. She's my mother's aunt. She must be three hundred years old by now, poor thing. Used to make a rum cake that could knock you on your ass. She'd sneak me a tiny bite every Thanksgiving." Reginald smiled, surprising himself. "Until I turned 13, and then she started sneaking me two entire slices. My mother, of course, said anyone who had wine with dinner was going to hell, but she liked to convince herself the alcohol in a rum cake would 'bake out.'"

Lewis snorted quietly. "Oh god, did your aunt not realize you're supposed to soak the cake *after* you bake it?"

"Oh, she knew. And she did. My mother simply told herself otherwise so she had permission to sin." Reginald let out a long breath through his nose. "Aunt Myrtle was always a little too cosmopolitan for this place. I've always wondered where she picked it up. I figure she must have lived up north at some point. At any rate, don't feel bad about the 'Bobby' thing. She hasn't seen much of anything beyond vague shapes and colors since, oh, I don't know, when was the Teapot Dome scandal?"

Lewis strangled a laugh, ducking his head.

Reginald went on as the next local approached. "Last time I saw her, I could tell she was on autopilot, addressing anyone she saw as some member of our family and rolling the dice on being right." Reginald shrugged slightly. "But that was years ago. These days she's in a home." He nodded around the chapel, which somehow managed to hold exactly enough people for Reginald to feel like they were too few in number and at the same time too many. Dorothea Voth had ruled her church, her family, and a couple of small charitable efforts with a fist of iron drenched in blood. Reginald was surprised more people weren't here to see her off into the wild blue yonder and at the same time surprised this many people feared her enough, even dead, to show up. "Hell, most of these people probably are. Maybe they all took the same cab and got a group rate."

The next person in line approached: a thirty-something woman with familiar eyes behind her zebra-striped mask. She was a little curvy, with hair dyed in streaks of bright colors against black, and she wore a somber pantsuit. Reginald knew he ought to recognize her, but he didn't. He offered a hand, though, and nodded at her. "Hi. Thank you for coming."

The woman took Reginald's hand and squeezed it fondly. "Reginald, it's your cousin, Candy. I'm so sorry about your mama."

Reginald relaxed visibly and gave an involuntary sigh. "Oh, Candy. It's so good to see you. Gosh, it's been a long time."

"Yeah, since we were teenagers, I reckon." Candy's smile made it all the way to her eyes, and Reginald's heart melted a little. Candy then turned to Lewis and offered her hand to him. "Reginald and I go way back. I'm his first cousin on his mama's side. I'm Candy. Candy Tompkins."

"I'm Lewis. It's a pleasure to meet you." He shook politely.

Candy's expression shifted a little around her eyes and she glanced back and forth between Reginald and Lewis. "Are you Lewis'… friend? I guess?" Reginald had heard the same sort of question asked a hundred thousand times, and he could tell the difference between a hopeful tone and a wary one. This was the welcoming variety.

Lewis jumped in. "Friend of the family. I live down the street from Mrs. Voth."

"I asked Lewis to stand up here with me." Reginald cleared his throat. "Honestly, I hate the receiving line thing and I couldn't bear the thought of standing up here by myself."

Candy glanced to make sure no one else was sneaking up within earshot. "Well, since you mentioned it, is Bobby not going to be here at *all*?"

Reginald's eyes narrowed and his scowl was obvious despite the mask. "Apparently not. Candy, I'm not going to lie to you, he hasn't said one goddamned word to me the whole time I've been here, and it's been two days." Reginald lifted one shoulder. "Whatever. He's probably getting revenge for me never being around when she was alive."

Candy shook her head, and her tone reflected a frown as she turned to gaze at the portrait of Dorothea. In the photo, Reginald's dead mother wore a gold cross on a thin chain, her hair arranged in carefully groomed curls and a bun. She looked like a dowager from a Bronte novel. "I hate to see people be like that. But honestly, Bobby was always doing for her when she could do for herself, and I think she got off on it. All she had to do was snap her fingers and he'd heel like a beat dog." Candy turned back. "I'm sorry. I shouldn't speak ill when I don't know the facts."

Reginald laughed once. "Oh, you'll never offend me by talking shit about Bobby." He hesitated, then went there. "Or my mother, for that matter."

Candy chuckled once, reached for Reginald again, and gave him a squeeze on the forearm. "Now there's the Reginald I remember. Couldn't keep that mouth out of trouble."

Lewis chirped, "Still can't," and the silence between the three of them strained like a balloon about to burst. They all stood stock still, afraid to laugh, and then Candy snorted aloud, a raucous, grating grind of air against her sinuses, as sudden and jarring as a pumpkin fired from a cannon.

"Oh, I *like* you." Candy pointed at him. "I like you *a lot*. Always said the only funeral worth showing up to is one where you get to laugh." She turned back to Reginald. "Listen, I'll find you online or something. We should keep in touch more."

Reginald surprised himself for the twentieth or thirtieth time in the last twenty-four hours by saying, "I'd like that," and actually meaning it.

Candy then nodded at Lewis. "A real pleasure meeting you, Lewis. Hell, I'll friend you, too." She turned to the portrait, fluttered her hand around like she was considering saluting it, then settled for a nod. "Fair journeys, Aunt Dor."

"I thought you said you hated everyone in your family," Lewis chided as Candy walked away.

"I honestly forgot she existed," Reginald replied, "but it's nice to see someone else managed to survive our family with their brains mostly intact."

The next person to approach was an older white man in worn overalls and a red, white, and brown plaid shirt of flannel. The shirt was buttoned at the collar and the man wore shining, square-toed dress shoes in place of work boots. His hair, streaked white and black, lay flat and sculpted by comb and hair oil. He held a cap over his heart as he stepped forward. Behind him were two much younger men bearing a strong resemblance and dressed somewhat but not overwhelmingly more formally: one wore an ill-sitting blue suit, the other wore black slacks, a white dress shirt, and a long black tie. Bringing up the rear were two young women: a redhead who looked to be 20-ish, her bright green eyes sparkling with emotion, and a 30-ish woman studying her phone. They were each wearing black ankle-length dresses and long sleeves with fairly high collars.

"I'd like to pay my respects and extend my condolences," the patriarch of the family said to Reginald. He offered a hand, and Reginald took it.

"Thank you. I appreciate that."

The man almost smiled, but not quite. "You don't recognize me, or remember me, but I'm Mr. King from around the mountain. You used to run into my kids up on Moriah Bald once in a while." He half-turned and gestured at his children. They each nodded at him and made sounds of sympathies being offered. "Isaiah, I'm sure you remember him." Mr. King introduced the other two, but their names flew right in Reginald's ear and back out the other side.

Reginald remembered the family now, though, and the eldest son with whom he'd run around in the woods on Moriah Bald when they were kids. "Oh, Mr. *King*. I am so sorry. I should have recognized you. And you, Isaiah, I apologize. We've been standing up here so long everyone's kind of turned into a blur."

Isaiah and the others nodded, but let their father continue doing the speaking.

The man did smile now. "No need to apologize. I'm just here to say

I'm sorry your mama died. I'm sure she's in a better place now."

Reginald smiled and struggled to respond. Plenty of counters volunteered themselves: *that makes one of us*, for instance. He pushed those aside. "Thank you. I appreciate y'all coming out today. I really do."

"We'll have a sing for her," King added.

"Oh, I'm sure she'd have appreciated that."

"Feel free to come join us if you like." Reginald felt like King's heart might not be in it when he said that, but the next instant he was as obsequiously friendly as ever. He turned to Lewis and offered his hand. "Are you Reginald's partner?"

Lewis coughed, and Reginald and he both turned bright pink. Lewis hemmed and hawed for a couple of syllables, then said, "I'm the neighbor. I'm Dorothea's." He paused. "Her neighbor, I mean."

King shook Lewis' hand, easy, friendly, welcoming. "If you're on the mountain then you're welcome, too. Gotta sing th'old songs when people die." He gestured at Reginald. "I'm sure he's heard it a few times."

The five members of the King family moved along, finally, and took their place along one side pew.

By the time Reginald and Lewis had received the fifty or sixty people in attendance, Reginald's feet were hurting from the beat-up dress shoes he'd worn and he needed a cigarette. *Why does the family never get five minutes out of the spotlight at times like this?* The minister from Dorothea's church—the same one to which Reginald was dragged as a child, but he never really thought of it as *his*—tried to pin Reginald down by offering to let him wait for the service in a side room rather than stand by the casket for the visitation. Reginald had turned him down, in part because he knew the preacher would also be trying to separate him from Lewis. Fundamentalists have almost as good gaydar as the people who legitimately need it, and Reginald figured it grated on the preacher's nerves to have two men do anything together other than pray, much less in public. Now, as the visitation part of the services concluded and people began to gather in the pews for the actual service, Reginald wished he'd taken the preacher up on the offer. Maybe he could've snuck out back for a smoke, at least.

The back wall of the funeral chapel had been lined with men of various ages dressed in somber black suits, white shirts, and black ties, since about twenty minutes before people started arriving for the visitation, and those same ushers were still there an hour and a half later when the funeral itself was due to start. Something about them struck Reginald as familiar, but he couldn't figure out why. They were as generic as any black-clad stagehand at one of these could ever be. *It's because they're watching us.* Reginald flinched at that thought and then, very consciously, one at a time, started on the left and studied the face and build of each of the eight of them until he'd gone all the way across the back wall and tried to memorize what each of them looked like. *What am I doing? I'm no detective. This is crazy. All this shit with my mother's house is making me all fucked up.*

Reginald turned to say something to Lewis, to crack a joke maybe, anything to distract himself and shift the mood, but he stopped short when he realized Lewis, too, studied the suited men standing against the back wall of the sanctuary. Just as Reginald opened his mouth to say something, the McLaren scion who'd greeted Reginald a couple of days before stepped up and invited the two of them to sit on the vast pew at the very front with its small velvet marker identifying it as FAMILY. Lewis hesitated, but Reginald nodded. No way was he going to sit up there in front of everybody and get stared at all by himself.

The memorial service itself was pretty standard fare with one exception: when the service commenced, the King family rose and went to the front. Each carried an instrument—banjo, mandolin, violin, harmonica, guitar—and Reginald realized they were a bluegrass band. *Are they about to perform?* He hadn't asked for this and he couldn't imagine his mother having requested it in any advance planning she did. But sure enough, instead of the funeral chapel's electric organ, all musical accompaniment to the hymns for the rest of the service was from the Kings' five piece band. To Reginald's great relief they did not turn everything into a rip-roaring bluegrass breakdown, but instead produced surprisingly pleasant tunes to support the singing.

Over the course of the service the congregation made it through a strangled and warbling rendition of *Because He Lives*, sat through a couple of readings from the Bible around the promise of a life eternal, then knocked out *If Thou But Suffer God to Guide Thee*. Dorothea's pastor, Preacher Owenby, gave a brief combination eulogy and sermon in which he extolled her virtues as a member of her church and community as if scolding others for not doing enough of the same. The overall theme was that all anyone had to do to have a chance of *not* spending eternity in Hell was to live every moment terrified of doing exactly that.

"Give unto Him your entire life," the preacher said at one point, "holding nothing back, and you shall be rewarded."

Rewarded how? With a pat on the head from the same sky-father who spent your whole life threatening you with a balled-up fist? Reginald puckered his lips like he'd eaten a lemon and spent the rest of the sermon looking at his phone.

Eventually, they all sang Amazing Grace with a melancholy violin solo under it, and the funeral was finally over. Dorothea had been the last of her siblings and cousins, the last one standing at all from her own generation or any before it, other than Aunt Myrtle, and Myrtle was too checked out to really participate in everything. Reginald had expected Bobby, his wife Sue, and himself to be the only family in attendance. Maybe a distant cousin of his mother's, someone whose name he wouldn't recognize. Candy had been a pleasant surprise. But other than Candy, there had been no one else at all. Just Lewis. Without him, Reginald would have been flying solo in front of a hundred people, none of whom he knew and each of whom he'd probably hated at one point or another.

Reginald kept waiting for Bobby to show up, to call him, to burst in the door and pick a fight, to stagger drunkenly out of a back room where they'd kept him buttoned up since he broke in the night before, *anything,* literally any sign. Bobby had always been the one concerned with the *appearance* of his relationship to their mother. That was one of the things he used to say to Reginald when they still talked: *I want people to see our mother was good to us.*

After all, seeing is believing.

And it's always the people for whom appearances are everything who make the biggest fucking mess when the chips are down. They're the people who burn everything down around them to show how much it meant.

But Bobby never showed.

At the very end, as the electric organ played an overwrought *Nearer My God to Thee* for the recessional, an usher from the funeral home appeared beside the end of the pew. Reginald stood. Lewis stood. The two of them walked beside each other from the front of the chapel to the back, flanked front and back by ushers as silent and serious as a Secret Service detail. The funeral home had to scare up pallbearers—normally a place of honor for minor relatives—from among their own staff, apparently, as the eight men who'd stood against the back wall moved into place with military precision and lifted the casket to carry it to the waiting hearse at the street outside.

Hemmed in by employees wearing McLarens name tags, Reginald and Lewis endured a too-slow and somehow also too-fast semi-march, semi-stroll from the front of the chapel to the exit at the back while the organist ran through the last six measures of that ancient hymn for what had to be the fortieth time. Reginald could *feel* people staring at him, at his too-big suit that he should have had cleaned and pressed but hadn't, at his Just For Men hair, at the place on his finger where he wore no wedding band, at the space beside him where his brother *wasn't*, and at the one beside him where Lewis *was*.

At the doors out of the chapel, Dorothea's preacher stopped him to shake his hand and look comforting. Reginald felt the weight of a tremendous amount of *obligation* as the man, whose raw complexion on a slightly puffy face made Reginald think of rehydrated beef jerky, pumped Reginald's hand up and down perfunctorily. "I'm sorry for your loss, Reginald, your mother was a great woman and a child of Eternity."

Reginald made a sound that was probably *thank you* but without all its parts stuck together.

"I hope we'll see you in church on Sundays now you're home."

Reginald cleared his throat and said with a small smile, "No thanks." Nothing more, no grand scene. What had been in Reginald's heart was a lot more complex, a lot longer: *No thanks, preacher, my life is more than a waiting room outside the court where Heaven and Hell collide,* but he didn't bother with the rest of it. No need for it, anyway. These people would take anything less than an enthusiastic yes as one step shy of pledging his soul to Satan right there on the steps of the funeral home regardless of what he did or did not say.

One of the ushers guided them to a limousine idling at the end of the long, concrete walkway.

Time to put Dorothea in the ground.

They didn't talk for the first five minutes of the ride out to the graveyard. Lewis eventually broke the silence by saying, "I liked Candy."

Reginald felt himself return from somewhere else, somewhen else, an almost physical sensation of arriving back in his body, back in the now. For half an instant he could remember the place he'd been—remote, vast, dark skies pricked with agitated stars—and then it was gone. He felt like in that lost moment he could have recalled it perfectly, what was said to him there, could have even returned to it had he wanted, and then the door to that place was closed on him. He felt like he'd been asleep. "I'm sorry, what?"

Lewis smiled and took his hand fondly. "I said, I liked Candy."

Reginald smiled and shook off the disorientation. "I feel like we clicked pretty well. We always got along as kids."

Now, Reginald could tell, Lewis asked what was really on his mind. "Do you think Bobby's okay?"

Reginald scoffed, though not too meanly. "Oh, I'm sure he's fine. He's going to milk this for the next forty years. *I was so mad at my brother I couldn't even go to the funeral and they buried mama without me*, that sort of thing. Don't worry, I'm sure he's home filling a notebook with lines like that so he can try them out on me later."

"Is he… I mean, doesn't someone have to clean out her house?"

Reginald groaned from across the back seat of the limo. "Yes. And fucking Christ, I was willing to give it a start last night but he'd better not think the whole job's on *me*. He loved her so much, he can pick through her underwear drawer. He's probably doing it right now, anyway, so he can bitch about me not being there to help or something. He's always wanted to get the good stuff, used to make a big deal out of which china would be his, that kind of thing. Maybe he decided to stay home and box up the good shit because he knows I'll just put it all on eBay."

Lewis didn't push it, and Reginald descended into a slightly deeper stew. *One more damned thing to worry about. Well, fuck Bobby, I'll go knock on his door when we get home.*

Reginald shuddered at having used "home" to refer to Dorothea's house.

Reginald, Lewis, and maybe two-thirds of the people who'd attended the memorial service piled out of cars at the cemetery and traced various paths between tombstones old and new to arrive at a rectangular platform tastefully bordered in astroturf. The eight pallbearers lifted the coffin with familiar ease and picked their way across the rolling, time-warped landscape of the old graveyard. It sat on the side of a low rise, facing east, bordered on three sides by thick and ancient Appalachian forest, trees bursting now with the reds and oranges and golds of their own demise, and on its fourth side by the dirt road they'd turned onto a half mile back in order to get here.

This was the cemetery where Dorothea's father had been buried, her mother, her grandparents on both sides, her siblings and cousins, and uncles and aunts. Reginald might have guessed there were five hundred graves in the place, and he'd bet a hundred of them had *Voth* engraved overhead. None of that modern shit of having stones flush with the grass so a riding lawnmower could pass over them, either. This was an old-school burial ground, the kind where the dead showed off how well-to-do they were, or weren't, even from beyond the veil. Some of the graves bore monuments the size of a large car, or were above-ground mausoleums, whereas others had only a simple stone slab or a cross. The cemetery was old enough that it predated bulldozers and backhoes.

The ground rolled and buckled, as creased here and there as the mountains themselves. The ground had shifted with what must have been two centuries of use, and tree roots had wormed their way in from the edges, and generations upon generations of spring rains and winter freezing had chipped away at the ostentatious immortality each grave had promised when it had been filled in. The effect was that the cemetery was not laid out in a neat grid pattern, and everything looked a little bit tattered. The shining new casket and the tidy precision of the movements of the pallbearers carrying it stood out in sharp contrast as they wended their way along to the plot where Dorothea would be, at long last, laid to rest.

A thick drape over the casket bore MCLARENS in white block letters. The bearers lifted her pecan wood final ride onto the complicated contraption that would lower it into the ground after they had gone, then moved to stand at the back of the gathering as they'd done at the funeral itself. A few chairs had been set up with the same black velvet FAMILY signs on them, but Reginald didn't want to sit. Instead, he stood. An usher indicated one of the folding chairs but he shook his head at the kid. A different usher leaned in and whispered, "Sir, we can't start until you're seated."

"I don't want to sit down," Reginald said in full voice. "I'd like to stand. Let somebody else sit if they're tired, it won't bother me one bit."

Lewis coughed to cover a laugh while the crowd shifted uncomfortably. *Good fucking God*, Reginald thought, *the gossip mill will snap its jaws for just the piddliest shit at times like these. At least she picked a nice time of year to die.* Reginald let his eyes roam over the brilliant autumn golds and reds and greens of the trees ringing the graveyard. It was a small cemetery off a side road off yet another side road, at least three miles from anything resembling a highway anybody would recognize. The gravel road to get here needed a fresh scraping, too: ruts and dried out puddles and old tree roots made for a bumpy ride even in the heavily cushioned comfort of the funeral home Cadillac.

Now that they stood in it, the graveyard appeared to be in no better shape. The grass had been mown and many—but not all—the headstones had been trimmed around, but the older ones were covered in black and green… algae? Moss? Reginald had no idea, but it obscured the names and dates on the oldest ones. These people didn't just have no one left who cared, they had no one left who knew they'd existed. Even their gravestones were being reclaimed by the earth. *So much for eternal anything.*

Reginald remembered his mother stopping off to "visit" relatives interred here a few times in his youth before she gave up that habit. When his grandfather died, his mother draped all the mirrors in the house and sat up with the body the night before the funeral. *It didn't even occur to me to do that until now*, he thought. *So old-fashioned. Always had to do things like the dead were still watching. But who needs to sit up with the body when her **fucking ghost** is running around **what the fuck**—*

A spike of terror shot through Reginald's chest and snapped him out of the spiral of resentful thoughts even as it started. He stood there, his heart pounding, breathing fast and shallow, sweat breaking out on his forehead, suddenly worried he might faint. He reached up to rub his eyes. Lewis gave him a comforting pat on the back. *Good, let them think I'm just crying instead of scared out of my fucking mind.*

Dorothea's preacher was giving yet another speech about eternal life and the rewards of faithfulness. That phrase he harped on in church came up again: *Give unto Him your entire life, holding nothing back, and you shall be rewarded.* No one seemed to pay much attention this time. Nobody ever does when there's a yawning grave in the middle of everything.

The service eventually ended, and that meant a second round of shaking hands and making small talk. *I live over in Quartz Gap, well near there,* and, *I do medical transcription from home,* and, *No, Bobby's not feeling well.* Reginald managed to get each little nicety out to the satisfaction of each person determined to touch death one more time, even if at a remove. That's what people want at a funeral, he knew: to get close enough to death and grief to touch them, physically touch them with their actual hands, paw at them like an old dog roughing up the carpet before it lies down, and then go back to the safe and sunlit world of the living. Reginald let them. It wasn't the first time he'd let strangers have their way with him so they'd leave him alone.

Eventually that was all over, too, and Lewis and Reginald found themselves alone with the funeral home staff, the preacher, and Dorothea's grave. Reginald reached into his pocket, pulled out his phone, and took a photo of the coffin.

The preacher started to say something, but then his jaw snapped shut when Reginald pulled a cigarette from the pack in his pocket, tucked it into the corner of his mouth, turned his back to the casket, and raised the phone high. Reginald made a little "V" with his fingers and smiled as he took a selfie. Then, around the cigarette, he said to Lewis, "Get in here. We're doing this."

Lewis let himself laugh once, though he blushed in obvious horror, and he pressed his left shoulder to Reginald's right. Another photo, this one with the preacher's angered expression visible in one corner, and Reginald and Lewis laughed together. It was the first natural thing Reginald felt like he'd done all day. Even getting fucked that morning had a surreal, as-seen-on-TV quality to it. After all, it was on the set of one of his favorite pornos. Reginald slipped the phone back in his pocket and took out the lighter. The cigarette, for which he'd waited two hours, felt like a million bucks.

"Mr. Voth," the preacher snapped, "I've endured your disrespect at every turn today and let it slide so that your mother could be buried in the dignity she deserves, but this…" He made a fist, but he didn't raise it. Reginald was a little disappointed he wouldn't have an excuse to deck a preacher over his mother's grave. "I have *never* in all my life seen someone behave like this at a grave."

Reginald took a long drag and spoke smoke in the preacher's direction. "Bullshit. My uncle's second wife's cousin died fifteen years ago, and her kids got in a fistfight before the service even started. Knocked her coffin right over in the middle of the church and, unless I'm mistaken, *you were there.* Don't come at me about me and my mother, and don't ever ask me again if you'll see me in church on Sunday."

Reginald and Lewis rode from the graveyard back to the funeral home in nearly total silence. Lewis sat beside him, Reginald's hand on Lewis' forearm, but Reginald stared out the window and thankfully Lewis left him to his thoughts.

When they got into Lewis' hatchback in the funeral home parking lot, Reginald let out a long sigh. "Oh, thank the fucking gods." He drew a deep breath, held it for a count of three, then let it back out slowly. "Christ almighty. I hate this shit so much."

"I'm sorry you're having to deal with it." Lewis put his hand on Reginald's knee and squeezed it.

Reginald reflexively took Lewis' hand and held it for a moment. "Thanks. And thank you for coming with me today."

"Of course. I mean, shit, I'll go anywhere to watch a preacher get told off."

By the time they got back to Moriah Bald Estates, it was half past two in the afternoon and the cops were parked in front of number 8: Johnny and Kate, across the way from Lewis' house.

CHAPTER ELEVEN – IT'S RAINING MEN

"Sir, I'll need you to step back for now. There are officers talking with the resident at this time." The sheriff's deputy was a big guy, plenty of well-marbled beef wrapped in curves, and Reginald hated himself a little bit for tucking him away under *Probably Yes* in the inner filing system used to determine whether he'd fool around with literally every man he met. It wasn't a conscious thing, it just happened. He didn't hate himself for that, not at all. He'd long since decided to savor the many times the internal bingo cage coughed up a *Probably Yes* or a *Definitely Yes* or a *Hell Yes* or a *Why Not*, not merely despite the world telling him it was shameful but *because* the world told him it was shameful. No, he hated himself a little because the guy was a cop. Reginald had known—intimately and otherwise—enough law enforcement to have figured out plenty of them join up with good intentions but the good ones usually quit.

"I live across the street," Lewis said. He gestured over his shoulder at his house. "We're neighbors. We actually run the neighborhood watch together." He pushed his hair back out of his eyes and Reginald thought it was the most beautiful thing he'd ever seen in his entire life. "Is everything okay?"

The deputy frowned and shook his aviators at Lewis. "I'm afraid I can't comment on anything at this time. I'd suggest you contact the liaison officer for a copy of any report, if there is one. And it's possible an officer will want to talk to you."

"Sure." Lewis chewed his bottom lip for a second. "Can you tell them I asked? And let them know I'm happy to help if they need anything?"

"I can pass that along, yes." He delivered that with the sort of finality that closes a door firmly enough to let you hear the latch rattle but doesn't quite count as a slam.

Lewis and Reginald walked away a few feet, up onto the grass of the big oval in the middle of the neighborhood. "Christ," Reginald said, "I hope nothing happened."

Lewis nodded in that direction. "Two cruisers and an unmarked car. She's in there with a detective." He looked back at Reginald. "Something bad happened."

Reginald nodded in the direction of the house. "Johnny seemed harmless enough last night. Kind of a big puppy dog. Did he have a bite?"

Lewis didn't look away from the house, but his brow did wrinkle.

"I mean, was he ever violent?" Reginald waved a hand vaguely.

Lewis shook his head and met his gaze. "No. Ha." He chuckled the once, but he didn't seem to find it very funny. "If either of them were an abuser I'd expect it to be her. She's the dominant personality in that relationship. She's the breadwinner, she's the one who picked the neighborhood, sold your mother on developing it, the whole nine yards. She's always been the one in the house with a master plan. I suspect she keeps that puppy dog on a pretty short leash."

"Well, given the way she made a move on my mom's shit five seconds after she met me, and Johnny's boldest move was to try to shake my hand, maybe that isn't so surprising. But for real, I hope everything's okay. They seem nice enough. I mean, they annoyed me, but almost everyone annoys me."

Lewis seemed lost in contemplation of what might have caused the sheriff to show up in Kate and Johnny's driveway. After a few seconds he said, "No, they wouldn't fit the profile for him to be a violent abuser."

Reginald tried to lighten the mood. "You watch a lot of cop shows?"

Lewis didn't laugh. "No, but I've sat through a couple of raids and I've known plenty of violent abusers."

Oops. "Oh, uh, I'm sorry?" Reginald felt as though the boat had tossed underneath his feet and he'd barely managed to stay aboard. "I wasn't, I mean, I didn't intend to—"

Lewis smirked at him. "Oh, you're fine. But the guys who ran the first two studios I worked at were decidedly *not.*" He shrugged once. "Sometimes it turns out the skeezy guy running the 'studio' out of a cheap apartment is in the mob and he gets mad when you see him beat up a model who owes him money, and sometimes he's 'just' selling fentanyl on Fredslist."

"They sell fentanyl on *Fredslist?*" Reginald scoffed and dug in his pockets for his lighter. "And here I was, telling myself I needed to spend less time on the Internet when the real problem was I just never looked in the right places."

Lewis chuckled, but his heart wasn't in it. "Oh, please, tell me you're not addicted to fentanyl."

Reginald laughed aloud at that. "Oh, honey, if I was, I'd have something better to do on nice days in autumn than bury my goddamned mother. Namely, fentanyl." He produced a cigarette with a flourish, a Virginia Slims 120. In college his friends had called them his Barbie cigarettes. "No, seriously, I am not."

Lewis stared at Reginald's hands as he lit the cigarette. "I'm in recovery." He waited a moment. "That's why I ask. They always told us, you know. In rehab? That two addicts just set each other off again. Like, we'd both start using again if we ever got together with another junkie."

Reginald took a long drag, held it, then blew it out to the side. "If you're worried I'm going to run screaming in the other direction, don't be." He took another drag. "Though I do have some questions. I mean, if we're just putting all our cards on the table like that."

Lewis nodded and walked over to one of the picnic tables in the oval of grass and concrete curb in the center of the neighborhood. He sat down backwards on the bench, leaning against the tabletop. "Okay. We can do that now." He offered a small smile that vanished quickly but he looked like he meant it all the same. "Just this morning a handsome guy told me I shouldn't treat him like the fine china, and I'm going to say the same thing now. I knew we would need to talk about this stuff eventually, one way or the other, and there's no such thing as a *good* time." Lewis licked his lips. "It was meth, it's been four years, I checked myself into a rehab facility in San Diego after the second raid. I got into it because the 'studio,'" and here he made air quotes, "was always on us to stay thin. They wanted us to do steroids, human growth hormone, work out six days a week, dehydrate for thirty-six hours before a shoot, you know, the whole deal. Whatever it took to have ten-pack abs and make our dicks look bigger, make our veins stand out all over, be able to go for hours and hours and hours. They actually used to inject something into our dicks at the start of a shoot to make sure we stayed hard all day." He shrugged. "It's so easy to get pushed out by somebody hotter and leaner, and it's especially easy to get pushed out when you're not white. I needed every advantage."

Reginald took another drag. "This is going to come out wrong, but I thought meth, like, made your teeth fall out and your skin turn weird. But I suppose for some things maybe losing your teeth is a professional advantage."

Lewis didn't laugh. "Sure, after years. I used it for eight months. At first just when I had a shoot, then when we went out and celebrated after, then all the time. Then he got raided for fentanyl and I checked into a program rather than get prosecuted myself."

"Did you flip on the guy?"

Lewis nodded. "That—agreeing to testify—and keeping my nose clean and doing a year of informal probation along with two weeks in rehab and a year of NA, that kept me out of a jail term."

Reginald's eyebrows bounced once. "I thought people only went to jail for having a *lot*."

Lewis clearly didn't love that response. "Not in California. It's a year of jail time or what they call 'informal probation.' No probation officer, but a judge could still tell me what terms I had to satisfy and every few weeks I had to show up in court and tell the judge all the stuff on the checklist I'd done so far. Community service was better than jail, I guess, but not by much. You go in thinking you'll just be bored raking leaves outside city hall, and the next thing you know you're forced to pick through a homeless camp after *it* gets raided, throw away these people's stuff, and try not to stick yourself with their needles if any of them were users. It was awful. Nobody wins, not on a day like that."

The wind picked up for a moment, and Lewis shuddered. "By the end I found an Elks club where I could tend bar and that was OK. I didn't get paid, though. In fact, I had to pay them. Anyway, I was terrified my family would find out about the arrest, about the meth, about the gay porn, all of it. That was the worst part of all. I stayed sober purely out of terror, to be honest, which made it possible and also much more difficult. Rehab seemed to think sobriety hinged on them getting me to make some huge personal discovery, find some single cause for all my problems, whatever had fucked me up in childhood, all that dumb shit. But none of them seemed to think, 'I needed to stay skinny *plus* fuck and get fucked for six or eight hours off and on whether I felt like it or not,' was good enough." Lewis sniffed once, one long inhalation to clear a nostril, and it sent a kitchen knife of hurt and sympathy through Reginald's heart with *don't ask obnoxious questions* written down the handle. "But NA has been good. I've gotten a lot out of that. There's bullshit, but for me, it's bullshit that works and that's all that really matters."

"Narcotics Anonymous?" Reginald had finished the cigarette and twisted the butt back and forth between his fingers to drop the cherry and a little leftover tobacco out of the end, onto the ground, before crushing it under the toe of his dress shoe.

Lewis nodded. "So, you know, you keep apologizing for being fucked up, but all I see is a guy who doesn't necessarily love his job, and definitely doesn't love his mother, but so what? At least you didn't have to satisfy the terms of a sentencing agreement before you ran away to the other side of the country, to the remotest place in it, where no one would look for you, only to realize you don't have any actual employable skills other than your mouth, your asshole, and your cock. At least this time I work for myself." Lewis looked away, at the trees beyond the houses in Dorothea's former yard, at the sky, at a few autumn clouds streaming past.

"My mother tried to molest me." Reginald blurted it out, something he hadn't said aloud to very many people at all. He didn't try to dwell on it very much, or even think about *thinking about it.* "I was in junior high. Way past, you know, the whole 'don't tell anyone' or 'this is our special game, keep it a secret' kind of shit."

Lewis turned and held Reginald's gaze and Reginald fought down the urge to light another cigarette right away. Instead he locked eyes with Lewis until he could *see* Lewis decide he believed him. "I'm sorry."

"It could be worse. Nobody died."

Lewis chuckled once, a cough of irony rather than amusement. "A life has many endings before it's over, Reginald. Don't kid yourself about the significance of them when they happen. And no kid should have to deal with that." He said it again. "I'm sorry you did."

"Well, I appreciate it, but it's not like it was your idea. She had me figured out. The gay thing, I mean. She told me later she realized it when I was a little kid and I asked a question that, to her, meant I didn't totally believe in God, or at least in her version of it. That question, by the way, was whether all the pre-colonial-era Native Americans went to hell since they didn't have a chance to hear about Jesus. She decided only a child 'possessed by the demon of homosexuality' would have asked 'such a perverse question.'

Anyway, puberty hit and I didn't turn into a big butch lumberjack of a kid, and I didn't get any girls pregnant in seventh grade, so I think she decided to 'fix' me herself. I believe the technical term is 'corrective rape.'"

Reginald went for the second cigarette. "To be clear, I want to emphasize that she *tried* to molest me. I didn't let her. I pushed her away when I realized what was happening. She told me never to tell anyone and immediately pretended it never happened. I mean, she woke me up for school the next day and drove me there and everything, and we didn't speak to each other for three days, and after that she just went back to normal, for all that was worth. So, I got away as soon as I could, and I stayed away as much as possible, and that was that. Thirty-seven miles might as well have been the other side of the country, insofar as my family was concerned. It was outside of 'random drop-in' range, 'closely monitoring your lifestyle' range, *and* 'why don't we see you in church' range. That was what mattered to me." Reginald shrugged before lighting the second Virginia Slim and taking a quick puff. "I'm kind of surprised you still drink. Is that bad to say? I mean, I don't know what I'm talking about. I'm just sort of assuming you'd have to stay totally off of everything."

Lewis had never looked away, even as Reginald did break their shared eye contact to light his cigarette and look back at the houses on the circle, the cops, their cars. Lewis didn't shy away from the topic or from Reginald's observations. He said, "So you get feeling terrified—of both things, I mean, your parents and also of what people think."

"And I get wanting to run away, and I get there never being a good time to bring it up." Reginald drew deep and burned the cigarette down practically in one go. "So don't worry, handsome. Everybody's fucked up somehow. I'm just glad you survived."

Lewis looked away and up the street, in the direction of Bobby's house. "Does he know?"

Reginald lifted one shoulder and realized as he did so it had been exactly the same body language he used with his mother as a resentful teen.

He'd even stooped a little when he did it, the beaten-down posture of disaffected youth everywhere. Reginald stood straighter and swallowed some of the bitter cocktail of emotions: sympathy and empathy for Lewis and his obvious embarrassment at his past, and Reginald's hatred of his own mother, and of whoever would shame Lewis for his body, and at basically anyone who'd go out of their way to hurt a kind soul just for fun. Reginald drew a breath and sighed it out. "I have no idea. He and I never discussed it anyway."

Lewis stood up. "Man, fuck these people. Well, let's go knock on his door and see what his fucking problem is."

"Oh, I do not want to inflict my family drama on you." Reginald waved a hand at that. "You've been too kind by far. I mean, you've got your own shit to tend to, right? And I've eaten up the last, what, sixteen hours of your life? Eighteen? Thank you, but please don't feel like you have to go be my bodyguard or anything."

Lewis gave Reginald a look that said a lot of things, none of which Reginald could totally read. "Huh-uh. No way. I'm not letting you out of my sight. I'm not going to push you to confront things you're not ready to confront, because that's a shit way to treat people. But if you're about to go ask your brother why he didn't go to the funeral then I'm down to go with. I want him to know you're not in this alone." Lewis blushed a little. "And I owe it to you for letting you walk into your mother's house solo."

Reginald felt a pang of something gentler than fear but just as surprising—real affection—shoot through him this time. After two seconds of consideration he tried to push it aside with teasing. "Well, if you insist. It's a public street, you can walk the same way I do if you want."

They strolled, and Reginald found himself fighting the absolutely ridiculous urge to take Lewis' hand. He'd known the man less than a day. *I'm getting sentimental,* he told himself. *Maybe I'm getting lonely. The first guy to show a little potential and I'm acting like a teenager all over again. God, I hate coming back here. Sets me back thirty-five years every time.*

Ninety seconds later they walked onto Bobby's short driveway. His house, a conglomeration of beige stone and gray siding, loomed over its own front porch like a face with a too-small mouth. The porch had a hyper-modern baluster pattern on the railing, something Reginald was sure had a fancy name and cost three times as much. Bobby had married into money and clearly didn't hesitate to spend it. *He's probably bought all her land already. I'll be lucky if I inherit half the house. A shit payout for a lifetime of being hated and feeling afraid.*

Bluegrass music blared from inside Sue and Bobby's house, muffled by walls, but audible once they got close enough. Reginald could all too easily believe Bobby would be in there kicking up his heels about leaving him to face the funeral all on his own. It fit in perfectly with the lifted pickup truck with a Confederate flag sticker: performative country-ness by someone who can afford to pay more for a pickup than Reginald made in a year. A part of him, he realized, looked forward to this. Reginald was sad and confused and vulnerable, and that always had him spoiling for a fight.

Realizing Lewis had stopped a few paces back, Reginald turned. "Cold feet?"

Lewis' tongue darted out as he licked his lips in a nervous flash. "No." His voice shook a little. "But I need to tell you something."

Reginald's stomach fell away, turning into a deep pit. He could only imagine what needed to be said now. Maybe Lewis had fucked Bobby, too, and he needed to confess. Or maybe Lewis had fucked Dorothea. He had guilt written all over him in bright red even as he turned a little pale. "I did see something in the woods last night."

Reginald's breath caught.

Lewis went on. "I was scared to admit it. Scared to confirm what you saw. But I saw the silhouettes of people, or at least what could have been people. They were just beyond the tree line, and their eyes glowed golden yellow. Tiny little eye shine, like an animal stepping in front of a light, but there wasn't any light on them. To me, it looked like they were peering around the sides of trees, like they were hiding behind them, spying on us.

They just watched us, never blinking, and then they were gone. Three of them. And when you asked, I just, honestly, I didn't know what to say. I was scared of what that meant. So I lied."

Reginald opened his mouth to say something, but Lewis held up his index finger to tell him to wait.

"I don't like lying, Reginald. I want to be really clear about that. Let's get that straight right from the start. I *hate* lying. I've done enough of it myself for three lifetimes. And if I ever do lie again, I hope you can trust that I'll tell you, as soon as I'm brave enough, and that I will own it. I'm not trying make any excuses by telling you how afraid I was. I just want you to know there's an explanation. And I need you to know how big a deal lies are to me so that you won't lie to me, either."

Reginald held out his hand.

Lewis took it without hesitation.

Reginald smiled a little. "It's a relief that you saw something. And I appreciate you telling me. I don't *like it*, because it means we have to do something about what's happened so far. It means it's *real*. But I appreciate honesty, too." *And given how casually I throw men out the airlock, this is fucked from the get-go.* But Reginald didn't say that part, even as it filled him with the dread of anticipated sorrow waiting for them down the road. "Now let's go kick my brother's ass."

Lewis let out a breath he'd been holding, a frightened little huff, and then nodded. "Okay."

The compound stench of decomposition hit them before they made it onto the front porch.

CHAPTER TWELVE – DOUBLE TROUBLE

Reginald had never experienced the garlic-rotting-egg-mothball-cabbage-baby-shit smell of decomposing bodies before, but some part of him, some ancient genetic memory implanted by the very first primate ancestor who happened upon a dead neighbor, recognized it and issued the safest possible command: to puke his guts out immediately.

Obeying, all he could do was lean his entire body over the top of the white-painted wooden railing and empty his guts directly into the shrub roses and azaleas clustered together in a narrow garden bed along the front of the house. He didn't even have much in his stomach, but he stood bent double, gasping for breath, then gagging on the foul taste of the air, then violently straining to empty himself again.

Lewis wrapped a hand around Reginald's left bicep when he half-stood between heaves, dragging him away from the porch, down the front walk, and out into the street. "Oh, *fuck*, Reginald, *fuck*," he groaned, but Lewis kept his wits about him better than Reginald did, at least. He got Reginald to lean against the mailbox—identical to every mailbox but Dorothea's—before turning and puking on the concrete driveway. "Christ," he gasped after, "Fucking Christ, Reginald, I am so sorry."

"Jesus fuck me," Reginald whispered. He drew a breath, almost gagged again but held it at bay, then blew all his breath out at once as though trying to expel that horrible smell and any memory of it. "What the fuck is going on around here?"

Lewis looked up, down the street towards Kate's house. "Do you… if…" He paused, drew a breath, stood up as straight as he could and tugged his shirt into place. "You need to call the cops."

Reginald took another shallow breath, held it a moment, let it out; then another, less shallow. Then he breathed deeper. His voice came out as a low moan. "I can still smell it, Lewis. I can *taste it.*" He didn't look at him, favoring instead some blade of grass approximately eight feet away from his left foot at the very edge of the lawn. "I can taste my dead brother."

Lewis very tentatively reached forward and put a hand in the middle of Reginald's back, not quite patting it, not quite rubbing it. "Do you want me to go get those cops down there?"

Reginald drew a breath through his nose and grimaced at the bitter stench and immediate burn: puke in his nose, puke running down the back of his sinuses. He hated throwing up. He'd hated it since childhood. It always made him feel *ashamed.*

"What. The *fuck.*"

"Reginald, believe me, when you find a dead body you need to tell the police *immediately.* If there's any suspicion that anything…" Lewis hesitated, "Anything *intentional,* you need to be the one to tell them and you need to tell them right away."

Reginald drew one more breath, then snorted hard, getting it all over with at once. He stood up straight, worked saliva around his mouth, then spit it out on the ground. "Yeah. Okay. Let's get those cops."

Lewis squeezed his shoulder once, then threw both hands in the air to wave at the deputy standing against his car at the end of Kate and Johnny's short driveway. When he shouted, the deputy jumped like he'd heard a gun go off.

Two hours later, Reginald finished telling the story *again*. "…But once we got onto the porch, we knew." He sat at a picnic table in the big green oval. He couldn't look at Bobby's house. He could only look at the officer asking him questions, who sat on the other side of the same table. Lewis and another officer sat on the other side of the little quadrangle of picnic tables being questioned separately. One corner of Reginald's brain supplied, *they haven't said "questioning" yet, but it's obvious what they're doing.* Another answered, *who the fuck cares?*

Reginald tried very hard never to look over the officer's shoulder at the tall, white van now parked in Sue and Bobby's driveway. It had SHERIFF DEPARTMENT emblazoned on the side.

"And what then? I know I've asked you already, but I want to make sure I have everything down." The officer was neither kind nor unkind. She was a stout black woman with eyes Reginald could tell caught every detail of his movements and demeanor. She wore a burgundy suit and clip-on earrings, and a clip-on badge that read "Investigator Hollingsworth." Reginald knew she was asking again—a third time, actually—to sift for inconsistencies. If he'd murdered his brother and his brother's wife, now would be an excellent time to catch him.

"Then, to be honest, I probably killed the bush roses by yakking all over them." Reginald sighed and shook his head. "I'm sorry. I'm just—this— everything is a lot to deal with. Uh, then Lewis," he nodded his head in Lewis' direction, "got me down off the porch and out to the street and he flagged down one of the deputies over at Kate and Johnny's."

"And you said your mother owned the house at the end, the original property?" When Reginald nodded once, Investigator Hollingsworth went on. "And Lewis is your partner?"

Reginald shook his head. The first time she asked it, he'd laughed. It had come out wrong: strangled, too sharp, too sudden. The second time he simply said *no, we just met.* This time he said, "I wish," and it was just as much too sudden and too sharp as the laughter had been. Reginald tried to cover for it, but badly. "I mean, like, you know. We just met yesterday."

Investigator Hollingsworth had poker face for days, but Reginald felt a little ping on the gaydar. Something told him she understood.

"Can you tell me what's going on with Kate & Johnny?" Reginald felt tired of being the center of attention, but also, to his surprise, he truly wanted to know.

"I'm afraid not, but don't worry, we're handling it." Hollingsworth made a note of something. "Now, let's go back over your and your brother's relationship. When was the last time you spoke to hi—"

Hollingsworth stopped speaking and looked up, over Reginald's left shoulder, and then stood. With a nod at a deputy and a gesture at another, she stepped back over the picnic table bench and looked at Reginald again. "Mr. Voth, I need you to wait here just a moment. Please don't go anywhere."

Reginald nodded, then twisted to look back up the block.

Johnny Spangler stood on Reginald's mother's front porch. He could just hear her screen door latch behind him. It was obvious Johnny had just walked outside.

Reginald couldn't help himself. He asked aloud, "What the *fuck?*"

Johnny's face opened up in a grin that made Reginald's flesh ripple with goosebumps. His teeth were too big. His lips were too narrow. He looked like his whole head could flip open on a hinge for just a moment, and then it was gone: he returned to being nothing more than a man in a place he shouldn't have been, wearing a smile too large by half.

Johnny waved at the deputies who started walking in his direction. With a few jaunty steps, he jogged down off the porch and went to meet them by Dorothea's mailbox.

"Is everything alright, sir?"

Johnny all but beamed at the man. "Oh, I'm fine. Feeling great. But what's going on out here?"

Hollingsworth caught up to them all now. "I'm more interested in knowing what's going on in there." She nodded in the direction of

Dorothea's house. "Sir, did you spend the night in that home?"

Reginald turned a little further and caught Lewis' eye. Lewis held his face very still, but the way he cut his gaze immediately back to Johnny made Reginald realize Lewis saw something terribly wrong in Johnny's demeanor. Everyone in the oval had stopped talking and each now listened to the conversation unfolding at Dorothea's mailbox. Lewis shook his head just a little. Reginald wondered what he meant: don't speak? Say nothing? A much worse interpretation occurred to him: *that isn't Johnny.*

Johnny shrugged and cranked his grin up another couple of notches. "I guess I did. Must have fallen asleep. It's a very, you know, cozy kind of home."

The shift of Hollingsworth's weight from one leg to the other told Reginald she didn't think very much of that answer. "Why did you enter Mrs. Voth's residence?"

Johnny waited a beat and then looked surprised, as though he hadn't expected that to be important. "Oh, I thought I saw someone in a window. And I figured maybe it was Reggie, except I think he stayed with Lewis last night. I didn't want to disturb them, but I wanted to come up and check. Found the front door unlocked, and at that point I worried maybe it was a prowler, maybe a burglar. That happens a lot with recent deaths, you know. The house gets broken into." Johnny gave her a ridiculous, shit-eating grin as he mansplained crime statistics to a cop. "And I figured, well, if I called 911, by the time anyone got here the burglar would be long gone. So, I came up here myself to check. But I didn't find anybody inside, and then I sat down on the couch just to kind of, you know, let go of the tension of having thought I saw someone? And then the next thing I knew, it was five minutes ago, and it sounded like a lot of activity out here, so I decided to come check it out." He waited another beat. "Sorry. What are you people doing here, anyway?"

Detective Hollingsworth shifted her weight back to the other leg. "Your wife reported you missing this morning. We've been interviewing her, getting your description, and putting together a bulletin we could release. Did you not tell your wife where you were going last night?"

Johnny's grin stretched ever wider, and Reginald felt his stomach tremble again. "She was asleep, officer."

"You didn't think to leave a note?"

"Time was of the essence." Johnny's grin re-sealed itself shut as he smacked his lips for a moment, then dawned anew. "I'm sure you know how that is."

Hollingsworth shifted again. "Do you have permission to be in Mrs. Voth's home?"

Johnny scoffed openly at her. Arrogance dripped from every word, every syllable. "I'm sure Bobby wouldn't mind. Let's go ask."

Hollingsworth took two steps backward from Johnny, turned halfway, and gestured for Reginald to come forward. Reginald stood, stepped away from the picnic table, and strode in that direction. He and Lewis exchanged a long look as he passed. Reginald wished he knew Lewis well enough to read his expression. He looked worried. Beyond that, Reginald had no idea.

Johnny's smile turned back into all teeth and stretched lips as Reginald approached. "Sure, we can ask Reggie, too, if you want."

Reginald didn't bother to correct him. It didn't even occur to him against the overwhelming roar of *something is wrong with his face* pounding in Reginald's mind. He managed to force his gaze from Johnny's bear-trap grin and look at Hollingsworth, but Reginald felt panic starting to ball itself up in his stomach, ready to uncoil. He had to work not to physically cringe and forced himself to speak. "Yeah?"

"Mr. Spangler says he saw someone in your mother's house last night. He entered to investigate on his own rather than call 911. Do you wish to press charges for trespassing?" Hollingsworth put a fist on her hip as she shifted her weight a final time. She was done considering Johnny's story.

Reginald could tell she just wanted to wrap this up one way or the other.

Reginald blinked at her. "Press…? No. Whatever." He glanced back at Johnny for a heartbeat. He, too, had seen someone inside his mother's home. But nothing about Johnny, in this moment, inspired the sort of trust it would have taken for Reginald to say anything about that in front of him now. "I don't really think that matters."

Johnny's grin somehow managed to get even wider. "I promise I didn't take anything worse than a nap."

Hollingsworth hated everything about that, but she looked at Reginald, right in his eyes, weighed whatever she saw there, and then nodded. She didn't so much as look at Johnny as she addressed him. "Mr. Spangler, I suggest you return home and let your wife know you're okay. She's very worried. And now I've got a missing persons report to make sure we *don't* add to the national database." She grimaced. "A deputy will *accompany* you." Now she nodded back at the oval. "Mr. Voth, if you'd be kind enough to accompany me back to the table, I still have a few more questions."

"Is something wrong, Reggie?" Johnny's grin, like a cat curling up on a ledge to watch the birds, wound itself down to an oh-so-innocent smile.

Now Reginald couldn't hold back. "It's *Reginald*, goddamn it, I told you that last night. And stop poking around my mother's house, Johnny. I promise you'll get pick of the litter for your FotoFeed, just stay out of my mother's goddamned house." Reginald's voice rose at the end, shrill and frightened, and he blushed.

Johnny's face became a dramaturge mask of tragedy. "You've got a lot to deal with right now, so I won't hold that against you. It's easy to lash out when you feel like everything's out of control." The corners of his mouth twisted in reverse to form something like a smile. "But don't worry. You're home now, Reggie. It'll all be okay in time."

Reginald's eyes bugged out in frustration, fury, and confusion, but he managed to say nothing. He simply turned and walked—slowly, angrily—back to the picnic table with Hollingsworth by his side. That killed a good thirty seconds, time he spent trying to sew patches onto his fraying emotions. He knew Lewis tried to catch his eye, but he didn't return the look.

Reginald folded himself onto one of the picnic table's benches one more time, but Hollingsworth remained standing. "Mr. Voth, I don't have any more questions for you. The forensics team will be done in your brother's home soon. When that happens, my team and I will go in and begin our phase of the investigation."

"I didn't kill my brother," Reginald said it quietly: all the exhaustion of the day, the night before, the last several days, all of it, hitting him at once. "It's probably *gauche* or something to say that part out loud, but I am very tired. I buried my mother today, her neighbor broke into her house, and my brother is dead. Maybe his wife, too. You've been very careful not to tell me what's in there, but I can imagine. I watched my share of *Unsolved Mysteries*. Both their cars are there. One of them killed the other and then themselves. I'm sorry you're having to deal with all that, and I am way too tired to keep dancing around it."

Hollingsworth reached up and rubbed her chin with the crook between her thumb and index finger. "I'm not confirming what you just said," she replied, but her tone shifted. It didn't exactly soften, but it became a little less institutional and a little more human. "I'm not making any formal statement. But I'm also not going to tell you that you're wrong." The last part, she said very softly, and the kindness in her voice nearly broke Reginald wide open. "I need to know where we can reach you for the next little while. I know you gave me your cell number. Will you be staying in your mother's home, or somewhere else?"

Reginald looked up, and now he and Lewis locked gazes for a moment. The deputy who'd been talking to Lewis had left him sitting there, and the two of them shared a long, uninterrupted look. Reginald doubted Lewis could have heard Hollingsworth's question, but he felt like Lewis' expression asked him the same thing. "I'll be staying with my… friend."

Hollingsworth nodded in Lewis' direction. "Mr. Gwan? That's very kind of him."

Reginald noticed Hollingsworth wore a wedding band but no engagement ring, and the band was wide and made from some dark grey metal in a matte finish. He looked up at Hollingsworth again and shrugged. "Yes, it is. And if he throws me out, I'll be at my mother's. I had a room in town but, I'm going to be honest, if I go that far, it'll be to get away from all this, and if I try to get away from all this, I won't stop at town. I'll just keep going. So, I'll stay here. Don't worry, I won't run off." Reginald drew a steadying breath. "Detective, will I have to identify my brother's body?"

Hollingsworth shook her head side to side very subtly. "Not if you don't want to. You can, it does speed some things up, but that isn't necessary anymore. That's more of a TV thing. We have options that don't involve you at all."

Reginald nodded at her. "Thank you. I'd rather not. But… I might want to see him anyway. At some point. Not right now."

Hollingsworth changed the subject. "I'm going to move on to the next steps in this, Mr. Voth. We'll be in touch."

Reginald watched Hollingsworth walk away, and then watched Lewis approach. "I'm sorry you got dragged into all this," Reginald said. "I hope they didn't give you weird shit about California."

Lewis smiled incompletely and for only a moment: a quick quirk of the corners of his mouth. "They didn't have to. I told them. They wouldn't know about that at this point, but if it came up when they ran me through the system later, and I hadn't told them, it would seem like I tried to hide it. So, I warned my cop that when they search my background they'll find all that stuff. And that's all we talked about for the rest of the time. When was the last time I used? Had I ever stolen to support my 'habit'? Had I ever become violent while high? All the most fun memories an addict can have."

Reginald put a hand to his forehead and then leaned his elbow on the table. "Lewis, I am so sorry."

"It's not your fault your brother died. Or whatever's happened. And it's not your fault cops are cops."

"Do you… can we go sit on your back deck or something?"

Lewis smiled. "Sure. Come on. I'll try to take your mind off of things."

Johnny Spangler finally strolled past them on his way to his own home. "Catch you fellas later, eh?" The grin he gave them looked like it had been cut into his face with pinking shears.

GENERATION FOUR – MARY

November, 1928

"I see you, mother. Yes, I see Grandfather with you."

Mary sat in a rocking chair in the corner of the room. Her father had said those words a dozen times in the last few hours. Mrs. King had been there for it once, bringing over a roast chicken and some cornbread. *He's at the gates of glory*, Mrs. King had whispered, but Mary had waited until Mrs. King's back was turned before she let herself roll her eyes.

If this was glory, Mary wanted no part of it.

Eber had not been a kind father, but she knew he'd had a hard life. He'd grown up in the last of the old world, old ways of living, and Mary had disappointed him at every turn by being distinctly a child of the modern age.

Eber had hated her for having Harvey in the first place and then doubly so for not giving him away, and Mary had lavished Harvey with affection as a form of revenge. She loved her little boy, so bright and playful, so eager to roam the woods, to catch fish from the creek that ran along the edge of the Voth place and to sing the songs he learned from Mary's old Victrola.

Eber wanted Mary to get married to a King, he said. He'd called Harvey *that little bastard* from birth, to the point Mary got scared her father might kill her child if she wasn't careful. She'd been so young, though, and had so little of her own, no way to make an escape on her own terms. She had Harvey sleep in her bed every night, kept either him or her father close at all times, stayed vigilant for years. She'd given up her whole life on the slim promise it would save her son's, and she'd do it again in a heartbeat. Soon, though, this would be over. She'd finally be able to relax. Mary spent just a moment wondering if she should feel guilty about that, then almost laughed at the very thought. The preacher said Jesus knew what thoughts and feelings lurked in every heart, and if so, that meant he'd had to stare into the lightless pit where her father's soul should be. If Mary was supposed to ask forgiveness after what she'd been through, well, that was too bad. Jesus might have to wait a while.

And yet, a part of Mary did feel sympathy for her father—well, more like pity. His mother had scraped a life out of the side of the mountain only to have it cut short. And her father had brought them here when the land barons ran him off their old patch. Eber said his grandfather never talked about that but his mother never *didn't*, bringing it up at every turn as part of her frequent litany of blame and accusations. The woman had spewed poison to the very day she died, and some of that poison had gotten into Mary's father from an early age.

Still. The man lived his own life, made his own choices. Maybe he and Jesus could talk forgiveness. Mary'd had to wait this long just to get some peace and quiet.

On the bed, Eber sat up straight, blinked twice, and then looked directly at Mary.

Stunned at his sudden clarity and strength, the way his knuckles cracked and popped as he gripped the edge of the quilt she'd had over him, Mary dropped the magazine she'd been reading.

"Go and get it, girl," Eber said.

Mary sat and stared at her father as her heart pounded in her chest.

Her father had spent the last three days mewling like a kitten, mumbling halves of conversations with dead people she'd never met, fading by the day and then the hour and then, for the last three hours, by the minute, and now, like a flash of lightning from a clear sky, he'd returned to the here and now and spoke with the voice that had blared chastisements her entire life.

"I said go and get the knife."

CHAPTER THIRTEEN – DEAD AND GONE

Reginald and Lewis didn't make it to the back deck of Lewis' house. They stopped in the kitchen so Lewis could pour them each a glass of wine, but before Lewis could walk to the bar, Reginald grabbed his shoulders, spun him around, and pushed him up against the cold, granite countertop of speckled gray and kissed him as though he wanted to be invaded by him—and that is exactly what Reginald wanted. He wrenched Lewis' suit pants open so hard the button flew off and rebounded off stainless steel elsewhere in the kitchen, forcing them down around Lewis' ankles as he sank to his knees. He had his face buried in Lewis' gray and black striped bikini briefs, huffing, snorting, moaning long monosyllables, their tone shifting up and down, as he hooked his fingers into the elastic waistband of Lewis' underwear and started to pull.

"Are you sure you want this right now?" Lewis was already panting, already hard as a steel rod, and Reginald paused just long enough to make eye contact.

"I want you to fuck whatever part of me you like until I forget my own name." His breath as he spoke was hot against Lewis, hot enough to reflect against his own face, and Reginald didn't wait for an answer. He nearly tore Lewis' briefs in two getting them down.

"My pleasure."

Twenty minutes later the two of them walked into Lewis' bedroom-sized bathroom upstairs. Reginald's jaw ached and his lips were numb, and he was ready for a shower followed by a long afternoon of debauchery to remind himself he was alive. He was going to ride Lewis' dick until one or both of them passed out, if Reginald had anything to say about it. As far as he was concerned, Lewis didn't get a vote at all.

"I'm afraid I can still remember my name," Reginald said to Lewis as they finished stripping off their suits. "So, I'm going to need you to work on that once we're freshened up."

"That's weird."

"Not really, most people know their own names." Reginald chuckled at his little joke, at the ease with which he let his guard down just a little to crack wise in front of Lewis, at how natural all this felt after guys like… what had his name been? Chris? No, *Clark*. Anyway, after so many guys who were fine men, easy on the eyes, gentle and rough in exactly the right measure, but also distinctly *nonstick*, it was strange that Reginald so readily fell into easy familiarity like this with Lewis. With men like Clark, Reginald had always, to some degree, performed a role: sometimes the butch bottom, sometimes the fem top, sometimes the cocksucking slut, sometimes the gruff voice on the other side of the glory hole. With Lewis, he didn't feel that need.

Reginald had gotten his undershirt off, slipped out of his boxer briefs, and peeled off his socks before he realized Lewis had stopped to stare out a window.

The windows in Lewis' main bathroom were regular-sized, just like the ones in the bedroom or at the end of the hall, but the panes on the bottom three quarters were frosted for privacy. The top row was plain glass, however, and Reginald and Lewis were both just tall enough to look out if they stood close enough.

Across the street outside, over the oval of green space with its picnic tables and charcoal grills, and across the other half of the neighborhood's circular roadway, Johnny Spangles sat on the steps up onto his own front porch.

He stared directly at the window in the bathroom.

He wore a lopsided smile.

"Jesus," Reginald said, "I didn't mean to piss him off *that* badly."

"When?"

"Last night, when he came over. I mean, I realize I was kind of an asshole, but it wasn't exactly more than my usual amount. Did I say anything *that* bad? Bad enough for him to be breaking into my mother's house and threatening me like this?" Lewis didn't say anything, just staring back, and Reginald groaned. "Oh, fuck, *was* it that bad?"

Lewis put a hand against Reginald's chest. "No. That's why this is weird."

"Well, I never thought I'd say this, but I wish the cops were still here."

Lewis snorted but his heart wasn't in it.

"Look, let's just take our shower and fuck some more. I'll go over later and apologize. I'll eat whatever crow or do whatever begging I have to. I'll bury the hatchet. I'm good at that."

Lewis and Reginald didn't move towards the shower, however.

Across the way, Johnny stood up without taking his eyes off them.

His grin widened as he turned and walked inside.

The two of them showered quickly and industriously, the playfulness of the moment gobbled up in Johnny Spangles' lopsided grin. Reginald's mood soured as he realized Johnny—a forgettably-featured 40-something doofus with brown hair going gray and the sort of body one gets from working in the yard all the time—was most certainly one of his *types*. Under other circumstances he would have gotten off on the idea of Johnny ogling the two of them as they went at it. But that grin had conveyed the wrong sort of interest: predatory, not passionate, and not even the fun predation of going cruising and making something happen. They stopped at the window on their way to the bedroom without either of them mentioning it.

Johnny was back on the front porch, but this time he was talking to his wife, Kate. He still had that grin, too, but now he had turned it on whatever he was trying to persuade Kate to do—and clearly they were having a "conversation" about that.

Reginald and Lewis couldn't hear what Johnny was saying but he gestured in the direction of Dorothea's house at the end of the street. As he did so, Johnny took a few steps down the walk, towards the street, backing away from Kate as he spoke to her.

She looked exasperated, throwing her hands out to her sides theatrically once or twice before folding her arms over her chest. The body language spoke volumes: Johnny wanted to go back to Dorothea's house. Kate clearly did not wish to join him. Johnny looked like he was ready go to back with or without his wife, but preferably with.

"Oh, Christ," Reginald sighed, "should we do something?"

Lewis drew a breath and pushed it out his nose in a huff. "Well, she and I *are* the neighborhood watch committee. Yeah. Let's go see if she needs help."

The two of them walked—Reginald was conscious they very much did not *run*, but that they both wanted to do so—to the bedroom and pulled on some clothes: a pair of gym shorts and a tank top with *I FEEL LIKE A NEW MAN* in large letters and *(You'll do.)* in smaller ones underneath. He slipped his feet into sneakers and checked himself in the mirror while Lewis finished yanking on a pair of burgundy joggers and a tee shirt with the logo for a seafood restaurant over his heart and *I Got Crabs in Calabash* in block letters on the back. By the time they got downstairs and out onto the street, night had just started to fall. The sun had set, but the sky behind Moriah Bald still glowed with the gloaming, the last light that lingers after the sun sinks beneath the horizon but before full darkness descends.

Kate and Johnny walked slowly up the street toward Dorothea's house, its windows dark, its porch light off. They'd made it maybe two-thirds of the way there.

"Kate! Johnny!" Lewis called out to the two of them.

Kate glanced back, her arms still crossed over her chest.

Johnny, still grinning as he spoke to her, ignored Lewis' cry.

"Kate! What are you doing? You guys going somewhere?" Lewis jogged ahead a few feet, and Reginald sped up in his wake.

"Y'all, if you want to go look around my mother's house, you can just ask." Reginald tried to sound friendly, even jovial, but neither Kate nor Johnny so much as looked at him.

The two reached the bottom of Dorothea's stubby driveway and walked into the yard, aiming for the steps up to the front porch.

Abraham—Reginald checked himself, *Ham*—came into view behind a row of low shrubs along the sidewalk in front of another of the homes. Reginald startled when he saw Ham there, then, hand to his chest, hissed, "Christ, kid."

Ham looked up at Reginald with the calmest, coldest, most resigned expression he'd ever seen on a child. He looked as though he might be about to apologize, then didn't. Instead he turned to watch Johnny and Kate as they climbed the steps onto Dorothea's porch.

"Fuck—*sorry*—but *fuck*, I don't want them barging in there again. What the fuck is wrong with people?"

Ham turned those all-seeing, none-saying eyes back to Reginald again and shook his head. "He isn't right."

"No shit." Reginald set his posture just so. *Christ, I hope we're not about to get our asses kicked.*

Lewis took two jogging steps toward Dorothea's house, then registered the conversation that had been happening behind him and paused to turn. "Get your moms, Ham. We might need a hand out here."

"That house did something to him," Ham said to Reginald, as though Lewis didn't exist. "He went in there last night, and when he came back out, he wasn't right." Ham shook his head, still watching Johnny and Kate. Reginald looked, too, just in time to see Kate put up one last attempt at resistance when Johnny placed his hand around the knob on the front door, but Johnny laughed at her. It sounded sharp and mean and violent, and Reginald shuddered. He'd had a couple of boyfriends who could laugh like that. It never meant good things were about to happen.

"You saw him go in?" Reginald couldn't look away from Dorothea's house, but Ham knew to whom Reginald spoke.

"Watched it out my bedroom window. Middle of the night. Went up there in his pajamas and everything. Had this dreamy look on his face."

Johnny opened the door to Dorothea's house.

"Oh, fuck. *JOHNNY!*" Reginald cupped his hands around his mouth to shout. "*STAY OUT OF MY MOTHER'S GODDAMN HOUSE.*"

Lewis retreated to join them, his voice pitching up a little. "Ham, please, go get your moms."

"He went in there looking like Johnny, but he came out looking like *that.*" Ham's voice was low and cold, frightened, doomed.

Kate walked into Dorothea's house.

Johnny walked in behind her, pulled the screen door shut, and looked back through it, at Reginald, at Lewis, at Ham, right next door and a million miles away all at the same time, and grinned.

Two women—one White and wearing an apron over yoga pants and a sweatshirt, the other Black with green denim overalls and a peach tee shirt—stepped out of the house onto the front porch. The woman in yoga pants spoke. "Ham, you okay?"

Lewis stepped closer to Reginald and waved. "Hey, Megan. Hey, Beck."

Still grinning at Reginald, Johnny closed Dorothea's front door.

Reginald broke into a run, tearing up the inclined street and Dorothea's steep drive and skipping two steps on his way up onto his dead mother's front porch. At first he could hear Lewis explaining it all to Beck and Megan, telling them who Reginald was, explaining about all the madness of this day from hell, but Reginald tuned it out. He put his hand on the screen door of the house, pulled it open, then placed his hand on the doorknob…

And waited.

Looking through the diamond-shaped windows in the door, Reginald saw nothing. The interior of the house wasn't merely dark. He could *feel* the nothing behind that door, as though it were set against the back wall of a deep cave and at the same time opened onto space itself. He heard nothing, felt nothing, saw nothing.

Reginald hesitated, his hand halfway to the knob. When he'd opened that door two days ago he'd stepped into a nightmare of memory and hallucination. *Not a hallucination.* The words rang through his mind. *A vision.*

"Hold up," Lewis said, jogging up the steps onto the front porch now. "Beck wants to come with us."

The Black woman in green overalls paused halfway up the steps. "Hi."

Reginald nodded at her. "I'd shake hands, but if I don't open this door right now, I swear I never will." Then he put his hand on the knob, turned it, and pushed open the door.

Light—bright, yellow-green, and shifting as though it shone from behind a drape that rippled in a breeze—spilled out all around them. As Reginald pushed the door open, that light yawned in a mirroring arc, casting stark shadows sharp as knives, dancing as the light twisted and shimmered and shook.

"What in the actual *fuck*." Beck's voice didn't shake, but the shock was real.

"Y'all don't have to come with me," Reginald said without looking back. "But I need to go in there and find out what's happening."

Lewis' voice was soft but steady. "No way am I letting you go in there by yourself *again*."

Reginald reached back. Lewis took his hand.

Together they walked inside.

Beyond the door to Dorothea's house stood an ancient forest. Where her living room and abandoned crochet and a kitchen with a half dozen broken dishes in it had been, Reginald found old trees, too tall to even see the tops of, too wide to put one's arms around. They stood so huge and high he couldn't even make out what kind they were. He'd never been much of an outdoorsman, admittedly, but he knew the difference between an oak and a pine, and these trees, their branches woven together so thoroughly, and branching out so low he couldn't make out the sky, were like none he'd ever seen. Their bark ran in long striations, vertical ridges crisscrossing here, parallel there, like a map of canyons and the ridges between them.

"Holy shit." Lewis stepped forward and picked up a seed pod of some sort. "American Chestnut." He stepped back and looked up. "They're extinct. Well, the ones like this are extinct, anyway. The big, old ones." He held out a leaf he picked up off the ground.

The ground where my mother's front hall is supposed to be.

"See this leaf? That serrated edge kind of look?"

"Are you… a tree guy?" Reginald didn't know himself what his uncertain tone was meant to convey. Mostly he couldn't believe they were having this conversation at this moment in this place.

"No, but Johnny told me about them. The original was native to this region, but it went extinct. He had illustrations in an old book or something." Lewis blinked and seemed to return to himself and the reason why they were here.

Reginald raised both eyebrows.

Beck spoke up from behind them. "Well, this is pretty *fucking impossible*." Beck let out a sigh. "Let's go find out what the fuck Johnny's doing to Kate."

The three of them stepped around and sometimes clambered over tree roots two and even three feet wide and high, radiating from the trunks of the trees. Lurid, glowing light of shifting green and yellow shot in thick rays from between the trunks of other trees further in: Some oaks, a few firs, a tulip poplar at least fifty feet high. They walked atop a thick carpet of fallen leaves and bare earth, their footfalls silent, and after a few dozen yards they realized the trees were thinning out and the light grew brighter.

Ahead of them, Reginald could make out two figures silhouetted against a light so blinding he couldn't tell its source.

Lewis breathed out a quiet *Christ*, but it might have been as much in terror as in relief.

Johnny and Kate stood side by side, his arm around her shoulders, their heads turned up to gaze at the light. It shone with blinding radiance from a point above the center of a small clearing. Reginald couldn't tell exactly what produced the light, but it came from something, somewhere, and it shifted in hue and intensity in a way that very much felt alive.

"Do you feel that, babe?" Johnny shouted as though the light produced a sound, as though its sheer intensity could drown out other senses as well. "That's the light of everything. That's the light of interconnectedness. With that light shining on us I feel like we can have anything. Do anything. You feel that, too?"

Kate's answer was swallowed up in Reginald's own mix of horror and wonder. Whatever was happening in his mother's house, *to* his mother's house, it terrified him and enticed him in equal measure. That light, whatever it was, whatever made it, called to him, invited him closer, even as it pushed him away. He wanted to stare into it until he went blind.

"Kate," Lewis called out, "Kate, do you need help? Are you okay?"

She didn't move, didn't seem to have heard him. Reginald and Lewis, still holding hands, both strode forward and up to within a few feet of Johnny and Kate. Now he could hear her response.

"I feel it," Kate murmured. "It feels like the whole world is singing to me."

"Yeah." Johnny turned and acknowledged Reginald, Lewis, and Beck with narrowed eyes and another flash of that knife-slash grin. "The light gave me these trees. It said I could take some back with me, even. Might plant them in the yard. Just think, babe: American Chestnut returns to Appalachia. It'd make for a hell of a series of posts."

Kate raised a hand as though about to offer the light above them a little wave. "It says…"

"I need to know what is happening here," Reginald said to them. "I need to know why there's a forest in my mother's house."

"Kate!" Beck stepped around Reginald and Lewis to stand on Kate's other side. She looked down at the blonde woman's face, upturned toward the light, and took her upper arm in her hand to shake it gently. "Kate, snap out of it. Whatever the fuck this is, we should go back out. This is Reginald's place now, and he doesn't want you in here."

Kate didn't turn away from the light, so Reginald couldn't tell whether she spoke to Beck, to Johnny, or to all of them. "The light says I can have what I've always wanted."

Reginald stepped closer, further around, and saw tears roll down Kate's face.

Beyond her, just the other side of the nearest trees, he could see people watching them, backlit by the blinding, burning emanation from between and behind the trees.

The figures' eyes glowed golden yellow.

The green and yellow light reflected in Kate's eyes, also. "The light says I can have it all."

"Okay," Reginald said aloud, his voice raised but not quite yelling,

"Well, excuse me, but *that* sounds like some obvious monkey's paw bullshit, so come on, party's over, nothing to see here, get the fuck out of whatever is happening to my mother's house."

"Johnny, it said you could have these trees?" Lewis looked down at the chestnut burr in his hand. "You're going to plant these?"

Johnny's voice was even, confident, firm. "It said the old ones had to go away to make room for the new ones. But now the old ones are ready to come back again."

Reginald gave in and shouted: "I SAID. *GET THE FUCK OUT.*" He spun on his heel and pointed at the light hovering over them: a yawning, silver-limned orifice in the air with green and yellow beams rushing out of it like a storm drain in a downpour. He shouted directly up at it. "You want to know what *I* want? I want us all to *go the fuck home.*"

Reginald sat up in bed, still shouting.

Lewis sat bolt upright beside him. "Holy *shit*," he said. "You wouldn't believe the dream I just had."

Reginald let the corners of his mouth draw down tight. "It wasn't a dream."

Lewis opened his mouth to say something, then stopped himself and looked Reginald up and down.

"Yeah." Reginald gestured at Lewis in turn. "We're still dressed. You weren't dreaming. I told the house to kick us out and it *did.*"

Lewis blinked slowly and shook his head. "No way."

"Fuck!" Reginald blurted. "Kate and Johnny and Beck." He leapt off the bed—they hadn't even been under the covers—and ran over to the window.

Beck walked out her front door, still in her green overalls and peach tee, causing Megan and Ham to utter a startled cry from the end of their driveway.

Reginald looked across at Kate and Johnny's place. The lights were still on, as they had been when they first emerged and went up to Dorothea's house. "Come on," Reginald murmured, more prayer than command, "come on outside, look around, look *normal*."

The lights in Kate and Johnny's house went dark.

Lewis had joined Reginald at the window and shuddered. "Okay, that's bad."

"Let's go check on them." Reginald used the words of a suggestion, but the tone of an intention. He was already halfway across the massive bedroom and headed for the stairs when Lewis caught up. "Let's just knock, see if they're okay, and then leave it be."

Lewis chuckled. "Leave it *be?*" He laughed louder this time.

Reginald put his hands up as he started jogging down the stairs. "Fuck yes. Leave it be. Sell the place—my brother's, too—and go buy a nice place somewhere far the fuck away from here." He stopped halfway down the steps and looked up at Lewis where he hesitated on the landing. "I'm not kidding, Lewis. Fuck it. If ghosts or monsters or extinct trees or aliens or whatever have taken over my mother's house, it can be someone else's problem. I don't give one solitary shit. I do not need to fix that. I need to get paid and go somewhere else." He started back down the steps. "But before that, I'd like to know if Kate and Johnny are okay or if they got eaten by whatever's up there in my mother's place. If nothing else, it could affect my asking price."

Lewis jogged down the stairs and caught up. "Reginald, you can't just sell that place and let somebody else blunder into it. That could be murder. That could be what it *wants*."

Reginald didn't slow down, making a line straight for the door. "Or maybe it wants *me*. Maybe the only way to get out of this intact is to break the cycle. Do you know how long a Voth has lived in that house? Since there've been Voths, Lewis. As far back as anybody remembers, anyway. Under all that white-painted siding there's an ancient log cabin that got expanded into a farmhouse that got dressed in planking and fresh paint and had some insulation put in, and pipes run, and a few other of the creature comforts of modern living. But under that, often no more than skin deep, the original house is lurking. An unbroken line of fathers and mothers and daughters and sons runs all the way back to whoever first pulled up here and decided they could handle a garden only *this* slanted. And maybe I just have to break the chain to make them all fuck all the way off." Reginald paused at the front door and looked Lewis directly in the eye. "But before that, I'd like to know if your neighbor-friend has murdered his wife."

Lewis locked the door behind them in silence, and the two walked across the central green oval of the neighborhood without a word. When they got to Johnny and Kate's front walk, Lewis put a hand out. "Let me ring the bell. They know me."

Reginald nodded. "You want me to wait out here by the street?"

Lewis shook his head. "Oh hell no. Just let me talk."

It took Johnny and Kate maybe twenty unendurable seconds to answer, and they did so over their doorbell camera.

"Hey, Lewis." Kate's voice sounded distant and flat despite her friendly tone. "Something wrong?"

Lewis cleared his throat. "I wanted to see if you're okay. It seemed like maybe you and Johnny were arguing earlier. You know, a few minutes ago. When he made you go into Dorothea's house?"

"He just wanted to show me something, Lewis." Kate sounded a little bit dreamy but also like she was trying to suppress a laugh at Lewis' expense.

"The trees?" Lewis asked it as if she might mean something else, but clearly, no one could even think of anything else.

"No, Lewis." Kate's voice took on a sly edge. "He needed to show me what gave him the trees. And now it's going to give me what I want, too. You know, it doesn't ask for much, Lewis. All it wants is your whole life."

He stepped away from the front door and turned to look at Reginald.

Kate went on. "Hardly anybody's using theirs anyway."

CHAPTER FOURTEEN – EVERYTHING SHE EVER WANTED

"What the hell happened back there?" Beck walked down the street, hands by her side, a look on her face that said very clearly she expected an actual answer. Her question was anything but rhetorical. "Did you know that was going to happen?"

Reginald barely turned to look at her. "My mother's house is haunted. Probably. Maybe. And I think whatever's haunting it messed with Kate and Johnny's heads."

Beck stopped a few paces away. "And you let me walk in there? I have a wife and a son, asshole. You could have warned me."

"I *said* you didn't have to go in there with me, didn't I? I'm sorry I didn't take the time to show you some infographics and produce an 'explainer' video first."

Beck nodded backwards, in the direction of Ham and Megan. They still stood in their own front yard. Megan had her hands on Ham's shoulders, and he looked like he was trying to press himself against her without anyone seeing him do it. "Okay, well, fuck you, too, then." She turned, and Lewis elbowed Reginald in the side. Reginald made a little noise of alarm.

At Lewis' continued prompting, Reginald called after her. "I'm sorry. I'm sorry, Beck! I really am. I didn't know we were walking into *that*. If I had, I would never have let Lewis or you go with me. I'm sorry. I swear to you." Reginald realized with surprise that his voice was about to crack as his eyes stung. "I would never have done that to Lewis, and certainly not to a stranger."

Beck stopped and turned back around. "Oh, shit." She looked Reginald in the eye, then up and down. "You two are serious that fast."

Reginald drew a shallow breath and worked his mouth without producing words.

"Reginald went in there last night and… saw things. But we thought maybe it was, you know, just interested in *him*. Since it's his mother's house and all." Lewis trailed off towards the end. "Or maybe that it was a hallucination," and here he looked at him, "though for the record I have *never* doubted your story. I'm just trying to remain open to all the possibilities."

Reginald tried not to sound annoyed. "My reflex is to say, I'm sure the fellas down at the lab will be really glad to hear about your objectivity, but I get it." He looked back at Beck. "But yeah. I thought it was my mother and that she would only… ugh, I don't even want to say it."

Beck cut her eyes sideways at Kate and Johnny's house and raised one finger to silence them.

The three turned and looked at the front door.

Staticky breathing came from the doorbell camera, then a click as it was turned off.

"Let's go talk about this inside *my* house. Right now." Beck gestured back up the street with her thumb. "I can see you already know Ham. Now *you* get to tell my wife what the hell just happened."

Two hours later they were sitting around Beck and Megan's dining table. Ham played a game on his phone in the living room. The four of them tried to keep their voices down, but they could tell the kid heard every word.

Megan had listened to them with moments of skepticism and alarm peppered throughout, then finally folded her arms and sat back. "First, I don't believe you." Beck opened her mouth to speak but Megan kept going. "I *do* believe my wife. But guys, I won't lie, I'm an atheist and a skeptic. I don't believe in *anything* supernatural. We're born, we live, we die, we're gone."

Reginald tried not to sound cross. He'd walked into a stranger's home—what felt like the four hundredth stranger to whom he'd had to lay bare some part of himself in the last three days—and told his story, and he had not enjoyed it. "Then how on earth do you explain it if you say you believe your wife? She reappeared in *your* house just like Lewis and I did in his."

Megan frowned briefly. "C'mon. Your mother's house has a gas leak."

Reginald produced a strangled blurt of sound, scoffing openly. "My mother's house doesn't even use gas. She's got baseboard heat, a fireplace, and an electric stove."

Megan unfolded her arms only to spread them open in a dismissive shrug. "And? Maybe it's radon gas." She kept talking over Reginald's exasperated *oh please* in response. "Maybe it's lead in the pipes, maybe you're tripping on mold spores, maybe… I don't know, but Jesus Fucking Christ, Reginald, your mother isn't haunting her house. Your mother's *dead*. Her house is *empty*. Have you considered maybe you hallucinated all this because it would be easier to confront some sort of supernatural infinitude than the fact you and your mother didn't like each other very much, and neither did you and your brother, and now they're both gone and you'll never be able to fix that?"

Reginald could feel his autonomic responses to this, both a plain statement of what he knew to be facts and an unthinkable intrusion into the personal space of his story of himself. A part of him leaned back against some interior wall of ice and felt the cold down his spine, and another part of him wanted to knock the table over and scream. His heartbeat stuttered, and he *felt* the erratic thudding in his chest so hard he actually started to lift a hand to clutch at it before stopping himself and cupping that hand in the other. He took a moment to feel himself, something a therapist had told him to do years ago. *Is my left arm tingling? Or am I just that mad?*

Those silent few seconds drew a deep breath and took up the entire room.

"I think I should go home." Reginald's voice shook when he finally spoke, and he stood from the table very slowly, very cautiously. "I'm sorry we intruded on your home and family."

"Oh shit no," Beck started to reach for Reginald's shoulder but stopped at the look he gave her. Still, she pressed her case. "Megan doesn't know. She wasn't there. You can't expect people to take this stuff at face value, Reginald. If you can't convince my wife, when I told her myself I saw some of it, too, then you can't convince anybody. And good luck getting any help *then*."

Reginald turned and looked at Lewis, who wobbled his head back and forth and spoke. "If you want to go back to my place, Reginald, I will totally understand. And if you want to stay here and talk more, I'm game for that, too. But no matter what anybody else says, *I* believe you."

Reginald could feel his flared nostrils straining to go even wider, as though all the anger and embarrassment—and that's what it was, really, just embarrassment at having had strange things happen, at yet again being the object of disgust and fascination, much less here, on *this* tract, *this* mountain, just like he'd been as a child and as a teen and when it finally dawned on him that his mother had said all those cruel things about *fairies 'n queers* not out of ignorance of who he was but because she knew him better than he'd known himself.

He remained standing, unsure what to do, torn between too many possible reactions, and tried not to look relieved when Beck turned her attention onto Megan. "Okay, babe, so you don't believe. No problem there, right up until today. Like I said, I get it, you weren't there. But I was. So, what would convince you? Because that lady's house was musty, yeah, but nobody went in there and started having mold spore hallucinations. And radon gives you *cancer*, not sudden-onset credulity. I don't *know* his mother's up there rattling chains and pod-peopling Kate and Johnny, but I do know I saw what I can't explain. And honestly, babe, whether you believe him or me or Lewis or not doesn't make any difference. Not to me, anyway. No offense. What matters to me is whether it's dangerous to you or Ham."

"It is." Lewis spoke without hesitation, and both Megan and Beck turned to look at him. Reginald felt separated from his own body, not entirely in control of what he did with it, but he sank into the chair and turned his attention onto Lewis with some effort. Lewis went on. "It freaked Reginald out. It freaked *me* out. It showed up in the woods outside my house. And I know it did something to Kate and Johnny. He went up there by himself, and when he came out he was *wrong*. The way he smiled, it was like, I don't know, Hannibal Lecter dressed up as the Joker on Halloween. It was evil, Megan. I know that sounds dramatic—" he had to put up one hand to stop her incredulous response before it started, "but I am here to tell you he came out of that house *different*. And then he practically dragged Kate up there against her will. And now they sit in their house and stare at mine? They made fun of us through their *doorbell?*"

Megan looked skeptical, but instead of speaking it aloud she tightened her lips into a thin line and gave Lewis the half-lidded expression of someone who is tired of being tired of a topic.

"And babe, I know it sounds ridiculous, but I was in that house and it *was* full of trees, like a forest, but like an old one, and there was light between the trees from nowhere, and it *had* Kate and Johnny. I can't say exactly what I mean but I could feel it, deep down. The looks on their faces? Jesus, they looked like something out of a movie. They looked like the thing that takes someone's place after it eats them."

Megan listened more charitably to her wife, and something about that, at least, started to make the knot in the middle of Reginald's chest uncurl itself. She didn't look happy about any of this, but at least she didn't leap to frame him as a lunatic.

"What if …" she started to say, but Ham spoke up from the living room and interrupted them. He muttered it, though, and clearly none of them could make it out.

"What, babe?" Beck turned halfway in her chair to speak to Ham, and the shift in her tone from partner-who's-had-debates-like-this-before to mother-whose-love-knows-no-bounds made a pang of sudden and unexpected sorrow shoot through that jumble of feelings trapped behind Reginald's sternum. It didn't make them go away, it tied sandbags to it and dragged it down. "Speak up, hon."

Ham only briefly glanced away from the game on his phone. As soon as his eyes were turned back to it and his thumb returned to flying over its face, though, he drew a breath and spoke. "They're right. The house does something to people."

Now Megan's objections fell to the wayside so fast Reginald could practically hear them clatter. "Why do you say that?"

"'Cause Bobby went up there the night his mama died. And when he came back out he was laughing."

Beck and Megan exchanged a long look, and in that interval Reginald finally found the ability to speak again. "Is there some reason why that was odd? I mean, I will be the first to admit my brother was an asshole, but I'm curious. The way everyone's looking at each other makes me think that's *special.*"

Beck wasted no time dithering. "Your brother was an asshole, Reginald. Just a pure-tee asshole: racist, sexist, homophobic, you name it. I never saw that man smile unless he'd just insulted somebody."

Megan and Beck this time visibly avoided exchanging a look. "He said some things to us, that's for sure." Megan didn't look at Reginald until after she'd said it, then she shrugged. "Said some things to Ham, too."

All the color drained out of Reginald's face, and he felt sweat break out on his forehead. "I am so sorry. Oh, fuck, I am *so* sorry."

"Thing is," Ham said, "I could tell it wasn't about *me*. He was like that with everybody. It wasn't that he hated certain people and was nice to everybody else. He tried to find something to hate about everybody he met. So, he said shit—"

Megan and Beck spoke in unison: "*Language!*"

Ham tried not to sound embarrassed and pressed on. "—*stuff* to me, yeah, but he also talked *to* me."

"I don't quite follow your distinction." Reginald fluttered his lashes, not really sure what the kid was saying.

"Nobody who really hates you ever talks *to* you. If somebody says mean sh—tuff but they also say other stuff? That's somebody who's just hateful to everybody. It's not personal. It's just *them*." Ham shrugged a little. "That's why I knew who you were. Sometimes Bobby'd talk to me about other people in the neighborhood but sometimes he'd talk to me about your family, your relatives. He'd mostly just talk about what he hated about everybody. That was the other thing that told me it wasn't personal. Some people are just like that."

Megan spoke gently, probing but trying not to sound like she was interrogating him. "And when he came out of his mother's house the other night he was smiling?"

"Grinning." Ham still didn't look up. "Like, stranger-danger grinning. Scary movie grinning. You know?"

"I do, yeah." Reginald nodded at him. "Like Johnny was, and then Kate."

"Yeah. And after he went back into his house, his wife went over to your mom's place and went inside. She was gone a long time. Like, an hour maybe. But when I heard her come back out, I looked out my window and she was grinning, too."

Reginald cleared his throat. "And I don't expect she was any more congenial a person than my brother, given they wed."

Beck murmured out of the corner of her mouth, but clearly intended them all to hear it. "She was a bitch, is what she was."

"And that was the night Reginald's mother died?" Lewis spoke to Ham, but he looked at Reginald.

"Yeah."

Reginald nodded at Lewis. "And today he and my sister-in-law are both dead, too."

Lewis nodded back.

"It doesn't do it to everybody, though." Ham still spoke as though addressing the phone in his hand, and as evenly as if he were reporting it'd been an uneventful day at school. "Her preacher went in there the same night, but when he came out, he just looked normal."

Reginald's eyes widened. "Owenby went in there?"

"Maybe being a preacher gave him, I don't know, some sort of protection?" Lewis asked it in a tone that indicated distinct distaste.

Beck rolled her eyes. "Just what we need, another Jesus freak thinking they're safe from everything because of the Bible."

"Kate said a thing earlier, through her doorbell." Reginald cleared his throat again. He felt like he could drink a gallon of water. "About how all 'it' wants is your whole life. Owenby said something about that, too, at the service."

Lewis shrugged faintly. "Did your mother particularly hate your sister-in-law?"

Reginald let out one short, sharp, breathy chuckle. "I have no idea, but she certainly went out of her way to mention now and again how glad she was to have them so close, how useful it was to have *both of them* there. I always kind of assumed that was her taking a dig at me being single."

"Tell us more about them showing up in the woods behind your house." Beck said this quietly enough that it sent up red flags.

All eyes turned toward the sliding glass door behind the head of the dining room table. With the overhead light on, and night on the other side, the door had become a giant mirror revealing nothing other than their own doubles staring back at them. Beck reached with one arm to flip the light switch. Their reflections in the glass vanished and they could see out into the yard beyond.

From what Reginald guessed to be the tree line, three pairs of gold-lit eyes stared back.

Beside them, a fourth pair appeared.

Then a fifth.

The four adults at the table sat in silence, staring back. When Reginald started to say something, Lewis grabbed his hand and squeezed. His meaning was clear, even if it wasn't rational: *quiet or they'll hear us.*

One pair of citrine-colored eyes blinked and then vanished; then a second; then a third.

Ham spoke from the living room again. "They started showing up the night your mom died, too."

"I want to go home and lock the door." Lewis' voice sounded strained. "I want to just *run* from here to my house, slam the door shut behind me, climb into bed, and wake up tomorrow and think about this in the light of day."

Reginald scoffed. "If there are strange, I don't know, beings? Creatures? Whatever those are? If they're hanging around out there, I don't want to go *anywhere.*"

Lewis shook his head. "If they wanted to break in and kill us, they could have done it last night. And this is getting too scary. Everything's moving too fast. I can't think about this stuff until I've gotten some rest. This has been a really hectic couple of days. Our brains are worn out."

Reginald considered for a long few seconds.

Megan spoke up, but in the sort of tone Reginald recognized as that of a parent who is trying very hard to contain panic in the face of everything they've just learned. "Ham, have you seen eyes in the woods every night?"

He shrugged in silence. The adults all exchanged glances.

"Okay, this is a lot to process," Reginald said. Finally he looked at Lewis. "Fuck it—*sorry, language*—I need some sleep to think about this stuff, too. Before we go, I guess maybe this is a question better asked on OneDoorDown or Neighborhood or something, but where exactly do y'all find a good exorcist around here?"

CHAPTER FIFTEEN – OUR VIEWERS ARE LISTENING

Reginald's eyes snapped open two seconds before Lewis' doorbell rang. It wasn't the usual *bing-bong* of a doorbell on television, and it didn't produce cascading chords of electronic tones. Personally, he'd always wanted a doorbell like something out of an '80s soap opera: a ridiculous arrangement of Bach or Beethoven, something weighty, as though he'd captured the soul of some hoity-toity university bell tower. At home, his doorbell made a faint, weak *bzzzzzzz* like a kitchen timer that's lost enthusiasm for its job.

Instead, Lewis' doorbell prompted a series of short, sharp buzzes from Lewis' phone.

I would never wake up for that, Reginald thought, even though he'd always been a light sleeper.

Lewis immediately lifted himself on one elbow to look at the face of his phone in the darkened room, and Reginald's peek over his own shoulder showed Lewis trying to turn the phone so the light wouldn't disturb Reginald's sleep.

"I'm awake," Reginald whispered as he rolled over to face Lewis' back. "It's fine."

Lewis gave him a little smile over his shoulder and then looked back at the phone as it filled with the fisheye lens' view of his doorbell camera.

A dark-haired White woman in a pantsuit so sharp it could draw blood held a clipboard. Behind her stood a man with a shoulder-mounted camera.

"Oh, *shit.*" Reginald propped himself up, too. "That's the station out of Asheville." Beyond the two people on Lewis' front porch they could see the back half of a news van with WSOL 11 NEWS on the side.

The screen filled with the hand of the woman in the suit and Lewis' phone buzzed again in his hand.

"I am so sorry." Reginald covered his eyes with his other hand. "Christ. They've got to be here about Bobby and Sue and..." Reginald hesitated, "and what happened."

"I'll tell them to leave."

Reginald made a nonverbal noise, something on its way to turning into *don't bother* or *just ignore them*, but Lewis' thumb was faster than Reginald's mouth.

"Hi, can I help you?"

The woman's face distorted further with a television grin. "*Hi, I'm Rowan Thompkins with WSOL in Asheville. I was wondering if I can ask you a few questions about events in your neighborhood in the last few days?*"

A text notification appeared at the top of Lewis' phone:

Beck

Reporter from WSOL is poking around, don't answer.

"Too late for that," Reginald muttered under his breath.

"*Hi, did you hear me? I said this is Rowan Thompkins with WSOL.*"

"I have no comment. Have a nice day." Lewis thumbed the big red X on the screen and the image went dark.

Reginald sighed as he lay back down. "I am so sorry."

"Why?" Lewis half turned and looked down at him. "It's not like you called them and invited them over. You apologize too much, you know that? If San Diego taught me anything, it's that reporters are a double-edged sword. They always want to tell a story. If you're lucky, it's one you can shape to your benefit. If they show up on your doorstep uninvited, they're trouble. Fuck that *sorry* business." Lewis smiled, though. "Also, good morning." His hand moved down to grope Reginald. "And, *good morning.*"

Reginald didn't let his brain complicate things. He pulled Lewis to him, and they were at it like teenagers in seconds.

Four minutes later, Lewis didn't even take Reginald's cock out of his mouth when he canceled the doorbell notification again.

Two minutes after that, as Reginald gasped a final time and his abdomen spasmed, his phone started to ring. Lewis took the time to savor the finish as the call went to voicemail.

Twelve seconds later, it rang a third time. Lewis looked up at Reginald. "Tell her to go away. It's the only way to make them leave."

Reginald, eyes rolled into the back of his head, pawed at his own phone for a moment and then wheezed, "Hello?"

"*Hi, is this Reginald Voth?*"

"Sp… speaking."

"*Mr. Voth, I'm Rowan Thompkins with WSOL. I'm so sorry about your brother and mother and sister-in-law. I was wondering if you have any comment?*"

"No com—" Reginald suddenly returned from the heights of ecstasy to the here and now. "How did you get my number?"

"*Your neighbor gave it to me. I hope that's alright.*"

Reginald thought of his neighbors back at the trailer: Mrs. Sweeney, who was very kind but he was pretty sure did not have his cell number, and the people who rent the old Meadows place, whose names he didn't even know and whose house was only barely visible around the curve. "Who?"

"*Kate Spangler, across the street. She told me you've been staying with Mr.*"

Gwan."

Reginald went cold all over his body, the way it feels when a fever comes on. Lewis rose to sit on his knees between Reginald's legs, one hand on his left thigh. Lewis' other hand swiped a string of cum from the corner of his mouth.

"*Mr. Voth? Would you be willing to talk about your family's tragedies?*"

Reginald hung up on her and looked at Lewis. "Kate gave her my phone number and told her I'm staying with you."

Lewis licked his finger and then frowned. "Oh shit."

"Yeah."

Reginald's phone rang again. This time he answered without looking. "I'm sorry, Ms. Thompkins. No comment." Then he hung up.

Lewis pulled up the doorbell camera on his phone, frowned, then clambered off the bed and walked to one of the windows with the peek-a-boo shades. "Oh great." He turned back to Reginald, who lay feeling absolutely spent in the middle of the bed and wanted nothing more than to go back to sleep and awaken in his trailer with none of this bullshit having happened. Lewis nodded his head to the side to indicate direction. "She's over there by the picnic tables and she's setting up to interview Kate." Lewis continued to watch for a few seconds, then sucked in a breath. "They're walking towards your mom's house."

Reginald yanked on his clothing—Lewis stopped him half-finished to suggest he wear something other than a stained tee shirt with *Live, Laugh, Loads* on it in curved lettering—and he and Lewis walked out into the street and up the circle towards Dorothea's house. The reporter and the cameraman were setting up for a shot where the viewer would be able to see the house in the background while Rowan Thompkins talked to Kate Spangler.

Kate wore an incongruous grin as they chatted before the cameras rolled.

"Reginald, you don't have to talk to those people." Lewis had been trying to slow—or stop—him the entire way through the house and up the street. "Just tell them to leave. It's your property now. Hell, even the street is privately owned. You can just throw her out."

Reginald stopped and let Lewis catch up the three strides he'd been lagging behind. "Lewis, you are goddamned amazing, and I'm pretty sure you just sucked all the sense out of me, because I am sick to death of having things happen to me in this place. I spent my whole childhood waiting for the next bad thing to come along, on the lookout for my escape. And for the last, what, three days? I've been doing the same thing. I'm tired as all hell of that bullshit. I know what Rowan Thompkins does: she ambushes people and makes them look guilty for things. I always figured they must be, or they'd sue her, but now here I am, getting ambushed, and I haven't done a goddamn thing wrong. But my mother is dead, and my brother killed his wife and then himself or the other way around, and this woman is here to make it sound like it's my fault somehow, or make me look helpless, or whatever her angle is. You said it yourself just now: these people want to tell a story, and if we're lucky it's one we can shape to our advantage. If they want to point a camera at me, I'm happy to use that. If they want some way to make me look like a victim or a criminal, I'd much rather make them think I'm a weirdo instead."

"Oh, *Christ*, Reginald, are you—" Lewis' eyebrows shot up as Reginald's intended course of action dawned on him.

Reginald held his hands out to either side. "I know, but I'm tired of doing nothing, and she's going to run a story no matter what. So it might as well be one I tried to steer."

Reginald turned back toward his mother's house and Rowan Thompkins had turned her full attention onto his approach. Kate still nattered away at her with that rictus grin she'd worn ever since she came out of Dorothea's house, but Reginald could tell Thompkins no longer heard a word Kate said. She wanted *him*, his story, his soundbite. He squared his shoulders and put a little sway in his hips as he clomped up to her in his jeans, the button-up shirt he'd worn to the funeral, and his combat boots.

"Hi, Ms. Thompkins." Reginald looked up at the deep sapphire blue of the autumn sky above them. "Nice day for it."

"Mr. Voth?" Thompkins managed to keep her smile to a polite, nearly-consoling twist of her lips as she nodded at him. "Thank you for speaking to me. I'm very sorry about everything you've been through."

Kate stopped speaking and turned her grin on him.

The cameraman turned his electronic eye on him as well.

"Is this good?" Reginald looked around. "For filming, I mean?"

Thompkins paused for a beat, and Reginald knew she had taken a moment to suppress her surprise at his sudden seeking her out. *I bet that doesn't happen very often.*

"Certainly. Would you like a moment to collect your thoughts?"

"That depends. What do you plan on asking me?"

"We don't generally do rehearsals." She let herself smile faintly, a *just between us that was funny I like you* sort of smile meant to put people at ease. It almost worked on him. Almost.

"Then what's the point of trying to collect myself?" Reginald manually unlocked the frown he automatically wore and waved a hand back and forth to slow or stop her. "Actually, yeah, give me a second." He reached up, rubbed the heels of his hands over his eyes and then up and down his cheeks, shook his head back and forth rapidly a few times, fluttered his lips to loosen things up, then took a deep breath. "Okay. Go for it."

Thompkins nodded at the cameraman. A light on his shoulder-mounted cyclops burned red and he gave a thumbs up. The reporter faced the camera. "I'm here with Reginald Voth, son of Dorothea Voth, deceased earlier this week, and brother to Robert Voth, who was found dead yesterday, as was his wife." Now she stopped, took a moment to shift as the cameraman walked a quick, small arc to reframe the shot, and held the mic between them. "Mr. Voth, I want to express my condolences for your family's many losses in such a short time, and I know our viewers feel the same. Thank you for speaking with us. Sources in the sheriff's department tell WSOL your brother and his wife died in a murder-suicide and that you reported it to authorities. Can you share anything with us to shed light on these events?"

Lewis stood off to the side, at least twenty feet away and actively remaining *behind* the cameraman to stay out of any shots. Reginald could hear his sigh at the question, but he doubted the microphone picked it up.

Reginald shook his head at Thompkins. "My family and I were not close, Ms. Thompkins."

"Please, call me Rowan."

"Okay. Rowan." Reginald drew a breath. "And I didn't see the scene itself. I could… I knew something had happened, so I called 911. Actually," and Reginald nodded off-camera, in the direction of Kate Spangler where she stood by Dorothea's mailbox, "the cops were already here because of these two."

The grin on Kate's face faltered for the first time, and Reginald felt a flutter of something like the adrenaline rush he experienced the time in 8th grade when he got pushed by a bully and, sick to death of bullies, finally pushed back. Kate managed to retain a smile, but her gloating grimace had finally vanished.

Thompkins turned to glance at her. "And why is that?"

"Her husband trespassed in my mother's house, night before last.

Actually, he broke in the day before then spent the night in there—doing God knows what, mind you. She called the sheriff to report him missing and he came staggering out of my mother's house. Maybe he was up there doing drugs, I don't know, nobody knows what he did in there. But anyway, the law was already out here so I called 911 and the same deputies who were questioning *them* went to investigate my brother's house. They found him and his wife dead, and only they know what things looked like inside. I can't tell you anything more about that. But I can tell you that whatever Kate over there had to say needs to be taken in context with the fact I plan to press charges against her husband for breaking and entering, trespass, and, once I've had a chance to inventory my deceased mother's belongings, possibly theft. She's got an incentive to make things sound worse than they are."

Kate's smile slumped all the way into a frown now, then she yanked it back up to a flat line across her face. "That's not true," she growled.

Reginald jumped on it before Rowan could respond. "You'll get your chance to talk in a minute, Kate." The cameraman was turning to get whatever Kate would say next when Reginald snapped his fingers to get the guy's attention. "Listen, I'm going to say something, and it's going to be controversial with some of your viewers."

That had Rowan Thompkins' full attention, and she and the cameraman turned back on him with the burning glare of a thousand watts of lights on a marquee. "Go on, Mr. Voth. Our viewers are listening."

"I don't know what made my brother and his wife come to such a terrible end. We might not have been close, but they were never bad people. Something *made* them do this. Something supernatural lurks on this mountain, and I need help to make it go away. There's something evil up here on Moriah Bald, and I need a professional to help me deal with it."

Thompkins blinked twice at him. "Mr. Voth, what do you mean? What sort of supernatural forces?"

Reginald shrugged. "Demons? Haints? Beats me. I'm not the expert in this stuff, but I plan to bring in somebody who is."

"Mr. Voth, are you saying you intend to perform an exorcism?"

"Exactly." He turned and looked directly into the camera. "I'm hoping my mother's long-serving minister, Reverend Enoch Owenby of Sparkling Branch Church, will come pray over their houses and drive out whatever evil forces have power over this place."

"And if he won't?" Thompkins held the microphone closer. "What then?"

Reginald turned to look back at her. "Then I'll have to find someone of great spiritual strength who isn't afraid."

Thompkins kept her face pleasantly neutral, but her tone revealed a touch of glee that left Reginald half-surprised even though he'd almost expected it. "Mr. Voth, that's a very unusual reaction to such a tragedy."

Reginald leaned into the microphone for this and spoke with a low and serious tone. "My mother, my brother, and his wife are all dead, ma'am. *That's* unusual. Acting like everything is normal when it isn't is what keeps most people trapped in bad situations. Trying to look good for the neighbors won't bring my family back. At this point the only responsible course of action is to make sure nobody else moves in here and suffers the same fate." Reginald looked directly at Kate as he said the next sentence. "Whatever did this to my family, I will drive it out. It won't get another soul if I've got anything to say about it."

The grin sprang back to life on her face, and that's when Reginald knew Kate Spangler was gone for good. Whatever lived *in there*, in his mother's house, lived in her now, too.

Thompkins turned quickly and pointed the microphone at Lewis. Her cameraman spun just as quickly. Thompkins called to him. "And what about you, Mr. Gwan? Do you have any comment?"

Lewis put both hands up to block the camera's view of his face. "You do not have my permission to film me, Ms. Thompkins, and this is a private street. On behalf of the home-owners association, I'm telling you to leave."

Once they were gone, Lewis suggested they walk around the house just to see if Johnny messed with it, took something, anything like that.

"I don't want to go inside," Reginald said, and he felt a little sheepish admitting it, but it was true. He didn't want to go back into that house without something resembling a posse, preferably one with some spiritual know-how.

"Then let's just walk around the outside, make sure he didn't, I don't know, leave the back door hanging open."

They walked around the near side. Reginald could see the work shed door was still closed and the old lock still looped and clasped through the latch.

When they got to the back yard, Reginald stood there looking around for a long time.

"See anything off? Anything not where it should be?" Lewis looked around the yard also, but obviously had no idea what would be strange or unexpected.

"Yeah." Reginald frowned as he studied the garden patch. "The garden's gone."

"What do you mean?"

Reginald pointed at a long rectangle of trimmed, even grass standing out from the hillside. "That's the garden. At least, it used to be. It was here the other night: two rows of tomatoes about done for the season, three rows of corn with beans climbing the stalks, some carrots, some onions, the usual. And now it's like it's been gone for years."

"I didn't spend a lot of time in her company," Lewis replied after a moment, "but I'd be surprised if your mother had a garden. She was in pretty good shape, but she couldn't possibly have planted or maintained something that ambitious."

Reginald studied the ground for long moments, then turned his back on the garden plot. "Come on. It's just her fucking with me. Let's go."

GENERATION FIVE – HARVEY

September, 1949

Mary Voth made Harvey dress her on her final day. "I'm going to meet the host of heaven looking good for the occasion," she said, and then she'd laughed, and when Harvey did not, she laughed again. "You've always been a good boy. I thank you for that, Harvey."

Mary had been sick for a while. The doctors in town said it was stomach cancer. They could feel growths in her abdomen, and now she was no longer able to keep food down. It wouldn't be long. Everyone knew that from the look on the doctor's face. So, Mary had Harvey take her to the department store in town to buy a nice new dress, something stylish for the times. She didn't have the strength to get her hair done. In fact, she'd had to sit down and have him bring dresses in her size for her to look at. But he found one she liked fairly quickly, because he knew his mother's tastes as well as she did. And then she'd had him take her home, cut off the paper tag, and help her put it on.

"I know this won't be easy," Mary said to him as they walked out the back of the house. She was so proud of the house. Her mean old bastard of a father had added a second story, but she'd had it insulated, had siding put on. She'd bartered with the King boys from around the mountain to paint it

173

a cheery shade of yellow in return for teaching them how to cheat at cards. Oh, Mary had savored this life. She'd spent her youth thinking herself too big, too loud, too bold for these mountains, and she'd been right. But here on Moriah Bald, with her brittle old records and her upright piano, with a little white whiskey from the Kings' still and subscriptions to magazines, she'd been able to taste the life she'd longed for. It wasn't the same as living it, but it had been as close as she could get. It wouldn't have been enough, but Harvey had been safe. Maybe he would figure something out. Maybe he would go somewhere and live a better life.

We all have to compromise, she'd said to Harvey when he was young, *and make little bargains with ourselves to get by. Don't spend your whole life feeling bad about it. Enjoy what you can instead.*

They had a victory garden out back now, a pale shade of the agrarian life her father and his people had needed in order to survive. It was fading fast. The soil wasn't as rich as her father said it once had been. Sometimes the tomatoes tasted sour. But it was hers—theirs—and maybe next year things would be better.

Maybe next year they'd be more blessed.

Maybe Harvey would get to live his own life.

CHAPTER SIXTEEN – HOWDY NEIGHBOR

"I think maybe it's time I went around the neighborhood and introduced myself to everyone else. All the folks I haven't met yet." Reginald shrugged with his glass of tea as he sat on Lewis' back deck. "They're going to see me on the news tonight, standing on their street. Seems like I ought to get out in front of that. And we can inventory whether *everybody*'s gotten eaten by whatever's in the house."

Lewis ran down the list of eight houses other than Dorothea's: Bobby's, Beck & Megan, Kate & Johnny, and his own. Of the remaining four, two sat empty most of the time. "Short-term rental investments," he said, and then he grimaced.

"Not a fan of SkyBNB and stuff like that? Where somebody rents out their house for a week at a time?" Reginald sat beside him in a reclining lounge chair of the style he always associated with beach trips from childhood.

Lewis stood up to get another glass of iced tea. He made it unsweetened, but preferring it that way had been just another way Reginald failed to meet the expectations of his forebears. "They hollow out a neighborhood one house at a time. They're predators. They tell you it's people renting out a spare room, or the apartment over their garage, but really it's that people with too much money buy up houses and hope to rent them out enough during tourism season—like right now—to cover the mortgage and turn a profit. It keeps real people from moving in. It makes a neighborhood feel like a ghost town."

Reginald smiled a little. "Careful, you're going to start to sound like a native." He shifted to a mocking hayseed accent. "*Ain't no dang outsiders movin' t'my culdy-sack.*" Lewis smiled, and Reginald grinned. He was still a little high on having spoken out when the cameras were here. They would have to talk about it, he knew. Lewis had been silent the entire walk back to his house, and conversation resumed once they got inside only in fits and starts. Still, seeing Lewis smile now was a good sign.

"The other two houses," Lewis went on, ignoring Reginald's comment, "are people I don't see very often. One is a retired lady named Patricia Something—I can't remember her last name right off. Seems nice, but I literally never see her leave her house. I went over and introduced myself—you know, Kate and me doing the welcome wagon thing we did for you—and she mentioned she'd moved here from somewhere in the Midwest after her husband died. Once in a while I see a station wagon in her driveway. I've kind of wondered if it's Meals on Wheels or something like that. Anyway, I think she's super-religious or something. Always keeps her lights off on Halloween, for instance, and one time she posted on OneDoorDown about, you know, *if my lights are off that means don't trick or treat!!!*, as though this were some sort of crisis."

Reginald rolled his eyes. "Okay, well, I hate her."

"Hey, be nice. I think maybe she's just afraid of strangers. She seemed awfully eager to get rid of us when we stopped by. She's far from home, hardly seems to know anyone or do anything. She's probably hurting." Lewis shrugged. "Anyway, the last house is the one down by the road, on the other side. They're a project manager, works from home. Named…" Lewis paused for a moment, freshly filled glass of iced tea halfway to his perfect lips, and Reginald got a raging hard-on. "Graham? I think? Really cool. Younger, which surprised me. I think they moved here to be close to the trails and stuff. They're always going somewhere with a bike or a kayak or some shit on the weekends. They drive up to Boone and go skiing in the winter, even."

"So why aren't the SkyBNB houses rented out right now?" Reginald gestured at the trees at the border of Lewis' yard, and the hillside beyond. "It's peak leaf season. This is when those people make bank."

Lewis' mouth quirked up for a second, as did his eyebrows. "Oh, there's drama *there*. The houses are owned by a couple, Ted and Fiona Barnes. Well, *ex*-couple. They're still arguing about who gets the houses, so they're not for rent."

"Two houses, two people, seems easy enough." Reginald grimaced.

Lewis grinned as he sat back down. "Gossip around the neighborhood is that one house is, like, four square feet smaller than the other, and their fight is about who's going to get the 'larger' house."

Reginald sighed. "Straight people are not okay."

Reginald rang Patricia's doorbell a second time. "This feels rude," he said to Lewis. "If she wants to be left alone, I should leave her alone." He turned halfway to face him now. "And if she's ultra-evangelical, she's going to have gaydar for *miles*. She probably clocked me when I was driving up the mountain *days* ago. What good does it do for me to meet her?"

Lewis arched one eyebrow at him. "Uh, it was *your* idea to go meet everybody before they see you on the news tonight. Not mine. If you don't want to meet her, let's just walk away."

Muffled by the thick door, Reginald heard a woman's voice from inside the house. "Yes?"

Reginald turned and faced the door. He looked at the keyhole as though addressing it. "Hi. Uh, ma'am. I'm Reginald Voth. Dorothea Voth, at the end of the cul-de-sac, she was my mother. I wanted to come around and introduce myself. I'm, uh, here dealing with her estate."

Silence from the other side.

Lewis looked at Reginald, who resolutely did not look back. Lewis spoke, calling out. "Hi, Patricia. It's Lewis, from the neighborhood watch? I wanted to come with Reginald"—Reginald stifled a laugh, Lewis did not react—"so you'd know he's… legit. I thought if a familiar face was with him, that might…" Lewis trailed off.

"I also wanted to let you know that I talked to WSOL this afternoon about, well, all the stuff that's happened. With my mom and my brother and my sister-in-law, I mean. And I just, I don't know, I don't want you to worry if you see that and then see me around the neighborhood."

Another long silence.

Reginald couldn't help but picture her in there: he ginned up a stooped, elderly woman in a shawl, her hair in a bun, two knitting needles poking through it. It would have been a little amusing, something right out of a cartoon, if he didn't also imagine her staring at him through the peephole. In his mind's eye, she glared, licked dry lips, and *studied* him. Reginald shifted his weight from one foot to the other. He could practically *feel* her judging him, finding him wanting in some way. He wondered if she worried he was a scam artist, or maybe a home invader. *Maybe she thinks I'm a demon. Maybe she thinks I, too, have been taken over by whatever lives on the mountain. Maybe she thinks murder-suicide is contagious.*

"Reginald?"

He turned and looked at Lewis. "What?"

"Are you going to answer her?"

Reginald blinked twice. "Huh?"

Lewis put on his most plastic smile. "Are you going to answer Patricia's question?"

Reginald studied Lewis' features for a moment—he didn't even know he had a "type" when it came to noses, but Lewis had the perfect nose, no doubt about it—and then smiled back. "And what was the question?"

Muffled, and said as if from very far: "*Did you grow up on the mountain?*"

Reginald did a brief double-take between Lewis and the door. "Uh, yes." Half a beat. "Ma'am, I mean. Yes, *ma'am*. This," and he gestured at the street behind him, "was my front yard for my entire childhood."

Another very long pause, so long Reginald thought perhaps she had gone away—or would have thought, at any rate, if he didn't *feel* her gaze firing at him out of that peephole like a laser in a sci-fi movie. She was still there, on the other side of the door. He *knew* she was.

"I'm sorry for all the trouble," he said, but it sounded limp, as well it should have. *Why am I apologizing for my mother dying and my brother—*

Reginald hadn't actually let himself think about it. For an instant, an image flashed through his mind: his brother pleading for his life, his brother's wife weeping as she held her gun on him. It had been her gun, one Bobby had given her as an anniversary present. They had that kind of marriage: performatively fucked up. It had been fun once, in the beginning, when they both laughed more easily and did little things for each other. He made her gourmet dinners, and she learned to bow hunt, and their life here, in this place, had been rich with promise. But then the babies they both so desperately wanted had failed to materialize, and trying for them had become a chore, and he'd stopped making gourmet dinners, and their easy laughter had faded away. And then, as they fought over his mother's death, what to do with her, what to do about everything now, *what to do about the mountain*, she'd said, *All I want is to be on my own*, and two minutes later she had been.

Reginald jumped about halfway out of his own skin at Lewis' hand on his elbow. "*JESUS!*" he shouted, and then he looked at the door and back at Lewis again.

Lewis, eyes wide with surprise, immediately let go and put both hands out in a *stay calm, it's okay* gesture. "Whoa, Reginald, I'm sorry. I'm sorry."

Reginald, wild-eyed, kept turning his head this way and that as though he had no idea where he was. "Did you see that?" But he knew, the moment he asked, as just the first sliver of himself returned to the here and now, just as he *knew* the scene he'd just watched with his mind's eye had been real, had *happened*, he knew Lewis had not seen anything other than whatever transpired here on this porch for however long Reginald's attention had turned inward and *through* to another time and place: his brother's house, just two days before.

"I'm sorry. *I'm sorry.*" Lewis' voice had dropped almost to a whisper. "You checked out all of a sudden. What a friend of mine used to call 'buffering.' I didn't mean to scare you, but to be honest, you scared *me.*" Lewis turned to the peephole and called out more loudly, "Patricia, sorry to be a bother. Just wanted to make sure you were in the loop in case you watch the news tonight."

Reginald, still a little wild in his expression, didn't budge when Lewis tried to usher him off the porch. "What did she say? What did I miss?"

Lewis's face turned hard. "I'm going to put my hands on you again. I'm just warning you this time." Then he took Reginald by his upper arms and gently steered him off the porch.

"What did she *say?*"

Reginald stopped again by her mailbox, at the end of the walk, and Lewis couldn't get him to move further. He drew a breath and glared. "She said you'd be in her prayers."

"Christ." Reginald twisted out of Lewis' grasp. "Well, thanks for nothing, *Patty.*" He frowned more deeply and shook his head. "Sorry. I guess that beats her calling me a faggot while she dials 911."

Lewis hesitated. "There's a problem, though."

Reginald arched one eyebrow. He'd cooled off from the initial shock of terror, and now he was the one to clasp Lewis' arm instead of the other way around. "Okay, tell me."

"This is going to sound crazy."

Reginald switched which eyebrow he held aloft. "Oh, just try me."

Lewis grimaced. "She didn't sound normal when she said it."

Reginald went pale and his faint smirk faded. He knew exactly what Lewis was about to say, but he waited for him to say it anyway.

"She sounded like your mother."

At the end of the cul-de-sac, no one answered at Graham's door.

"Their 4x4 is gone." Lewis nodded at a paved parking spot to one side of the single-bay garage. "Usually that means they're off on a hillside hoot somewhere."

"Well, good." Reginald looked down at his phone. "That means they won't be watching the news tonight, at least."

Lewis nodded. "Good point."

As they walked across to Lewis' house, they heard a familiar voice call out, "Hello the house!" Isaiah King stood on the walk, by the street. Reginald had been happy to see Isaiah and his family at the funeral, had even surprised himself later by realizing he had enjoyed their accompaniment to the hymns, but seeing him show up in the neighborhood like this put him on guard. He lifted a hand and, uncertain what to do with it, offered a weak wave.

Isaiah lifted his baseball cap to greet them. He stood even taller than Reginald, and even thinner, like a thin-bodied man stretched out to cartoon lengths. He had enormous, spider-like hands and wore a flannel button-up over a plain white tee and well-worn jeans. His boots had a little mud around the heels. Reginald's inner dial turned to *any time he likes* and he frowned.

"Evening, Isaiah."

Lewis nodded at him. "Can we help you?"

Isaiah removed his cap now and said, "I just wanted to come and talk about your mom, see what plans you've got for the place."

"Christ, Isaiah," Reginald said, "I've barely had time to think the last few days. I have no idea. Probably sell her house. And Bobby's."

Isaiah nodded. "Understandable. We'd wondered if you might decide to live here yourself. Carry on your family's presence on Moriah Bald."

Reginald lifted one shoulder in a shrug. "I've got a home of my own. And I'm not exactly planning to have kids who would live here after me."

"I'd figured that," Isaiah said. "The Pride sticker on your truck's back window 'n all. Didn't know, though, you might be looking to settle down, adopt, make a family here like your kin did before you."

Reginald blinked at him. "Isaiah, I really valued your friendship when we were kids. Not a lot of people were terribly nice to me. So, I'm going to give you the most honest answer I can, not because I'm trying to be rude but because I want to be straight with you. Uh, no pun intended."

Isaiah flashed a small smile. "I appreciate that."

"I hated it here." Reginald held Isaiah's steady gaze, and the man didn't flinch or show surprise. "My mother used kindness and cruelty to keep everyone off-balance. My father vanished when I was a child. My relatives all tried to turn me into versions of themselves and, when that didn't work out, stopped noticing I existed. When I came out to my mother, she demanded to know who 'did this' to me, but she was the only person who ever tried to fuck me when I was a kid. I'm sorry if that sounds like I'm trying to be an asshole, but it's the truth. I'd rather watch this place burn than spend another night in it. But if instead I can sell it off to someone who wants to renovate it as a historic property and flip my brother's house for cash while they're at it, that's *almost* as good."

Reginald paused and glanced at Dorothea's house, brooding in the shadow of the mountain, then turned back to Isaiah. "I'm going to get whatever money I can for this place from people too stupid to realize how much they're overpaying for it and then I'm going to go back to my little trailer thirty-seven miles from here and I'm going to buy myself a very nice television, pay off my credit cards, buy a new car, and book a vacation to somewhere the weather's warm and the guys are hot. *That* is my plan. I started collecting brochures from travel agents *years* ago. Sometimes those brochures were the only way I got through a phone conversation with my mother. But if you're asking because y'all want to buy it instead, own this side of the mountain *and* yours, then by all means I will cut you a friends and family discount. Not *too* deep, but I'd do it to be neighborly."

Isaiah studied Reginald for a long moment, then took a step in the direction of the beat-up Corolla parked nearby. "Much obliged if you do, Reginald. I think we'd be interested in taking you up on that offer. And I'm sorry she was not the mother to you that she seemed to be to the rest of us." Isaiah hesitated in his backing away. "We'd still like to do a sing for her. Would you be interested in hearing some of the old songs? Or joining us in them?"

Reginald hesitated for some reason. His reflex was to say no, but something about Isaiah's politeness, the way he responded with something compassionate, stayed his hand. "Right now?"

Isaiah gestured with his hands in a vague way. "I could grab my guitar from the car, sure. If Mr. Gwan here will allow us to sit on his porch."

Lewis spoke up. "Back deck, actually. That would be better. You know, don't want to bother the neighbors." He looked at Reginald, then flicked his eyes for half a second in the direction of Johnny and Kate's house across the street.

"Wherever's the least imposition on you," Isaiah said it with such ancient manners, even Reginald found himself a little charmed.

Lewis, Reginald realized, had discreetly taken his time getting each of them something to drink so that Isaiah and Reginald could catch up briefly on the back deck. They'd been playmates, sure, but they'd essentially never had a conversation as adults. They were practically strangers. Reginald reflected it was more like meeting someone and knowing you'd been friends with them in a past life than simply earlier in this one.

Isaiah worked construction part-time. His brother had a job in IT for the county. One of his sisters was in college at UNC Asheville, home on fall break. Another did something for the phone company, but she wanted to become a park ranger. There were a lot of parks around there, but ranger jobs required a lot of school and work experience, so she had a long road ahead of her if she wanted to land that as a career. In the meantime, they all helped their father around the farm. They all still lived with him. It had been a long-standing tradition in plenty of families in that area. Reginald knew one of the problems many families faced was dividing what had once been enormous properties full of economic potential down into halves, quarters, eighths, sixteenths, and so on for children, grandchildren, great-grandchildren. Eventually people wound up inheriting a postage stamp with no road to it and no one willing to let them cut one. Their success in reproduction resulted in diminished opportunities for each generation. What ancestors had managed to scrape out of a holler or off a hillside got spread too thin to make a meal.

"What will y'all do when your father dies?"

Isaiah greeted that with a smile. "Oh, I reckon we'll do what Kings always do: there'll be some caterwaulin' and at least one fight, then the funeral, then we'll work out some way for one of us to stay on the land. Probably the rest of us will build somewhere else on the property. Kings've had that whole side of Moriah Bald as far back as we've been here. It'll be the same when daddy's gone. We won't let it drive us apart. Gotta keep the music going."

The Kings had always been a family of musicians. As a child, Reginald now remembered, he'd sometimes gone up onto Moriah Bald and crossed to the other side to listen, down through the woods, to the sound of the Kings making old-time music together. Reginald had always assumed they were ignorant, but now he wondered if instead this were a conscious act of curation.

"Does your family know shape-note singing?"

"Like always. Don't you?"

Reginald shook his head. "My mother never taught me. She knew it, but she never took the time to share it."

Isaiah clucked his tongue. "Well, if you did settle here, that'd be something we'd fix right quick." He flashed another of his signature here-

and-gone smiles, lips pressed together, no teeth, and then nodded at Lewis as he took the can of Coke offered to him. "Many thanks, Mr. Gwan."

"For like the third time, please call me Lewis."

Isaiah nodded. "I was raised to call everyone Mister, Miss, or Missus, but I'll allow as you're a friend of Reginald's, so it's okay for me to call you Lewis. Please also call me Isaiah."

Lewis returned the flashed smile, but Reginald noted it looked strained. There was a limit to how long good manners remained charming. Eventually, they turned into unresolved tension.

"What song did you want to play for us?" Reginald tried to redirect the moment to something else, advance this strange visitation by the man who'd once been the child he'd thought a friend.

"For your mother, Reginald. And also for you, I reckon."

Reginald blinked, but he bit back whatever snide remark he'd normally make.

Isaiah strummed the guitar, produced a couple of chords to test it, cleared his throat.

Reginald lit a cigarette.

Isaiah opened his mouth and began to play quick, staccato licks, as much percussion as melody.

My home is in the Blue Ridge Mountains
    My home is on Moriah Bald
    My home is under twinkling starlight
    And I never expect to be there anymore.

How can I keep from crying?
    How can I not cry out?
    I'd thought that when I'm dying
    I could always expect to be there evermore.

I thought I heard a freight train blowing

> *Thought I'd seen a gate on high.*
> *But instead I lay down knowing*
> *That the pathway to heaven's shut behind a door.*

I leave here this Monday morning.

> *Gonna go back to those hills.*
> *Gonna rest my weary body*
> *Set my burdens down upon a river's shore.*

Isaiah pitched his voice high with a key change and the tempo slowed.

It's a river through those mountains

> *Water deep and crystal clear.*
> *'Gainst the rocks of that old river.*
> *My soul will fly back to these hills of yore.*

Isaiah played a few chords, buttoning up the end of the song, then popped the top on the can of soda and drained it in one long, unsettling go.

Lewis let out a gust of breath. "Wow. Isaiah, that was beautiful."

Isaiah ducked his head, half thanks, half humble aw-shucks-ing.

"That was such a sad song," Reginald said.

"The tune was written a century or so ago by a gentleman called Clarence Ashley. Been a lotta versions of the original song. We like to tinker, though, so we wrote new lyrics along the way. I apologize if it seemed inappropriate to your mother's memory."

Reginald shook his head. "No, it isn't that. It's just... I can see why you wouldn't sing it in church. I mean, it's a song about suicide, right? Or at the very least it's someone choosing where and when to die. I can't imagine Pastor Owenby liking that one too much. That isn't a criticism, mind you.

And normally I do *not* go for the old-time music or bluegrass or anything, but I liked that a lot."

"It isn't a joyful tale, no. Or is it? The singer gets to go home in the end. There are worse endings." Isaiah flashed another of those smiles. "Your mama always loved good music, and she considered old music one of the best kinds of good. So, I thought it'd do her memory some honor."

Reginald opened his mouth, stopped, closed it again.

Lewis reached over and put one hand over his.

Reginald drew a new breath and nodded. "I have a lot of feelings about whether I care what she would have liked, and how I feel about the things she would have enjoyed, but I also know that song somehow helped me with all that."

Isaiah rested the guitar in his lap. "Sometimes that's the best work the old songs can do: Shine a light on what we're feeling. It's up to us to sort it out."

"If I told you my mother's house was haunted, what would you say?" Reginald didn't look away from Isaiah's guitar as he said it, and he kept his voice very low.

Lewis held his breath.

Isaiah pondered for a few seconds, his face serious. "I'd say the whole mountain's haunted, Reginald. It wouldn't surprise me to hear she's got unfinished business. And maybe finishing it will keep you here. We've had magic here aplenty, and I reckon we always will."

"Magic?" Lewis raised one eyebrow and looked from Isaiah to Reginald and back.

"It might sound silly to somebody not raised here." Isaiah didn't sound embarrassed as he spoke, and he didn't seem to be trying to *other* Lewis, either. "There're a lot of old ways we keep up here."

Reginald surprised himself by grinning as he tossed out some examples. "Stuff like dowsing for water when you're going to dig a well, or plugging a tree to make something happen, or checking how many acorns fall to see if we'll have a hard winter."

"Folk magic, right?" Just as Isaiah had spoken with no belittlement, Lewis likewise asked it without rancor or obvious judgment.

Reginald nodded at Lewis. "And other superstitions. There's a lot of stuff that was, you know, common knowledge when I was a kid. But a lot of it was only common around here. Old-fashioned beliefs the rest of the world left behind a long time ago."

Lewis cut Reginald a look. "You think Koreans don't have their own version of the same sorts of things? You're not the only one who grew up in a culture most of America only *thinks* it understands." Lewis smiled at Reginald's obvious surprise and gave his hand a squeeze. "You don't have to be embarrassed by that stuff, Reginald. I think it's interesting. Don't worry, if you start feeling too uniquely siloed, I'll tell you a few stories about *dokkaebi* to curl your toes."

Reginald laughed once. "What are they?"

"Think of them as goblins that either kill you, possess you, or, if you're lucky, make do with eating all your jelly." Lewis winked.

Isaiah grinned now as he stood. "Gentlemen, I hate to sing one song and go, but I do need to get to the house. I just wanted to stop in on my way home from town and ask after you. Thank you for the chance to sing a song in your mother's memory. I'm sorry to hear this is even harder for you than I'd thought.."

"Thank you." Reginald surprised himself by how much he meant it. "Don't be a stranger, Isaiah."

"You say that like you'll be around after all." The man held the guitar in his left hand and offered to shake with his right. Reginald took it, they shook once, then they each let go. Isaiah turned to Lewis. "Kind thanks for your hospitality. Coca-Cola's my favorite, but daddy's got diabetes so we can't keep it around. I always appreciate it as a treat."

Lewis didn't seem sure what to say. "I'm glad you enjoyed it. I hope your father's well."

"Oh, he'll do alright as long as he needs." Isaiah touched his hat. "But I do have to go."

"We'll walk you out."

Lewis and Reginald stood on Lewis' front porch and watched Isaiah drive away in the old, gold-colored Corolla.

"Well, *that* was fucked up." Reginald reached into his pocket, produced his phone, and squinted at his screen in the late afternoon autumn light. After a moment he made a small sound of displeasure.

Lewis halted, having started to go inside again. "What's up?"

Reginald held up his phone. "An account named PattyDoodles just followed me on OneDoorDown *and* Yearbook *and* PhotoGram." Lewis leaned in and then pointedly looked in the direction of Patricia's house without saying anything. Reginald went on. "Yeah. Exactly. So, whoever they are, whatever they're doing, they're keeping an eye on me for sure. I thought maybe, when I was at the coffee camper, when you called me? I thought it felt like the stars were watching me…" Reginald waved it off. "Water under the bridge. Should've trusted my gut." *But then you wouldn't have come back to Lewis and be standing beside him now, would you?* Reginald shut that line of thinking down immediately. A person who spends his whole life never trusting, and then trusts too quickly, will wind up hurt immediately *and* forever, and he wasn't quite ready to pass that sentence on himself. He pushed ahead. "*And* I missed a call from Pastor Owenby while we were talking to Isaiah. And unless the voicemail transcription got it completely wrong, he wants to come over tomorrow night." Reginald's eyes went wide. "Oh shit. Of course."

The light went on for Lewis as well. "They posted it on their website already."

"Right. WSOL must have edited the segment as soon as they got back and put it online in advance of tonight's broadcast. Oh, *fuck*." Reginald shook his head in frustration with himself.

"Isn't it what you wanted, though? Getting Owenby out here, taking the fight to…" Lewis gestured at Dorothea's house. "Whatever's in there?"

"Yeah." Reginald nodded, but he didn't look up from his phone. "Yes. Not that. I mean, oh fuck *this*." With a sour expression, he held up the phone for Lewis to read. "When it rains, it pours. I got a message on PhotoGram from some account called @Th3H3xorcist." Reginald thought for a second. "Oh, 'the hexorcist.' They say they're in Asheville and they want permission to film inside my mother's house tomorrow."

"What are you going to say to them?" Lewis nervously adjusted his glasses.

Reginald shrugged. "I've already poked the bear. Worst case scenario, he's just another person on the side of whatever the fuck is happening." Then Reginald's face broke into a grin. "Best case, he's a legit paranormal weirdo and I get to use him to piss off my mother's ghost *so bad*."

Lewis awoke a little past 3:00 AM, aware with perfect clarity that the house—Dorothea's house, Reginald's house, the house at the heart of everything—called to him. He cleared his throat, rubbed his eyes, and put a gentle hand on Reginald's shoulder. "Wake up," he murmured. "Wake up, something's happening."

Reginald breathed softly beside him but did not stir.

Lewis heard music from outside, faint, distant, the sound of stringed instruments and soft voices, and he shook Reginald's shoulder harder. "Wake up." He spoke with his full voice, then repeated it more loudly. He pushed Reginald once, rolling him over from his side onto his stomach, and he said it a third time, nearly shouting it.

Still, Reginald slept.

Lewis pressed his lips into a line.

The house would not *allow* Reginald to wake up.

"I guess it's my turn to meet whatever's in there," he said aloud.

Lewis got out of bed, slipped on a pair of crumpled jeans from the floor and a tank top with the logo of a gay bar from California. It was the first place he'd ever gone dancing. He'd bought a succession of shirts and hoodies and hats from it over the intervening years. The bar's logo—an old-fashioned paper matchbook, the kind that folds closed and tucks into itself, with one match bent to extend beyond the cover, struck and burned to a blackened cinder, a line of smoke wafting from it—had become for Lewis a kind of sigil of freedom and of self. He occasionally reflected on the irony of having a brand logo as a personal emblem, but the emotional truth of it defied the way his mind attacked all sentimentality with persistently and viciously skeptical logic.

Such are the thoughts of three o'clock in the morning.

Lewis walked down the stairs, put his keys and his wallet in his pockets, slipped out the front door and locked it behind him. A week earlier he wouldn't have bothered to lock it if he weren't driving somewhere, but now the neighborhood didn't feel safe. Lewis allowed himself a little smile. Funny, that it would start to feel unsafe now that it also had a reason to feel like *home*. But then, the two effects had one cause: the man asleep in Lewis' bed upstairs.

Outside, the music was louder, but still distant.

Lewis did not have to wonder whence it came. He could hear it clearly. It came from Dorothea's house.

Lewis wasted no time on terror or some pretense of shock. But he also for fucking sure was *not* going to walk into that house. He harbored no action hero fantasies. He did not wish for a gun, or for a baseball bat, or for some other implement of destruction. He *did* briefly wish he owned a flame thrower, but that, too, fell into the realm of the patently silly. He would not march into the house and do battle with whatever engine of hatred and need gave it such presence as a malefactor. At the same time, it had put Reginald in an unresponsive state and he had to assume it did so to gain Lewis' attention. Well, it had succeeded. Even now, he trod slowly up the sidewalk toward the ancient home that sat in the lap of Moriah Bald like an old cat filled with territorial malice. He could *feel* it watching him as he walked. He could practically hear it purr. It wanted to sink its claws into him, and he was about to step within reach.

Lewis saw his choices in the moment in simple terms: he could refuse to go to the house and hope it released Reginald; he could go to the house and be consumed by it in whatever way it consumed his neighbors and former friends; or he could go tell it he refused to participate. And he could do that from outside, certainly. It made no sense, but it was a better option than falling into the trap and it was a better option than waiting to see if they ever let Reginald wake up again. The house wanted Reginald, that was clear, but Lewis knew he would never use Reginald's life as a bargaining chip. He would take his own risks with his own life, and certainly had plenty of times, but he would not gamble with another's..

Lewis arrived at the foot of the driveway, the place where the ancient gravel from the road emerged from the asphalt like a bone jutting from a makeshift grave. He looked up at the house. The music coming from inside had been slow strings and vocals he couldn't make out, but now he heard them and could comprehend. The melody did not sound familiar, but Lewis could tell it must be another ancient Appalachian ballad. It sounded both distant and muffled, even from here, mere feet from the front door. The house stood before him, immediate, real, but the music sounded as though it came from far away and on the other side of thick and heavy walls. It had the same quality as the one Isaiah had sung, but a different melody, one Lewis did not recognize:

> *Down in the deep green holler*
> *There thee and thy love did meet*
> *When you ceased cavorting*
> *Your love fell off to sleep*
>
> *Blue hills and hollers have never been thine*

And your true love they can't let go
We've plans long laid for your true love
But you need not live in woe

The music grew to a swell with the last line, a bluegrass ballad about to shift gears into something more driving, more active, and Lewis put up a hand. "You can shut the fuck up now." He said it quietly, careful not to sound perturbed or particularly affected. If a career in porn had taught him anything, it was how to sound enthusiastic when not and how to stay calm when agitated. He applied the latter now. "I'm not going inside. You're not going to do to me whatever you did to the others. I'm only here to tell you that I know you—whatever you are, Dorothea's ghost or something else—are up to something and I'm not going to fall for it that easily. When I get back to my house, I'm going to wake Reginald up. If you keep him asleep, or put him in a coma, or anything like that, I'm going to come back with two cans of kerosene from my garage and I'm going to burn this fucking house down."

The music shifted to one note held impossibly long on a fiddle.

"Good. You're paying attention. This is the home of Reginald's ancestors, not mine. It's his fight to win or lose. But if he fights you, I will fight beside him. And if you take him from me, I *will* burn you to the goddamned ground. You have a knack for knowing our desires, so I trust you realize I mean it. And now I'm leaving, because we have nothing more to say." Lewis turned around and walked down the sidewalk toward his house. He refused to look back, refused to give whatever evil crouched in that house--and over it, and behind it, and *beyond* it--the satisfaction of one ounce of his own fear. He let himself back in his front door, slipped off his slides, and crept back up the steps. As he slid the jeans back off, Reginald stirred and rolled over.

"What's up? Did something wake you?"

"The house tried to zap me," Lewis murmured with a shrug.

Reginald blinked at him. "What?"

"I told you, I hate lying, so I'm telling you right now: your mother's house called to me. It used music to wake me and draw me there, and it sang me a little song about how it has plans for you but maybe it would let me off easy if I don't get in the way. So, I told it to leave me alone or I would burn it down. I didn't go inside."

Reginald seemed at a loss for what to say. "It did?"

Lewis smiled softly. "Yes."

Reginald put a hand on Lewis' bare shoulder. "Would you really burn my mother's house down?"

Lewis leaned over and kissed Reginald's hand. "Of course. If you said you wanted to burn it down right now, I'd go siphon gas out of my own car."

"Lewis, that's the sweetest thing any man has ever said to me." Reginald yawned. "This is the weirdest fucking dream in the world."

Lewis grinned. "I'll tell you again in the morning, so you'll remember."

Reginald sat straighter and looked at Lewis for a long moment. "This isn't a dream, is it?"

"No."

CHAPTER SEVENTEEN – THE HEXORCIST

Th3 H3xorcist, it turned out, was an oversized slice of tanning-bed-baked meatloaf named Vincent Hargrove. Lewis and Reginald had enjoyed an extremely vigorous fuck in Lewis' ridiculous shower, then eaten a late breakfast. Two hours later, right on time, Vincent AKA Th3 H3xorcist drove up the cul-de-sac in a well-kept sport coupe from ten or fifteen years ago. He drove slowly, and though Reginald wasn't a gear head by any measure, he guessed the car could probably melt asphalt if the guy breathed on the pedal.

"Wow, a 2007 GT Spyder?" Lewis gripped Reginald's upper arm as though to steady himself through a swoon.

"Is that what he's driving?"

Lewis fluttered a few fingers. "It's an unusual trim level on one of the last Mitsubishi Eclipses."

"Oh, I remember those." Reginald's mouth turned downward. "Or at least I remember the asshole jocks who drove them in high school."

They'd been able to hear Th3 H3xorcist coming from half a mile away: he sounded like a rolling dance club right after someone screams *ALL YOU FUCKERS ON THE DANCE FLOOR!* To Reginald's surprise, however, he'd cranked his music down the second he turned into the neighborhood. Reginald nodded in the direction of the car. "I'm kind of surprised. Car like that, PhotoGram handle like his? I'd figure he'd want to advertise his presence."

Lewis chuckled once, only a little grimly. "People whose career is online and on camera get pretty good at curating their presentation. Everybody edits before they post."

Reginald lifted a hand to wave at The Hexorcist, and the Eclipse wheeled into the driveway of Dorothea's house as the windows went up and the sunroof closed.

Vincent climbed out, all six-foot-five of him. *Christ, that's probably how wide he is at the shoulders, too.* He had buzzcut hair and a barely-visible beard with no mustache, a shirt at least one size too small, and muscles like a Thanksgiving turkey. The first words that sprang to Reginald's mind were *it's been a long time since I got bred by a brick wall like that*, and he blushed hard. Lewis apparently had noticed, because he stifled a chuckle and cleared his throat.

"Hi. I'm Lewis. This is Reginald."

"I'm Vincent Hargrove." He walked over with the odd grace a lot of gym bunnies have from time spent squatting and turning and lunging with huge weights across the backs of their necks. He extended a hand and said, "Which of you is @mountainqueen?"

"Oh, uh, hi. I'm Reginald. This is my mother's house."

Vincent smiled with genuine friendliness. "Oh, I know, I saw the segment online. I just wasn't sure which of you I was talking to on the G. Sometimes couples have shared accounts."

Reginald reached out and took the enormous man's hand, shaking it once. "Of course. Duh. So, you're Th3 H3xorcist?" He tried to pronounce it as regular words, but somehow when the sound came out of his mouth he could tell it represented something more complicated.

Vincent grinned so that dimples appeared. "And a lot of other things: Hargrove Media, Vincent Hargrove Personal Training, FApp by Vincent, and I'm Vince the Prince in the Asheville chapter of Hometown Wrasslin'. But you can call me Vince." The smile on his face was wide, sparkling white, his teeth perfectly aligned. It caught both Reginald and Lewis by surprise, though, when Vincent winked at Lewis. "I'm also FitFeet on InterFans. I mean, I'm straight, well, mostly straight, but I've followed your journey. Mad respect to anybody who can make it on their own, y'know? Really love your content."

Reginald thought Lewis looked as though he'd just farted in church: his face went perfectly still, his eyes wide.

Vincent produced a business card from his back pocket, bent and crumpled from being sat on, and held it out for Lewis. "Fifty percent discount on a single purchase of a used wrestling singlet or a signed foot pic. You know, a little discount from one pro to another." The card had a QR code and a petroleum-jelly-on-the-lens photo of truly gargantuan Chuck Taylor high-top sneakers.

Reginald tried not to laugh. He really did. It happened anyway: a sudden, high-pitched yelp and then he positively cackled with both hands over his mouth. He laughed so hard and so suddenly that he fell into a coughing fit and had to bend double as Lewis, as though in slow motion, reached out and took the card.

"Uh, thanks."

Vincent—Vince—continued grinning, unfazed by Reginald's hysterical reaction. "You know how it is, bro. Always be hustlin'. Right?"

"Right." Lewis did not sound as though he agreed, and Reginald laughed all the harder.

Lewis visibly tried to suppress a smile, failed, and then let himself laugh a little, too.

Vince slapped him on the shoulder. "That's the spirit. And remember that *mostly* if you ever wanna collaborate, bro. Could be good for both of us. Get a lot of cross-promotion out of stuff like that." The look on Lewis' face sent Reginald into another fit of giggles and coughs, but Vince kept the train on the tracks by clapping his hands together, startling both of them. "Speaking of the spirit, let's see that ghost, bro."

It took two more rounds of sniffling and wiping tears from his eyes before Reginald could intelligibly respond, but eventually he put his sunglasses back on and breathed deep, let it out, took another in, and then stood up straighter.

"I have to admit, I kind of expected more of, I dunno, a Tally Johnson kind of guy." Lewis said it very politely and plainly. "Do you know him?"

"Great storyteller, bro, of course I do. Went to a library thing he did. Super polite like your grandma at Sunday dinner, and he knows his stuff backwards and forwards, up and down." Vince nodded and put a hand to his own massive, sculpted chest. "It's an honor to even have my name and his in the same sentence, bro. I'm a little more punk rock, y'know?"

"Yeah, I love what he does, and I hope it isn't taken as a criticism of either of you when I say that, honestly, you seem to be his polar opposite." Lewis' tone was congenial, and Vincent seemed to take it the same way. They shared a grin for just a moment and Reginald could feel a spark.

Reginald brought things back to matters more at hand. "Okay, so, uh, what exactly are your qualifications? Because I'm not totally sure it's a ghost—or *only* a ghost, fuck if I know—we're dealing with here."

Vince grinned down at him, and Reginald would have lied if he said he didn't feel attraction stir in his groin. *What the fuck is wrong with me, why am I suddenly crazy for dick?* Vince's answer snapped him out of it, though. "Oh, I trained as an exorcist. Did a two-year course online, got certified and everything." He shrugged. "And I'm mildly psychic."

"Only mildly?" Lewis arched one eyebrow.

At the same time, Reginald asked, "You're… a priest?"

Vince's grin widened as he waggled his hand back and forth, up and down. "Sorta. I did an online thing to get ordained, then I took a real online exorcism program. Didn't wanna waste, you know," here he tapped the side of his head, "*the gift.*"

"An online exorcism program. I had no idea the Roman Catholic

Church was so tech-savvy." Reginald himself wasn't even sure whether he meant that to be sarcastic, much less whether it came out that way.

"Oh, no Catholics." Vince used the same hand to wave that off by brushing his fingers low through the air. "I don't do the religious dogma thing. If you want a Catholic priest, I'm not your guy. But I do have a paladin-level certificate from the Institute for Responsible Exorcisms, and I brought with me everything I'd need."

Lewis managed, "Paladin level," very quietly.

Reginald surprised himself with his response to Vince. "Honestly, I'm a little relieved. If you were a Catholic priest I'd probably already have my pants off." He smiled when Vince gave him a guffaw as sharp and loud as a one-gun salute. Reginald went on, "So, you saw the segment. But what you don't know is, whatever's in there is changing people." Reginald said it before he could let himself overthink it. Now that it was outside of his head, it was easier to keep going. He nodded down the street, then looked back up at Vince. "Those people I said went in there? That afternoon? They came out wrong. Weird grins and saying creepy shit and everything about them *off*. Like, Invasion of the Body Snatchers levels of off. I don't want you to go in there without knowing something bad could happen."

Vince nodded back at him. "I appreciate that. Any prohibitions on what I do while I'm in there?"

Reginald blinked at that and turned to look at the house. He started to say, *no, as long as you burn it down after*, but then he shrugged. "Should there be? Nothing destructive, I guess? I don't really know what's involved. What will you do once we go inside?"

Vince shifted his weight, shoulders, and expression exactly as would a car mechanic about to explain why a special-order part would be both so small and so very expensive. It was the body language of *I'm trustworthy but you will never in a million years understand what I say and we both already know that.* "Well, Reg,"

"Reginald."

Vince didn't even trip over the correction. "Reginald, thanks, I mean that, mostly I go in there and try to determine the intention of the spirit, spirits, or manifestation. If it feels like a non-confrontational residual haunting by an unsettled spirit, I may talk to it to see where it's at in its journey and help it to the other side. If it's actively hostile and my time in there could present some danger to me or to either of you, I'll try to bind it so it can't harm us and then contain it or drive it out. Sound good?"

"It's going to be that second thing." Reginald's expression soured. "She was a bitch in life and I don't think dying's improved things." He pushed his hair back. "But I also don't think she's *it*. I'm not even sure it's her, to be honest."

Vince rested his chin in the crux between his left thumb and index finger. "So, what do you think it is?"

Reginald shrugged after a few seconds. "I'm not sure. But I think it's older than her. Bigger. I think it's something that lives—" Reginald gestured with his left hand and looked in that direction as he did so. "Up there. On top of the mountain."

"But the first time you saw it was in the house."

Reginald nodded.

"Do you see it if you go up there?" Vince pointed by rocking his head back and to his right once.

"Yes."

Lewis raised a finger to correct him. "Actually… whatever you saw up there you saw *after* you went into the house. Right?"

Reginald reflexively began to correct him, but stopped short. After a moment, he shrugged. "I guess so."

"We know it showed Johnny and Kate something other than the house itself. And it showed *you* something other than the house in its current state in reality. And it probably showed your brother and then your brother's wife something, too, when they each went over there." Lewis chewed his lower lip for a second. "I mean, I'm not trying to tell you what you did or didn't see, but it's worth taking a second to be *very specific* before engaging directly with it."

Reginald gestured at the backyard of Dorothea's house. "But when it was over I ran down the hill."

Lewis shook his head. "But maybe that was *all* a vision, at least until you really came back through the front door at the end. We just shouldn't assume."

Vince clapped Lewis on the shoulder again. "Sounds like I need to start by going inside, one way or the other, double entendre *fully* intended, bro, ha ha. Seriously, though, I've got my tripod and lights, but if y'all are good with a camera it might be best to have you handle the rig, otherwise I won't have full freedom of movement to investigate." He paused and added, "Also, FYI, I keep it PG, maybe PG-13 when the camera's rolling. Gotta make sure the algorithms don't bury me where the kids can't see it."

Lewis sighed quietly. "Well, I do know my way around a camera."

"Bet that ain't all," Vince said with another wink. "Am I right, Reginald?"

Reginald cleared his throat. "Is this going to cost me money?" The other two paused, surprised by the question, but Reginald turned down the corners of his mouth. "Do you charge money for this? I need to know before I let you do anything."

Vince squeezed Reginald's shoulder lightly. "Nah, bro. I do this to help people." He smiled easily, readily, even eagerly. "TikTok and YouTube *pay* me. I get enough viewers, the content monetizes itself."

Reginald cleared his throat. "Okay. Sorry, I had to check. Let's go inside."

Dorothea's house smelled like a stranger's slept-in sheets: the aroma of a person no longer there, of skin oil and hair product and sweat and old deodorant and someone else's Crisco cooked into the walls and carpets.

Reginald was struck by how *dead* it felt. The other night it felt like a room someone had just walked out of. Now it felt like a room where no one had been in many years, not exactly a tomb so much as an old diorama he might have made for school, rediscovered years later at the back of a closet.

Vince gave brief directions to Reginald and Lewis as they set up lights, connected them to battery packs, and placed them in corners. Lewis set up a camera on a tripod and then fired up a handheld video recorder of some sort. Reginald knew nothing about these things. He knew there were tiny cameras people used to make porn or record themselves skateboarding, stuff like that, things people posted on the Internet, but he'd never owned one nor wanted to own one. He had an old shoulder-mounted VHS camcorder in the back of his storage unit in town, and that was as close to this as he ever really wanted to get. He spent enough time trying to forget his life, he didn't want to start recording more of it.

As they did the final setup, Vince pushed Dorothea's coffee table to the side. Vince gave the direction to start filming and Lewis pressed buttons on cameras then gave him a thumbs up from out of view. Vincent stood in the center of the living room, arms extended, face uplifted, eyes closed. He turned in a slow circle, pausing here and there, his lips moving as he silently spoke. Reginald assumed it was some sort of invocation, maybe a blessing or a protection charm, something they'd taught Vince in his *goddamned online exorcism school what the fuck am I doing* and then Vince opened his eyes and looked at the camera. "Hey, gang. I'm on location at the home of a really great friend's mom's place. She sadly passed away, and my friend here is worried she might need help getting to the other side." Vince turned to Reginald, who also stood out of view of the cameras, his arms crossed. Vince spoke up to make sure the cameras heard him. "I'm definitely getting some vibes, bro. Did you have a happy childhood?"

"Is that what the vibes are telling you?"

Vince raised both eyebrows. "Uh, not exactly, bro."

Score one for the vibes, Reginald begrudgingly granted. He made a vague motion with one hand. "It wasn't great, but there were certainly worse. The bad parts were all," he waved the same hand up and down his own chest, "internalized. I spent a lot of my youth wondering how bad it would be when my mother found out I was gay. Turned out she'd known all along. That's *why* she was so vicious in her homophobia. So, you know, not great, but I never got beaten and there was food on the table."

Vince looked at the camera in Lewis' hand and said, "We think of childhood as a time of protection, safety, caring. We get told we should look back on it with nostalgia, that we should long to return. But a lot of us don't get the one thing every child needs and deserves, and that's love. Listen up, Sexy Hexies, if you've got kids, you gotta love 'em no matter what, for exactly who they are, and make sure they know it. Whenever somebody tells me they can't love their kid if they're this way or that way, whatever, they're really telling me they weren't cut out to have kids in the first place. I bet you know some people like that. Maybe you got raised by 'em. If so, I'm gonna give this guy a hug right now, and I want you to know I'm sendin' this great big bear hug to you, too." Vince walked to within a couple of feet of Reginald—Lewis turned the camera to follow—and opened his arms. "Bro, do you consent to a hug?"

Had Reginald watched this in a video, he would have mocked it without mercy. This was exactly the kind of bullshit performative sympathy he'd expect from an oversimplified little homily like that. *No shit, a lot of parents are terrible*, Reginald would have said, and then he'd have scrolled on to watch a video of whatever car crash or cat cafe was next in his feed. But in this moment, hearing those words said *to* him, *about* him, in his dead mother's living room, by a man who could have wrestled a hundred-year oak into submission in the first round, Reginald felt emotion well up inside him. The rage he felt at his mother, at his childhood, at life in general, melted away and sloughed off, leaving behind the real problem: how very lonely and afraid he'd always felt, from childhood until now.

Reginald tried to speak, couldn't, so simply nodded. "Yeah," he managed.

Vince leaned in and pulled Reginald to him, burying Reginald's face against his own massive, rock-hard chest. He wrapped his arms around Reginald's shoulder and put one hand on the back of his head, running it through his hair. "I'm sorry you had to go through that, bro. I bet it wasn't easy."

Reginald clung to Vince for dear life until Vince finally started to relax, a much more intense and long-lasting embrace than Reginald had expected. He reached up to wipe his eyes, sniffling hard, and Vince wrapped one ham-sized hand around his shoulder. "You're not alone in this," he said, nodding in Lewis' direction. "Remember that somebody loves you no matter how hard it is to find that love for you within yourself."

Reginald's eyes widened momentarily and he blushed harder than he had in many years. "I, uh, thank you."

Vince turned back to the camera. "Now let's get that ghost b-word out of this house!" He clapped his hands like thunder and then half yelled, half howled. "AWOOOOOOOOOOOO, LET'S GET HEXY."

CHAPTER EIGHTEEN – FACE-OFF

"Dorothea Voth!" Vince had returned to the center of the living room and now spoke in his full, projected baritone. "By the five saints and the seven stars that guide the dead to the next world, I ask that you appear." He spoke again, this time slightly more loudly. "DOROTHEA VOTH! Your kith and kin are here, and they wish to escort you across the threshold to your next incarnation!" Vince lowered his voice and waved at both Lewis and Reginald, inviting them into the center of the room to stand with him. "Bros, let's meet up here in the middle of your mom's living room and do some talking with her."

Reginald's eyes nearly popped out of his skull, and he shook his head back and forth. "No, I'm good over here. We talked plenty when she was alive."

"I know it's rough, bro, but it's part of the mantle of your heritage."

"The mantle of my *heritage*?" Reginald's tone was open disbelief, but Lewis set the camera down on the edge of the piano against the back wall of the living room and stepped forward.

"You can feel however you want about it, Reginald," Lewis said, "but we invited the man here, and he's the only certified exorcist in the room." He spread his hands in a gesture of surrender, then walked over and stood by Vince. "What do you need us to do?"

Reginald clenched his fists and muttered, "Oh my *fucking gods*," but after two seconds of standing there, shoulders hunched, he realized what a child he was being. *Just like a toddler about to throw a tantrum. This is what my mother's house does to me. I have to do something. I have to change things right now. I didn't come here to do nothing about this.* He made a conscious effort to relax, shook out his arms and shoulders, and then took another deep breath, in through his nose, out through his mouth. "Okay," he said, then breathed deep in and out again. "You make a good point."

He stepped around the wing-backed chair reserved for his mother's guests and over to Lewis and Vince. "If we're about to make a porno, this is the weirdest opening I've ever seen."

Vince smiled in a way Reginald couldn't help but classify as "fatherly" despite being an easy dozen years younger than Reginald himself. "Reginald, I feel your mother's spirit present with us in the room. Do you feel it, also?" He took Reginald's hand in his giant paw and held it up.

Reginald started to say some smartass thing in reply, but stopped. Lewis was right. Vince was probably their only help. Pastor Owenby would be there the next day, sure, but so what? What good could *he* do? He'd probably hum a few bars of *Onward Christian Soldiers,* sprinkle a little water on the carpet, and tell Reginald the rest was between him and Jesus. Vince might have a fake online degree, and his entire career trajectory might be three dodgy side hustles in a trench coat with a porn site in their pocket, but he was the best thing they had. Reginald told himself he didn't *know* this wouldn't work. And he did *know* whatever was in this house had taken hold of Johnny and of Kate, and that Patricia down the street had spoken with his mother's voice, and that it had tried to take Lewis from him last night, and he didn't know what any of this meant, but he wanted it gone from his life.

"Okay," Reginald said. "I feel it." He didn't, but it was obvious he had to play along.

"What do you feel?"

Reginald boggled for a moment but kept his expression mostly neutral. "I'm not sure."

"That's natural." Vince drew Reginald's hand up and placed it on Vince's chest, over his heart. Reginald could feel the thump behind all that muscle and the ribs beneath them. Then Vince took his own hand and placed it over Reginald's heart. It felt warm against Reginald's chest. "Close your eyes, Reginald. Open your mind. Imagine your mother standing here in the room with us. Take a moment to picture details: her hair, her face, her dress. What's she wearing?"

Reginald closed his eyes and let his mind wander, and as soon as he imagined himself stepping back and looking around the room *without* the cameras and lights he saw Dorothea standing in it. She stared at him from the other side of the room, her expression blank with a hint of benign interest: not quite welcoming, not quite concerned. "She's wearing a white dress with tiny blue flowers all over it. It's one she made when I was a child. And she has an old sweater vest. Her mother knitted it for her decades ago. She lost that thing when I was a child. It fell apart in the wash." Reginald heard wonder in his own voice and a part of him recoiled. This wasn't a place for wonder. This was a prison to escape.

Vince's voice was soft. "Tell us about her. Is she saying anything?"

Reginald felt his own eyes turn under his closed eyelids as though he were looking back and forth between Vince and his mother. Even in his imagined version of the living room, Vince's voice had a presence.

"She's gesturing at me to approach." Reginald gulped air. "She's trying to get me to come to her."

Vince tapped Reginald's chest with his fingers in rhythm as he spoke. "Don't do that, Reginald. Here is fine. Tell her she has to speak up, you can't go with her. Tell her you're there to let her speak her piece and then to open the door."

In his mind's eye, Dorothea shook her head at him.

"She says no." Reginald squirmed a little, but Vince's hand on his chest was like an anchor. "She keeps gesturing at me to come closer."

"Go open the door. Show her the way, bro."

Reginald imagined himself turning and walking to the front door. His hand gripped the familiar knob and twisted. The door opened.

The imagined became the real, and Reginald realized he was *there*, standing at the door, and had opened it. This imagined scene was happening.

Beyond the open front door of Dorothea's house, the inky shadow of endless night yawned where her yard used to be. Lightning flashed in that bottomless pit, silent, no thunder, as though he were watching it on a muted television. Lights twinkled into being like stars he did not recognize, stars beyond counting, too many of them, and too bright, unknown to him or to any human eyes, unmapped and uncaring. The night beyond that door was ancient beyond eons, long dead, eternal, one left behind uncountable lifetimes ago and waiting for something—anything—to return to it at the end. It hung open before him, a gaping mouth that swallowed up all its own sound, all its own texture, its own air, very nearly its own light, and still that darkness spasmed and pulsed, eager, searching, questing, *probing* for more to consume. Reginald had the brief fear that a giant tongue of night might emerge and run itself over him, that its teeth might close behind him, and that he felt as though it were already happening. "Beyond the door…" Reginald's voice was barely a whisper. "*They are beyond the door.*"

"It's okay, bro, we're here with you." Reginald felt a hand on his shoulder. It caught him by surprise to recognize it not as Vince's giant paw but Lewis'. The realization did not push him out of the moment, though. He felt himself supported, emboldened.

"Mother," Reginald said aloud to the Dorothea in his mind, "you need to go through this door now. You need to move on." He cleared his throat. "It's time to leave the world of the living, mother."

Dorothea's face in this realm, this inner reality truer than the merely physical, it was nothing he would imagine, nothing that would come from within. Her face split into a grin that could eat the world in a single bite. She took a step towards him, towards the door, and he realized abruptly he stood *between* her and the gaping maw of eternity beyond that threshold.

"Mother, you need to go through this," Reginald said, and he sounded just a tad hysterical. "Mother, no, *you* need to go through it, not me. It isn't my time yet, Mother, it's yours. *Go through it, goddamn you.*"

She was closer to him now. He didn't recall her moving more than that one single step but now she stood beside him, by the door, their toes on the threshold, having crossed the room as he envisioned it—*yes, in-visioned it*—and her grin got impossibly bigger. "Reginald, dear." Her voice was that of Dorothea, yes, but it wasn't his mother. It was his mother *and something*, two voices coming out of her at once, the Other's more a chorus of moans melted together than merely one living thing. "You have to help me across," it sang at him, "you have to push me. I'm far too frail to do it myself." She held out her arms as if to be picked up like a child. "I can't walk across on my own, Reginald, that isn't how it's done. *You have to make me go.*"

"Why, mother? Just walk across the fucking threshold allgoddamnedready!"

"Don't hold back, bro, tell her, bro!"

Dorothea strained at him with frail hands, her skin yellow-white like old typing paper, veins blue like faded jeans, and gripped Reginald's arms with strength that could snap his bones in two if she felt like it. Her face turned hard and cruel, and she looked down her nose at him from impossibly *below*. "Reginald Carlson Voth, get off your abominable homosexual ass and push me through that door right this goddamned minute or I'll never have a moment's peace, and *neither will any of you.*"

Reginald felt her nails dig into his biceps and he cried out in pain. His own arms shot up reflexively to fight back, and he grabbed her shoulders. "Listen, I may have hated you but I didn't want you to die!"

Dorothea leaned in, fury embodied, a creature of living anger, rejection personified, and roared at him. "You have to *push me*, you little shit, what part of that didn't get through your fucking head? They want my whole life, Reginald, do you understand? My whole life, and I cannot simply give it to them! *It has to be taken from me, Reginald, now grow some balls and do it.*" Her hair lifted as air gusted through the door and was swallowed up by the ancient and impossible night beyond it. Dorothea's voice dropped and she leaned close. "I swan, Reginald, if you don't push me through that door I'll haunt you and your little butt-boy friends and everybody else you ever meet, everyone you ever lust after, every date you ever have, every coworker, every truck stop trick and dime store hookup, every car mechanic, every cashier, everyone and everything and every place you ever meet or fuck or work or live, every square inch of earth you ever touch or tread, until you come back here and call me up and push my dead ass through this goddamned door, do! You! *Under! STAND?*"

It was her tone, in the end, that did it. He couldn't count the number of times she'd talked down to him like that, but not a single time, not *once*, that he'd really deserved it, and four decades of suppressed fury ran up his spine like lava. Reginald tightened his grip and flexed his arms.

Dorothea's face broke out in a mad grin, eyes wide and rolling, froth at the corners of her mouth, her tongue dancing as she cried out, "YES PUSH ME THROUGH FULFILL MY PROMISE YOU MISERABLE FUCKING F—"

Reginald screwed his face up, eyes squinted in fury, teeth bared, and pushed his fucking mother through the door and into the void, relishing the thought of feeding her to some uncaring universe in revenge for all the little ways she did not care for him, and he looked with terror at the serene satisfaction that washed across her face, the way her mouth split into a too-wide, gaping grin, and knew at once he should not have done it and that he would do it again in a heartbeat given a chance.

Shocking him, the vision ended, vanishing like someone turning off a television.

Dorothea was gone.

The ancient and starving sky at the other end of a dead universe was gone.

The door stood closed.

Reginald screamed in terror and frustration.

From somewhere far away, he heard a voice too much like his mother's ask, very softly, *Was that so hard? Next time, we'll do it for real.*

"Bro," Vince said, "you okay, bro? Oh shit, did something bring you out of the trance?"

From some faraway place, Reginald heard the *idea* of laughter echo around inside his skull.

Silence fell across all of them.

Reginald felt his features start to untwist and the rage drain away as quickly as it had come upon him. His hands started to shake first, and then his legs, and then his knees buckled.

Lewis was by his side in an instant, feeling his forehead, checking his eyes. "Reginald, can you see me? Can you hear me?"

Vince looked at them, then turned to the camera on the piano. "You see that, hexies? This shit gets real sometimes. Looks like this is going to be a long night."

"Reginald," Lewis said again. "Please answer me, Reginald. Please, it's me. He's right, you know. I do love you."

Reginald opened his eyes just a sliver and weakly patted Lewis on the arm. "For the love of God," he moaned, "can't everybody just shut the fuck up?"

Reginald awoke—or possibly regained consciousness, he couldn't tell—to find his head in Lewis' lap and his feet in Vince's.

"Bro," the latter said, "good to see you back." He gave a cock-eyed grin and Reginald found himself thinking, *am I tired of men who want to fuck me?*

"Hey there." Lewis' tone was much gentler, and he smiled at Reginald. "No, no, don't sit up just yet. Take it easy. You passed out."

"The spirit realm really did a number on you." Vince patted Reginald's calf.

Reginald looked around his mother's living room—they were on her couch. He'd never touched another boy on his mother's couch. He tried again to sit up, to break connection with this boy and this man. "We have to leave immediately. The house was fucking with me."

Lewis put just enough pressure on Reginald's shoulders to keep him down. Reginald had a shockingly multi-sensory memory of him doing the same in bed the night before and felt a wave of dizziness for half a second. He felt unstuck from reality, as though either that had been a dream and now he'd awakened, or now he'd found himself at large in a dream that wouldn't end.

"Seriously, y'all, we need to leave." Again, Reginald stirred.

Again, Lewis kept Reginald from trying to bolt upright. "Honestly, if you sit up like that you're just going to faint again."

"Well then help me up." Reginald reached up and took hold of one of Lewis' hands. "I promise to take it slow, Nurse Ratchet."

"Who?" Vince offered one of his hands as well.

"Oh, good *grief* that makes me feel old. OK, I'm going to sit up now. Everybody hold onto your garters."

Lewis and Vince buffered Reginald as he rose to a sitting position and swung his feet from Vince's lap.

"Thank you. Both of you. I'm sorry I've been such a bother." Reginald flushed deep pink all the way into red. "That's never happened before." He paused. "Well, one time, but it involved a lot of poppers."

Vince's meaty chuckle sounded like an encouragement, and Reginald found himself less put off by his directness this time. He filed that emotion away in some bulging drawer in the desk of his mind to be examined later. To his surprise, he felt a cold slither of guilt at being attracted to Vince in Lewis' presence. He'd never been much of one for exclusivity before.

"If we're leaving, we're doing it slowly. I admit I was a little worried the house would try to fuck with you the way it did Johnny and Kate. But we didn't want to move you, so we just…" Lewis shook the hair out of his face. "It sounds so dumb, but we stood guard, and everything seems okay." Lewis stood from the touch and offered Reginald a steadying hand.

Reginald stood, very slowly, then tested shifting his weight from one foot to the other. "For now. But it did try to fuck with me. It showed me a vision. Not something I wanted." Reginald reflected on the memory of Dorothea screaming at him, taunting him, daring him to push her into an eternally starving maw of night and stars. "Okay, maybe it was something I wanted a *little*."

Vince gave Lewis and then Reginald very serious looks, clapping a hand the size of an oven mitt over each of their shoulders. "Bros, real talk, I've never seen somebody dip out like that during a spirit experience. Before we go any farther, Reginald, Lewis and I need to hear what you saw."

Reginald told them, word for word, his eyes never leaving Lewis' own.

When he finished, they both looked at Vince for guidance.

"But you said you didn't even like her, right?"

"I think…" Reginald cleared his throat. "Vince, *bro*, we're not talking about a classmate with whom I do or do not get along here. Not some coworker I can maybe avoid if I move to a different shift. It's more complicated than that. I hated my mother and she was still my mother. And I'm sad she's dead. And I'm *glad* she's dead. And I don't think I can explain it in a way that will ever make you *feel* it, so take me at my word when I say I did not *want* to push her through that door, and at the same time I absolutely did and I loved it. It felt horrible, and it felt like I'd waited my whole life for the chance."

"Then it seems like a win-win, bro." Vince shrugged.

Reginald's face went slightly slack, and he considered for a moment. "Okay. So, the house had its laugh. It let me scratch an embarrassing itch so it could make me feel guilty about it. Well, fuck the house. But before we go, there was one more reason to come up here. We know my mother's preacher was here the night my mother died. I want one quick look around to see if there's anything obvious he left or took, something I might not have noticed when I was here the other night and focused on starting to clean up. And then we're getting the fuck out of this place."

Ten minutes later, the three of them had been all around the downstairs, all around the upstairs, and stuck their heads out the back door.

Nothing jumped out at them.

"He wanted something." Reginald's voice was low, accusatory, angry. He wondered how much of that was a lingering effect of the vision of his mother taunting him. "He came here so he could get something he wants. Right?"

Lewis ran a hand through his own hair. "Like what?"

Reginald halfheartedly wobbled his forearms around. "I don't know. Probably, like, the Necronomicon or whatever book all this shit comes from. If we were in a horror movie, that's what it'd be: he'd need some artifact she had, maybe a knife, maybe the goblet they used to drink virgin blood, maybe the book where they signed a contract with Satan, I don't know."

Vince turned the corners of his mouth down while he considered. "Why would he want that?"

"Because he's in on it, obviously." Reginald's cynicism didn't give him time to consider any other answers.

Lewis made a sound of uncertainty. "Or he's trying to stop it—look, I know from that expression you think that's bullshit, but come on, if coming here as an outsider has given me the perspective to realize anything it's that every Bible-thumping weirdo is just waiting for their chance to go three rounds in the ring against The Great Deceiver. If he thought your mother was in, I don't know, a cult? Something like that? If he thought so, he might be coming here looking for something he could use against it. Or maybe just something that might tell him who else was in it with her. Or maybe he's trying to steal her good silver so he can hock it for the church. My point is, don't leap to conclusions."

As Lewis wound down, so did Reginald's nervous excitement. Much of the energy of the night drained from him all at once, and he deflated just a bit where he stood. "Okay. Maybe you have a point."

Vince reached out to put a hand on Reginald's right shoulder and Lewis' left. "Hey, want to hear an idea for something fun we can do to piss off your mom before we go?"

Reginald didn't have to look at him. He could *hear* the horny grin. He raised his eyebrows at Lewis.

Lewis raised his back and gave the faintest hint of a smile. "I mean, if we were quick, it would be kind of funny."

"Not in my mother's bed," Reginald said. "But we can fuck like wild all over her couch."

At the moment of orgasm, Reginald melted into the usual erasure of all thought, all sound, all existence outside his own perfectly blank mind: earthly carnality transmuted into an experience of pure spirit. That wasn't all this time, though. From so far away he *knew* it must be the impossibly distant un-place from which he'd returned in that moment of disorientation on the ride to the graveyard, could in fact recognize it as that place even though he could not remember or describe it, Reginald heard something like trumpets sound and the whispered boom of a not-voice offering, very simply, *This, too, we would allow.*

GENERATION SIX – DOROTHEA

December, 1979

Dorothea Voth stood and stared in open horror at her ancient father. He held in his left hand the old corn knife he'd kept hanging up in the shed, the one he sharpened every autumn. He'd gone out the back of the house and gotten it, brought it in, and now stood in the back door with a look of shame and embarrassment.

Tears welled in her father's eyes. "I'm sorry," he mumbled. "But I always figured I'd tell you some other time."

CHAPTER NINETEEN – STRINGS ATOP MORIAH BALD

Vince went home two hours later, after they'd all gone two rounds, and then the three of them had spent a few minutes sitting in the rocking chairs on Dorothea's porch just to put a bow on their desecration of Dorothea's living room. He'd always wondered, in some part of his mind, if he'd be able to get off in his mother's house like that. It turned out it wasn't any problem at all.

Once Vince was gone, Reginald said to Lewis, "Now we're going to find whatever Owenby wanted out of here if we have to tear the place apart."

They did tear the place apart.

They didn't find a thing.

Eventually, Lewis and Reginald strolled—somewhat gingerly—down the street past Bobby's house, past the rentals, all the way down to Lewis' place. The tryst with Vince had been a refreshing break from all the weird melodrama of the last few days, another banked curve of intense pleasure on the roller coaster of everything else going on. Reginald was almost able to relax, but then he realized he and Lewis had each caught the other glancing at the trees beyond the houses to see if they spotted any golden glowing eyes.

They did.

They kept walking.

When they got back to Lewis' place, they stripped off their clothes, climbed into bed, exchanged one languid kiss, and then passed out like drunks.

In the morning, they shared the shower again while talking about how much fun Vince had turned out to be. A couple of texts later, he'd agreed to come by midday to "plan for what to do when Owenby arrived."

Instead, they spent the bulk of the day shaking Lewis' bed or drinking coffee on his deck.

"I really ought to get started on cleaning out my mother's house, start planning to have an estate sale, a yard sale, something," Reginald said at one point, and Lewis' responded by leaning in for a kiss that developed into a nicely distracting variety of *more*.

"We should keep an eye out for Owenby," Lewis said after, but instead Vince suggested they all adjourn to Lewis' shower.

Around 6:30 PM, just as the sun started to set, Reginald noticed Owenby's old Pontiac was parked in Dorothea's driveway.

Reginald tried Dorothea's front door and found it unlocked. He turned it very quietly and pushed it open just barely, one hand twisting the knob to make sure the latch didn't spring back and the fingertips of the other giving it the tiniest amount of force to open. The muscle memory of coming home late in high school flooded back at the first invitation. Reginald was a little embarrassed at how readily he remembered how to sneak back in.

He, Lewis, and Vince stood in the living room, straining to listen, hearing nothing. With mouthed words and a few simple hand gestures, they agreed to stick together and start their search. The three of them walked the house, starting on the first floor. Pastor Owenby wasn't in the kitchen, he wasn't in the dining room in the back corner of the house, and he wasn't in his mother's formal sitting room, the one with the good furniture that never got used except for very special occasions. *Every stick of this is mid-century modern and worth a fortune.* A part of Reginald noted that down for later evaluation. *This place could set me up for life.* But then he thought of Kate offering to "make him a deal" two minutes after meeting him--long before the house had gotten hold of her--and the idea turned a little sour in his head.

And yet, turning a profit on his mother's death was the foundation of his desire to do anything at all involving his family. He knew in his heart he'd have cut her and everyone else off entirely, never returned a phone call, changed his number, blocked theirs, gotten a post office box, the whole nine yards, except he wanted a little compensation for all the work he had to put in as a kid: the effort and self-restraint required to survive childhood in a family openly and actively engaged in his eradication. Why *not* sell every stitch and spindle he stood to inherit? That was the instant retirement fund he'd never build on his own. His job was okay, it got him by, kept him in store-brand salad dressing, and resealed the roof of his trailer every third year (instead of every other, like he knew he *should*). He was bound and determined to go to his grave driving the last running Geo Tracker on hill or in holler rather than ever have a car payment again, and he got paid just enough to do preventive maintenance and then some.

You've got it a lot better than kids these days. Sometimes he told himself that in bitter irony, envious of their easy queerness, their body positivity, their knack for converting any binary into a spectrum. Most times, though, he meant it with perfect sincerity. He owned the roof over his head and the wheels under his ass, he had health insurance even if it wasn't great, he could go to the dentist every year, he could afford the cigarettes everyone told him not to smoke. A lot of people worked as hard or harder and had it a lot worse.

And I want more than 'a lot of people have it worse,' goddamn it. The part of him that wanted to sit back and take a small measure of pride in something like self-sufficiency was instead engaged in shaking its head at the part of him that would always grasp for more, always resent that he had to do it on his own in the first place. *A lot of people get help along the way, too. And one day I'll get mine.*

Lewis and Vince stood at the foot of the stairs. Lewis cleared his throat gently.

Reginald blinked rapidly and focused on him. "Oh, shit, did I pass out again?"

"No, no. You just kind of, you know, drifted off for a second." Lewis smiled, and Reginald thought it was a *generous* smile, a kind smile, one that tolerated Reginald's absentmindedness. He hated feeling *tolerated.* He drew a sharp breath. "It won't happen again. Let's go." Reginald put his hand on the banister and started up the stairs.

At the top, the gallery lights were off. Even in late afternoon, the upstairs was gloomy and grim as midnight. The curtains were drawn in the windows at either end of the overhanging hallway, and the bedroom doors were all shut.

That was odd. *Why would Owenby shut himself in one of the bedrooms?* Reginald put a hand up behind him to halt Lewis and Vince as they followed. He turned halfway and nodded in the direction of the foyer as he spoke in the softest possible whisper. "Go back down and keep an eye out for him. Maybe he's in the back yard or something. I'll check upstairs."

"Bro." Vince gave him a very serious look. "No splitting the party."

"Just… trust me."

Vince and Lewis exchanged a glance. *Christ,* Reginald thought, *how did I wind up getting fucked by these two in one week? It's like I'm 20 again except now I'm on PrEP.*

Lewis turned back to Reginald. "Vince will check the back yard. I'll check the front. But I'm not leaving the foyer, and we're both going to be right here at the bottom of the steps. Okay?"

Reginald gave him a thumbs-up and looked first to his right, then to his left.

He strode over to his mother's bedroom door and put his hand on the knob.

It turned, and he opened the door onto near-perfect darkness.

Reginald gasped aloud, certain for a moment he had opened the door of Dorothea's bedroom onto that same alien night from the vision before, as his eyes strained to adjust and faint light appeared at the edges of indistinct forms and shapes. It turned out simply to be his mother's bedroom, though, without any stars and—importantly—without his mother screaming epithets at him. He reached to the wall and felt for the light switch, then flicked it.

The bulb popped and burned out.

"Oh, you piece of shit," Reginald said aloud.

"Hey!" Lewis sounded frightened. "What's wrong?"

Reginald heard footsteps on the stairs and called out in equally full voice. "Oh, it's nothing. Just a lightbulb. I'm good." He had to reassure Lewis a time or two that he really was okay, then Reginald reached into his pocket and pulled out his phone. He hit the flashlight button and bathed the room in bright LED glow.

Reginald advanced across the small room to the narrow door to his mother's bathroom. He hesitated, knocked once, waited ten seconds, then opened it.

The bathroom stood empty.

The bedroom across the hall, the one where his father's clothes had been, along with immeasurable other junk, was likewise untouched and held no crimp-faced Protestant ministers.

The last bedroom, of course, was Reginald's own. He hesitated to open the door to it for some reason, stepping back a few paces.

He opened the hall bathroom instead.

Nothing. No one. Just a bathroom.

"How're you doing up there?" Lewis sounded worried.

Reginald didn't blame him. "I'm fine. Almost done."

Something about the exchange bolstered his spirit, and Reginald strode forward with purpose, hand out. They'd talked aloud repeatedly now. If Owenby was up here and wanted to shoot them or stab them or preach at them, he'd had his chance. No more pussyfooting around. Reginald put his hand on the knob to his childhood bedroom, turned it, and opened the door.

Pastor Owenby sat inside it, on the edge of the bed, looking at a framed photo of Reginald from the third grade. His younger self wore a black and blue striped rugby shirt, though they hadn't called them rugby shirts then, and he had a gap between his two front teeth.

"Can I help you with something, Pastor Owenby?" Reginald tried to sound casual, like finding his mother's preacher silently studying a portrait of himself in childhood in his mother's haunted house was the most normal possible thing. "Or is this part of your… process?"

Owenby didn't take his eyes from the photo. "I was considering, Reginald." He paused. "Pondering, if you will."

"Okay."

Owenby still did not look at him. "I was wondering when it was you went so wrong?"

Reginald crossed his arms and leaned against the doorframe, casual, yes, but blocking Owenby's escape. He wasn't going to back down on his own turf. "Okay, preacher, well, that's nice, but trust me, I've heard it all. That's the first thing you need to get. Second, it's never made a damn bit of difference. Third, I didn't invite you here to make me 'like' girls the way God supposedly intended. I invited you here because I think my mother's spirit needs to be put to rest and I figure since you, y'know, *her preacher*, were theoretically responsible for getting her aboard the express train to the Promised Land, you might have a professional interest in helping her reach her next destination." He considered adding, *and I know you've been poking around for something, and I want to know what the fuck it is*, but he held off. No need to show all his cards right now. Something told him to hold that back. Still, Reginald's voice dripped with venom and he raised both eyebrows. Owenby still hadn't looked at him, but Reginald wanted him to see just what he was dealing with here: a mean queen who couldn't give a *shit* what some preacher thinks.

Owenby set the portrait down carefully and then turned toward Reginald, resting his hands atop a bible which sat, in turn, atop his left thigh. "Oh, I'm not interested in lecturing you. I don't think you can change."

Reginald shifted his weight and opened his mouth, but Owenby kept talking.

"The devil has hardened your heart, Reginald. I think some of you can change, but you? You're too far gone. You've decided to wear your damnation as a badge of honor—of *pride*, if you will, how fitting you people have taken a sin and turned it into a shorthand for obstinate identity—and I've got better things to do with my remaining years than try to teach you otherwise." Owenby gestured lightly, in a *that's just how it goes* way. "But your mother's soul is of great importance to me. As you say, I was her spiritual advisor and leader for many years. If she still needs to cross over, and it falls to me to guide her to eternal light, then so be it."

Reginald flipped Owenby an unceremonious bird. "This is for all that hardened heart bullshit. Now do your thing, Bible guy, and make my mother go to bed." Reginald was too mad to hold back the final tidbits, though, so he went on. "Or whatever it is you're here to do. I know you were here the night she died, and you're going to tell me why. Did you lead her up the path to the top of Moriah Bald? Given how casual you're being, I'm going to go ahead and guess you're in on whatever the fuck is happening already. Did you root around in her house looking for some unholy text or the receipts from the Satanic bake sale, or what?"

Owenby offered Reginald the most perfunctory and fleeting of artificial smiles, just a twist of his cheeks. "I'm sure I have no idea what you're—"

"Hey, Reginald!" Vince called up the stairs from below. "I just saw Owenby go into the woods out back!"

Reginald's eyes barely narrowed.

Owenby raised his eyebrows.

Without taking his gaze from Owenby, Reginald called out, "How sure of that are you?"

Vince hesitated. "Well… guy with a suit, carrying a book… Pretty sure."

Reginald nodded his head in the direction of the back of the house. "You're coming with us, reverend. Right now. Somebody's yanking my chain and I don't like it."

Owenby rose from the bed without protest. Reginald stepped aside so the pastor could go first as they walked to the top of the stairs.

At the bottom of the steps, Vince's face fell, and his mouth opened when he saw Owenby, with Reginald behind him. "Bro…"

Reginald waved it off. "Yeah, yeah, fucked up, et *cetera*. Let's get up the mountain and see what the fuck we're dealing with."

Lewis gave Reginald a very intense stare, his lips flat, features blank, and Reginald found himself wondering what Lewis wished he could communicate: *don't trust them*, or *I didn't see anything*, or even perhaps *I saw it, too*. Reginald felt certain at least one of the two strangers was lying, either Owenby or Vince, whom he lumped into that category despite having had Vince inside him multiple times in just the last 24 hours. He wondered where that certainty came from. The forces at work on Moriah Bald had shown him other things that were illusions, had tricked him into going to places and doing things he would not have voluntarily done. The same was true of Kate and Johnny: that the house had lured them to it so it could pod-people them in some way. It had done so to his brother Bobby and Bobby's wife, Sue, as well. It had tried to do it to Lewis, too, or so Lewis said. What did it want? If it wanted to kill Reginald, it could do so any time. It could just take over Lewis, and he'd die without ever knowing. And if it wanted to get him into the house so it could pod-people him, too, well, it had ample opportunities and had done nothing. Instead, it was all glowing eyes from the tree line and visions of his dead mother.

If whatever's atop the mountain is trying to hold me or someone ransom, it's doing a lousy job writing the fucking note.

Something in Reginald's brain snagged on that, and he hesitated at the top of the steps. No time to pursue that thread, whatever it was.

Vince and Lewis still looked up at him from below. "Well?" Reginald prodded Owenby in the shoulder. "I said let's go."

The four of them filed through the kitchen and went out the back door.

The garden was back, exactly as Reginald had seen it the other times he walked through the house and out the back door: tomato vines threadbare and emaciated, stalks of corn being slowly strangled by bean runners, sprays of yellow silk at the ends of finished ears of corn-like tongues hanging from toothy, sneering mouths. Lewis made a sound, something less than words, but a recognition the yard looked different this time. He and Reginald caught each other's eyes, and Lewis nodded. His meaning was clear: *I see it, too.*

Across the yard, on the other side of the rows of spindly plants and neglected tomato vines, the gap in the trees where the trail started stared back at them, an oval of emptiness inviting them in.

Vince looked around for a second. "Bro… you guys hear banjos?"

As the four stepped, one at a time—Reginald, then Vince, then Owenby, then Lewis—into the woods, they could hear far above them the sound of several voices in harmony:

The Lords come down to seek for thee
> *Their quarry and their servants we*
> *Behold the heavens dark and wide*
> *Salvation's found on th'other side*
> *The Lord's a-waiting, weary friend*
> *The doom they spell is not your end*
> *Salvation's found on th'other side*

From the Lords' gaze you cannot hide

"Christ," Reginald said aloud. "That's some grim shit." It occurred to him they were singing *lords*, plural, rather than *lord's*, the possessive.

Lewis tried to sound casual. "This is the stuff my mother warned me about when I moved here." His voice shook when he said it.

"That's an old song," Owenby spoke softly. "Heed the wisdom in it."

The wind carried snatches of further lyrics to them, incomplete, jumbled:

The Lords come
> *Weary friend*
> *Heaven's*
> *Salvation*
> *Other side*

Sooner than Reginald would have expected, they emerged from the trees at the top of Moriah Bald. The night sky unfurled above them, a deep purple-black dotted with diamond-dust stars and the gemstone sparkles of planets he was pretty sure he recognized: Venus, Mars, Jupiter, Saturn. They were not particularly aligned, but they shone so bright he thought if he looked hard enough at them, he'd be able to see them close, discs instead of sparkling pinpricks, and then again perhaps he would be able to zoom in, see them up close as if in orbit from nearby, watch them turn in silence against the backdrop of the soundless universe, all of time and space crowded in behind them, peeking around the edge of each to stare back at him.

Reginald blinked and looked around.

A bluegrass band, three men and two women, wielding a banjo, a guitar, a mandolin, a violin—*fiddle*, some inner voice corrected Reginald— and a harmonica, stood in an arc around the other side of the huge, flat stone in the center of Moriah Bald.

"The Kings," Reginald murmured. Isaiah, his siblings, and his father sang and played with the same energy he imagined they would offer a packed honkytonk on a Saturday night. Their fingers and arms worked in rhythm, and they sang in a harmony that hooked itself into the listener's mind.

Pastor Owenby--a second Pastor Owenby--stood halfway between where Reginald and the others had emerged from the forest, his back to them, Bible in one hand, both arms raised to the sky, his face uplifted. His back was turned, but Reginald knew instantly who he was. He turned to the other three—

The Owenby who had walked up the trail with them was gone.

Lewis and Reginald looked at each other, then both turned and looked at Vince, who shook his head.

"Reginald," the Owenby ahead of them said as he turned slowly to face them, "heed the words of the song. The lords are here now." Owenby's eyes shone glimmering black, the velvet of the night sky and the twinkle of alien lights far away sparkling against it. He looked back up at the sky and outstretched his arms, beseeching. "They've come for thee, Reginald, just as they came for your mother and for her father and for his mother and for her father, and on back to the very beginning, to the very first Voth to drag his blessed daughter to the top of Moriah Bald and offer himself to the sky so that his children might prosper. You said you thought I'd come here for a book, or to steal, or to otherwise get my hands on some artifact of a faith, but this is not something that comes from a book, Reginald." Owenby swept a hand around and over himself to take in Moriah Bald, the sky over it, and what might live beyond it. "This is a faith you *feel*, not one you *read*. I did not come here to scrounge for some fleeting scrap of material proof or connection. I came here to reassure The Powers Beyond the Mountain that we have not *all* forgotten the bargain your ancestors made. I want The Powers to know some of us still fear them. And they have rewarded me richly for it, Reginald, just as they will enrich you. They gave me exactly what I wanted, young man, just as they've given it to you as well." He nodded at Lewis, at Vincent, then met Reginald's gaze again. "They only want our whole lives—*your* whole life. Is that so much to ask?"

Reginald's own face lifted to the heavens, wondering what Owenby saw there, whether Reginald might again hear that clang and roar of the horns and hooves of titans beyond the sky. What Owenby said made sense, Reginald realized. He thought again of the stories of his mother spooning bowl after bowl of oatmeal or soup or stew into her father's mouth, changing his diapers, wiping his ass like a baby's, while he clawed at the air above him—at the sky beyond the ceiling—and conversed long and loud with ancestors who'd gone before. As Reginald stared at the heavens above, the light from the stars seemed to grow and shimmer, painful to look at, as though too much light forced its way through tiny holes in the dome of night, and Reginald lifted a hand of his own to shield his face from the burning radiance. "There's something…" Reginald tried to speak, but he found it difficult, as though some great and invisible fist had wrapped itself around him and squeezed. He struggled to draw a breath and tried again. "Something wrong… with the sky…"

The bluegrass band had never stopped singing, and they now burst into a long, loud chorus in half-time:

The Lords come down to seek for thee
    We beseech them, let us be
    They want to steal a life away
    Another's take we humbly pray

A bolt of lightning shot from a clear sky, not a cloud in sight.

Reverend Owenby stood in photographic negative as the blade of the gods ran through him from head to toe.

Arms extended in adulation, the reverend burst into flames.

He dropped to his knees.

He kept his arms up until they fell away from him.

In seconds, Owenby's corpse burned to ash.

CHAPTER TWENTY – RUN BOY RUN

Reginald might have said something—*run* or *go* or *fuck*, he would never remember—but the next thing he knew he, Lewis, and Vincent were tearing ass down the old trail from the top of Moriah Bald all the way to his mother's back yard. Some part of him remained sufficiently removed to notice he didn't trip, didn't stumble, and seemed to know the way in the dark despite having been up and down that trail for the first time in twenty years just a couple of days before. Lewis did nearly trip and fall, but Reginald reached and grabbed for him, caught his weight, and Vincent and they managed to keep each other upright as they bounded down the hill, leapt over roots, slipped on leaf-covered stones. The woods around them smelled sweet and fertile and rotten, the leaves already giving up their material selves to re-enrich the earth beneath, and there was a sharp tang on the mountain air that told Reginald it might be a hard winter.

All this flowed into his mind, across it, and back out without any real examination or intention on his part. The only part of him that functioned at all blared one command: *get the fuck away from here.*

As they reached the bottom, the trail opening into his mother's garden and sloped grass, Reginald gasped and wheezed at the others. "Gotta go gotta get somewhere call somebody tell that cop," but by the time the three of them half-ran, half-tumbled out of the tree line and straight through

Dorothea's never-to-be-harvested corn, miraculously restored to its rightful place in her garden patch, decades of cigarettes and a desk job had reasserted themselves, and Reginald could barely make a sound between wheezing gasps for air.

"Bro, you okay? You good?" Vincent's hands-on Reginald's back and shoulder felt good, warm, pleasantly intimate, and Reginald shook his head. *Mountain's fuckin with me gotta get outta here.*

Lewis patted his own pockets. "I've got my keys, come on, we can take my car. Let's *go*." He grabbed Reginald's hand and tugged, and the three of them started moving again, yanking open the door to Dorothea's kitchen and staggering through her house and out the front. At the bottom of the steps from the front porch, Lewis turned as if to angle his way across the yard into the street, to run to his own house, his own car, to freedom, but at least a dozen figures stood at the edge of the yard and in the street beyond it, waiting for them.

Kate and Johnny were there, and an elderly woman Reginald figured must be Patricia stood with them.

The women wore long, black dresses, and Johnny wore a black suit, white shirt, and black tie. They looked just like the pallbearers at Dorothea's funeral.

Backlit by streetlamps in the neighborhood, a silhouette Reginald instantly recognized as his brother stood there also.

As did his wife Sue.

As did Dorothea.

Shining gold eyes blinked at him from their otherwise featureless, unlit figures. They were made of shadows come alive, and he could feel the cool, light pressure of their attention on him.

And there, around them, behind them, reinforcing them in whatever work they were about, were other figures some part of Reginald checked off from family photo albums: his mother's father, and beside him what had to be his mother, and on and on.

They were like figurines cut from darkness itself, soft-edged and shifting, flickering when they stepped in front of the light.

Their eyes shone gold, the eyes of the figures who had watched Reginald and Lewis from the edge of the woods, and had spied on Beck's and Megan's the night after. They stood silent, merely watching them now as well. No one held weapons, no one obviously threatened. But Reginald knew the moment he saw them that he and Lewis and Vincent would not be allowed past.

Reginald drew a breath that scraped. "What do you want, mother?"

The silhouette of Dorothea Voth looked up, golden eyes shining wider, and met his gaze but said nothing.

Reginald gestured around them. "You and the rest of this little reunion obviously want me for something. Am I supposed to take you up to the mountain and sacrifice you now? Is that why you appeared to me when you died? Did you try to sacrifice yourself or talk your way out of the bargain or something?" Reginald cleared his throat, coughed twice, spat phlegm the color of a cigarette filter. "Am I supposed to do something? Did you promise *them*," and here his eyes glanced up at the stars for a split-second, "that I'd follow in the family's footsteps?"

Reginald sagged for a moment, the exhaustion of running and of watching a man die catching up to him. Lewis leaned in and put a shoulder against Reginald's upper arm. "Go away and leave us be," he said to the Dorothea shadow, but it lacked oomph. It sounded frightened rather than brave.

Reginald looked at the other figures, and then at Kate and Johnny, and presumed-Patricia beyond them, and then out across the little neighborhood, the houses too large for their yards huddled together like people in a crowded elevator all aware they must touch and terrified of it.

"Oh," Reginald said.

Lewis put a hand on Reginald's elbow. "Come on, babe. Let's go. What are they going to do? Rush us? Let's just keep walking."

Vincent put a hand on Reginald's shoulder. "Oh?"

Reginald didn't look at either of them. He simply said it again: "Oh."

"Let's go to your motel. Or back to your house. Or just, I don't know, let's just drive down the mountain and go *somewhere*, I don't care, anywhere else. They can't follow us. They're a part of this place."

"That's what the houses were about." Reginald said it, but not exactly *to* anyone. "Substitutes. Backups."

Vincent made a *hmmmm* sound that, frankly, struck Reginald as far more thoughtful than he'd anticipated out of someone like Vincent, who chose to present as a kind of dumb jock with a cock of gold.

Lewis tugged on Reginald's elbow again, but with less effort this time. "Reginald."

Reginald didn't look at Lewis, but obviously addressed him. "They figured out I wasn't going to continue the line, so my mother tried to draw in new stock. She parceled off the land, let people build fancy houses here, figured someone *else* would live on the mountain and have kids who could carry things forward." He looked at the shadow-Dorothea. "You hated Bobby that much, didn't you? And probably because he didn't require any *effort*. He wasn't a struggle. He just did what you said when you said it, everything *except* for when you ordered him to have a kid, and you hated him for that. And maybe you knew it wouldn't make *them* happy if you had him kill you when the time came, because he would so readily do *anything*. There would be no hesitation. They wouldn't get to savor you *making* him do it. They want lives, like Owenby said, like Kate and Johnny said, like everyone has, and Bobby didn't have a life, so he wasn't all that interesting to them." Reginald laughed, and it was short and sharp and sad.

He gestured around. "Were you going to, I don't know, adopt someone in one of the other houses? Or designate someone to do it if I wouldn't? I imagine you hoped it would count as good enough to have *some* kid brought up on this land and have them continue the pattern in the absence of Bobby producing an alternative for you. I don't know how transferrable the contract with The Powers might be. I don't know if whatever agreement our forebears made with the things that live in the sky over the mountain is necessarily something we can really understand anyway." He shrugged a little at her, a gesture she'd always said annoyed her. Now the shadow of her showed no reaction at all. "What mattered was maintaining some semblance of a line. Like a family tree, with a branch that's been grafted on rather than grown, right? Oh, fuck me Jesus, imagine the look on that poor kid's face forty or fifty years from now when they realized their parents needed them to take them to the top of the mountain and, what, kill them on the rock? Is there a special tool for that? Or are we expected to do it *by hand?* Choke out our own parents, one generation at a time, atop a stone under a leering sky?"

The Dorothea figure's glowing golden eyes blinked once.

"But what'd you get when you parceled out the neighborhood?" Reginald nodded his head at her. "Your son and his wife hated each other too much to have a kid. Or maybe they couldn't, and that's *why* they hated each other, I don't know. And Kate and Johnny don't have kids. Two houses got bought by 'investors' so no dice there. Patricia's old. Graham's single and it sounds like their life doesn't have a lot of room in it for a kid. Lewis is gay. So am I. The only family around who might qualify are Beck and Megan, and I bet you didn't *like* them enough to try to feed them to whatever gods your parents and grandparents were keeping happy one dead ancestor at a time." Reginald smirked a little. "So, the whole plan to find someone else and push it off onto them was a bust."

He stepped back and looked her shadow form up and down. "And then you died. And all you could do was try to rope my gay ass back into the family—or what? Or they torture you forever in some place beyond death? Or maybe Moriah Bald caves in on itself and slides halfway to South Carolina? Or do they bring back all those ancestors of yours and torture *them?* I don't really think I could comprehend it no matter what, even if you *could* talk. But here we are. Lewis and Vincent and I are leaving, mother. You can sit here and haunt your old house, haunt the top of the mountain, haunt the neighbors, whatever, I don't give a shit, haunt or don't haunt whatever you do or don't like, because my new boyfriend and I are going to get in his car—which is both very reliable and *very* new, because he makes an absolute *fuck*ton of money committing sodomy on camera, which is one of my favorite things about him—and we're going to drive away."

Vincent squeezed Reginald's shoulder lightly.

Reginald hooked a thumb backwards at Vincent. "And we're taking this hot piece of beef with us just for kicks."

Vincent again rubbed Reginald's shoulder with his slab of a hand, and Reginald turned and looked back at him.

Vincent's eyes were black like the night sky and glittered with strange stars. "Bro. All they want is your whole life. Is that so much to ask? It's not like you're doing anything with it anyway."

Silently, flickering and fuzzing around the edges, the spirits of Reginald's many dead ancestors drifted forward and surrounded them.

Vincent went on, and his voice dropped a little even though he retained some of his goofy rhetorical style. "The mountain can give you whatever you want, bro. All you have to do is ask. And all you have to give it back is everything—and not until the very end. Just imagine, bro." Vincent leaned close and sniffed Reginald's hair, ran a hand along his jaw. "And until then? Whatever pleasures you can imagine. The mountain can make your *every* dream come true. Look what it's done already. In fact, I think it kind of *likes* that about you: that you'll show them something *different*. I think they find you exotic. And the more you enjoy yourself, the more richly you'll feed them in the end. Why do you think they gave you Lewis here?"

Reginald turned from Vincent and met Lewis' gaze.

Lewis shook his head. "I'm not… whatever this is, no, I'm not part of it. I'm *me*, Reginald. I'm Lewis fucking Gwan, not some goddamned sex robot or whatever it is he's implying." Lewis pointed at the house. "It's just saying that because I told it I'd burn it down."

Vincent went on, his thumb and forefinger pausing to lift Reginald's chin. "The great thing is, maybe he's telling the truth, maybe he isn't. Will you ever really know? It won't change a thing either way. We'll still fuck you morning, noon and night, as long as you want it, as hard as you want it, for the rest of your life. We'll do *anything* to keep you here, Reginald. We'll make staying feel *so* good. The choice is pretty easy, bro. Seemed easy to me, anyway. It's another win-win."

"What… do I have to do?" Reginald very nearly whispered it, unable to meet Lewis' eyes.

"Reginald, no, we can *just. Fucking. LEAVE.*"

A string of obscenities poured out of Beck and Megan's house as more of these shadow figures emerged from it, half-dragging, half-carrying Beck, Megan, and Ham. "*What the fuck are you doing you let my baby go you let my wife go I swear to fucking God I am going to kick all your asses you sons of bitches you goddamned redneck hillbilly motherfuckers I swear I will—*" the rest was muffled by the hand of a being of night.

The part Reginald registered with surprise was that it was Megan screaming at them—soft-spoken, always calm, cool in a crisis Megan.

Beck glared at everything and everyone, but also turned her gaze on Ham, making sure he was not hurt by the two figures escorting him.

"First, you go up there—with all of us—and you take care of your mom. That satisfies the first requirement." Vincent sounded so calm, so reassuring.

Reginald nodded at Ham. "And then, what, I adopt him? You kill off Megan and Beck, and he becomes my son?"

"We don't have to hurt anybody." Vincent spoke very close to Reginald's ear, his breath caressing Reginald's earlobe, one of his hands on Reginald's ass, his fingers beginning to knead, to dig in. "You and Ham make some promises at the top of the mountain. That's all. And then… we're all one big happy family."

Reginald realized abruptly his dick was hard as steel and throbbing.

He could barely speak as he whispered back. "And then what, we just... live out our lives?"

"One... delicious... night... at a time..." Vincent pressed himself against Reginald now. "The gods..." He huffed abruptly, shifting his weight, forcing the two of them against each other. "They don't know what to do with you, Reginald. You broke the mold. But they figure there's a way to set things right again. It isn't perfect, bro, but nothing ever is. And they're happy enough to look the other way while you suck and fuck anybody you like as long as they get a slice when it's over. They'll even help out. Tell them a guy you want and they'll make it happen." Vince's hands had crawled forward and down, sliding beneath Reginald's shorts, and he now pressed two fingertips against the very heart of Reginald's ass.

Reginald's body shuddered once, reflexively, and he shifted his own weight just a bit. He drew a panting breath. "Get fucked yourself, Vince the Prince. *No deal.*" He pushed against Vince's chest, trying to break free—

Beck saw her moment and kicked, not at the shadow figure on her but at the one leading Ham around. The kick landed, and Ham broke free. Megan opened her mouth and tore at the one holding her back with her bare teeth, rending whatever stuff they were made of, the skin and flesh of shadow and night, so that it jerked away from her and let go. The three of them immediately circled together and the situation which it seemed the Powers and their servants so thoroughly had in hand moments before abruptly was *not.*

Reginald remained in Vincent's grasp, but Lewis, Megan, Beck, and Ham were free and clearly ready to fight or to run or *something.*

"Let go of me, Vincent." Reginald's voice shook. "Or I think my friends are going to hurt you."

Vincent considered, and the shadow people shifted around to try once again to block the others' escape. They could still get around them, but what then? If they made it off the mountain, perhaps they'd be beyond the figures' grasp. They could get a hotel room. They could go back to Reginald's trailer. Lewis had been entirely correct, they could just fucking leave.

Reginald called out, "Run for it, right now. *Go!*" Pressed against Vincent as he was, Reginald brought up a knee and caught Vincent right in the dick. The giant made a sound like a tire exploding and doubled over.

Reginald grabbed Lewis' hand, and the two of them pushed right past the shadows of Reginald's dead relatives, as soft and malleable now as gelatin molds. Reginald registered, at the edge of his vision, Beck and Ham and Megan yanking open the doors of a Subaru wagon. Reginald and Lewis let go of each other's hands to run faster and *tore* down the street, down the hill, toward Lewis' driveway and the souped-up hatchback waiting for them there. Lewis had the keys in his hand, and the blinkers beeped as the doors unlocked from thirty yards away.

Reginald's view of Lewis' car twisted, swirled, and tore open like a curtain on a stage. Behind it, a night sky filled with angry stars stared back at him, waited to embrace him, promised him nothing but cold oblivion. Reality unzipped itself top to bottom right in front of them, and their next footfalls carried them through.

The next moment, they were stepping back into reality in Dorothea's yard, surrounded again by the shadows of Voths long dead.

Kate and Johnny stood with them, grinning, teeth bared as if to take bite from the world.

Vincent stood, his face visibly pale even in the dim light of night. He adjusted his crotch and drew a shaky breath. "Nice try. But it's not that simple. Once you're here, Reginald, you're theirs. They're in control."

Reginald looked at Megan and Beck's driveway. Their car sat there, doors open, but Megan, Beck, and Ham stood encircled alongside Reginald and Lewis.

That's when Reginald knew the mountain would never leave him alone. His mother had haunted him his entire adult life and she hadn't even been dead. Now he faced a real possibility that even if Lewis, Megan and Beck, Ham, Reginald himself ever managed to escape, they would be hunted as well as haunted, and that it would last *forever*. He couldn't do that. Lewis had been right: this was Reginald's ancestral legacy. It was his battle to win. If it had just been him, maybe he would have tried a second time to run away, hoped for the best. *It worked for my father.* Maybe if it had been just Megan and Beck and Ham. But not with Lewis there. Not while there was a chance Lewis was for real.

"You want me to go back up the mountain."

Vincent nodded. His voice sounded strained when he spoke, and he put one giant paw around Reginald's spindly bicep. "Yeah, bro. That's the only option. And we all go with you."

"Let go of me first."

Vincent did so and stepped away, hands in front of him, palms out.

Reginald drew a breath, and this time it hardly shook at all. "Alright. Let's go. Let's *all* go."

CHAPTER TWENTY-ONE – NEARLY THE END OF EVERYTHING

Reginald, Lewis, Vincent, Beck, Megan, and Ham, and even the mob of shadows all traipsed back into the house, back through the kitchen, and back out into the yard.

Reginald understood now, of course: the back door to the house didn't go into the backyard, or at least not into the *right* one. It went into a shadow of the yard, a memory, a reflection. It went into a version of that yard from an earlier time. The Powers Beyond the Mountain would have Reginald make whatever deal he could make, and they'd have him do it on a version of the mountain from before the whole agreement got totally fucked, a version where and when they held sway, a version where they were powerful, immediate, and in control.

"Out of curiosity, bro, what made you see sense?" Vince walked behind them, moving easily up the trail from the memory of Dorothea's back yard how it once had been, as they all climbed the winding, slanted path to the peak of Moriah Bald.

Reginald lifted one shoulder, huffing from the exertion of climbing and talking at the same time. "When the house tried to zap Lewis," he said. "They put me under in order to do it. He told me about it the next day. I realized then, whatever this is must *require* me. Otherwise, they'd have just killed me off, gotten someone else to do whatever's next. That's what made it take so long for me to figure out about the houses being meant to draw in new blood." Reginald chuckled wheezily at himself. "If they didn't just kill me, they must need me. And standing there in the yard, I realized that makes me the only bargaining chip I have. I could have tried to make you promise to let everyone else go, but they can make us see what they want. Why would I believe anything they said about anyone else? I can only offer myself, and trading myself is the only way I can be sure they'll do it." He hesitated as he navigated one of the handful of stone steps built into the mountain here and there to ease the way. He didn't say it, but he certainly heard it ring from the rafters of his mind: *And if Lewis isn't real, this is the only way to keep him.*

At the top, they found the sky had opened to bathe Moriah Bald and the stone table at its center—an altar, Reginald now knew—in the stuff of naked eternity.

Stars sparkled and twirled in patterns no one could recognize. They formed obvious constellations, but ones Reginald had never seen, could never name, in shapes defying their own geometry. The patterns one might trace between them made no sense, twisted back on themselves, shifted when studied and at the same time beckoned from his periphery when he looked elsewhere.

What might have been the arm of the Milky Way arced across the sky like the nave of a gothic cathedral, too thick, too bright, painted in speckles of vivid purples and greens and blues. A meteor shower erupted from one corner of the night and sprayed glitter in long, straight, slow lines at its opposite.

"It's beautiful." Lewis turned his head this way and that as he studied it.

Reginald's answer had no meanness to it, only a statement of fact. "It's a kind of hell."

In the center of the bald the stone table squatted, broad and wide and brutally plain.

Beside it stood Dorothea, dressed again in her clashing nightgown and bathrobe, arms extended, face twisted in a silent scream. A shaft of light shined down upon her from no particular origin other than *up there*. Reginald took it in for a long moment, then turned to Lewis. "This is what I saw when my mother died."

One of the shadow people stepped forward, and Reginald instantly recognized the body language, height, and mannerisms of Owenby. It looked at him through glowing amber eyes and with some effort, and as though carried on a distant wind, it bade Vince to come stand beside it. He stepped forward and the shadow of Owenby placed a hand on the wrestler's shoulder. Vince turned his star-sparkling eyes on Reginald and spoke in Owenby's voice. "You cannot escape your fate, Reginald. This is not a negotiation. This is destiny. There's no advantage for you to seek. There's no means by which to best us. But we are glad you believed yourself capable of facing us, for it made bringing you here much easier, and we will relish your strength of spirit when we taste it in the end."

The shadow of Reginald's mother broke off from the group that had carried him halfway up the mountain, then followed the rest, and went to stand beside his mother's frozen figure. It lifted its arms—she, hers, Reginald didn't really know which to think of as "really" being his mother, if either— and tilted back its head to become a perfect mirror of his dying mother's stance. It had been her but made of shadow, and now it stood as though it had reattached itself to become her shadow again.

As if struck by a spotlight, a second pool of illumination spontaneously framed an old corn knife atop the stone table in the center of Moriah Bald.

Reginald looked at them. "Okay. So, what now? I drive that through my mother's heart, and you call it close enough for horseshoes? And then you make Ham and me, I don't know, sign our names in blood or something, and then he's my 'son' for the purposes of all this, and Beck and Megan stay in their house, and I stay in my mother's for the rest of my life so that Ham can one day drive that through me in turn?"

Vince again spoke with Owenby's voice and cadence. "Yes. The shadow of your ancestor will reanimate her form long enough to satisfy what is required, and you will destroy them both with the blade. It's simple. It's clean. It satisfies the spirit of the bargain. That's all that matters." Vince and Owenby both cocked their heads to one side a little as though noting an interesting bit of trivia. "This is a good time to transfer the agreement to a new line, anyway. Like many of the ways of your people, this burden has been handed down from man to woman and from woman to man, and now you are the seventh generation. Each of those factors adds to its power. Combined, they signify an ending and a new beginning." Vince and Owenby each turned to nod at Ham, who glared back at them. "He will be a new first generation. He will hold a place of great honor in his line."

Reginald chuckled once, bone dry, one half smoker's cough, the other half naked emotional exhaustion. "And what do I get out of it?"

Vince smiled, and somehow it was Owenby's expression instead of his own. "We keep telling you: you get whatever you want. We've certainly provided you with reason enough to stay here."

Reginald glanced over at Lewis, who shook his head. "It's not worth it. They want to take the life you've made for yourself."

"A life has many endings, Lewis. Just like you said." Reginald smiled at him and gave his hand a sincerely affectionate squeeze, then let go to take one step closer to the altar and to the knife upon it. Without looking away from that blade, he continued speaking to Lewis. "I've spent my whole adult life avoiding getting an attack of romance because it's a one-way ticket to disappointment, and in, what, three days? I've fallen completely in love. Maybe I want a life here. Maybe I don't want to go back to my lonely house."

"Your mother's house is lonely, too, Reginald. Anybody can look at it and see."

Reginald gazed out at the night and considered. "At least *this* lonely house has you right down the street."

Lewis worked his jaw uncertainly. "I think this is horrible, Reginald. I wish when I called you at the coffee shop that I'd come down there instead of you coming back up here. Maybe we'd have gone to your place instead. Maybe none of this would have happened. Maybe we'd be in your bed right now and I'd be entertaining a fantasy about selling my place and moving in with you and absolutely terrified to tell you about it so soon after meeting you."

Reginald arched one eyebrow. "As opposed to what you've been fantasizing, which is that I'd sell *my* place and come move in with *you?*"

Lewis shrugged with one shoulder. "I won't lie. Yeah. I think I want to try to make something special happen with you, Reginald. With some preconditions. I still have to work."

"Of course." Reginald tried not to laugh despite their circumstances. "Honestly, having a boyfriend who's so good at fucking that people pay to watch him do it is a pretty amazing concept. I would *insist* you keep doing what you do for exactly as long as you want." He smiled wanly. "What a weird time to be having this conversation."

Lewis grinned and then it twisted into a grimace. "Reginald, I'm scared."

"So am I." Reginald's face went blank. He looked back at the shadow of Owenby beside Vince. "What if I say yes, and then the first chance I get, I just climb in my shitty car and leave?"

"Then the bargain is not kept," Owenby-Vince replied.

"And?"

"The soil turns sour again. People are driven away." Shadow Owenby's other hand swept across the horizon, and Vince's opposite arm mirrored it. "Plants wither, animals starve. The trees return and crowd out all other life. The Powers Beyond the Mountain remember the trees, Reginald. They remember when there were trees so wide ten people could not have clasped hands in a ring around them. You may think of this place as old-fashioned, stuck in time, but there is an older version still, one waiting just beneath the thin soil of memory. *That* world will be restored, and then the mountains will wait."

"For what?"

"For the end of humanity. They were here before us, here before any of our ancestors, here before mammals, before dinosaurs, before bones. They have awaited us. And if we fail them, well, perhaps what comes next will be more capable. They can clear the field and try again."

Reginald let out a ripple of laughter. "You're not exactly convincing me to stick around. Out there? Down the mountain? We're staring at a century of hotter summers, more turbulent winters, the whole nine yards. The ecosystem of yesterday? Jeez, Owenby, don't threaten me with a good time. And if your desire is to appeal to my deep sympathy for my fellow man, I'm afraid you've got the wrong guy. Cashing out and taking off sounds better the more you tell me."

Vince smiled with Owenby's sour expression. "If you leave, well, that's that: for you, sure, and also for everyone, everything. And if you stay, why, you'd have *decades* to figure out how to beat Us at our own game. Perhaps there's a loophole in the agreement you could exploit. Perhaps there's a test you could set before Us that we'd fail. There's always an escape clause in every contract, Reginald. Perhaps there is in this one."

"You just thirty seconds ago said there's no way to beat you. And I get the feeling this whole thing was never exactly written down. More of a spit-on-it-and-shake thing, I reckon." But Reginald knew he sounded too intrigued. "Is that what kept everyone else here, too? The idea that maybe they'd be the one to figure out a way off the mountain? It's not exactly an unfamiliar story in these parts. I could name a dozen families up and down the road who've stayed put one generation after another and gotten by on a promise to themselves they'd find a path out." Reginald hooked a thumb in the direction of the Kings. "Case in point. But why even bother with telling me what'll happen if I leave? You've proven they can stop me."

Owenby-Vincent smiled as they spoke. "Because a willing sacrifice tastes better."

Lewis shook his head. "Reginald, don't do this. Don't give up your whole life, your future, everything. We can leave together! Fuck this place, these people! You didn't come back here to give up the life you made for yourself. You came back here to see the one you escaped get lowered into a grave and covered over."

Reginald turned and looked at him. "That's true. And if I did stay and try to take on whatever these assholes are, all by myself?"

Lewis' eyes glimmered with unshed tears. "I don't know that you could beat them. You're great, Reginald. You're smart, you're sharp-tongued, I said I love you, and I meant it, I don't even know what's up with that, with how fast this is moving. But I don't know that you're smarter than some ancient power that lives in the sky over the mountain where you spent your childhood being abused. That—*that*, the whole idea of coming back here to *beat it*—seems like an obvious trap. Don't fall for it."

Reginald studied Lewis for long seconds. "What if we outsmart them together?"

Now a tear did run from Lewis' left eye. "Reginald, I swear to you, those things Vincent said down there about me being one of the things the mountain used to draw you here—I will not vanish if we drive down the mountain together."

"And if we stay here, I *know* you won't." Reginald turned back, not to Owenby, and not to his mother's frozen form, but to the stone table at the center of Moriah Bald. He walked the remaining fifteen paces to it, Lewis keeping up beside him.

The Kings stood on the other side of the table from him, instruments at the ready. Mr. King wore the same or very similar overalls as he had at the visitation. The others wore work clothes for farm life: each in jeans that had seen their share of times in the laundry, the women in hoodies, the men in layered tee shirts and light flannel jackets.

Reginald reached for the corn knife but paused before touching it. He looked at Mr. King. "What exactly is y'all's role in all this?"

"Music helps them sleep," the man said, then he glanced up.

"Ah. So, when you said the 'old' songs, you meant the *old* songs."

"There's one we sing at times like this."

"I imagine you sang it when my mother used this knife to kill her father, then?"

"I was young, then. My daddy led the band. But yes, I was there."

Reginald looked at the King children, all adults, some his own age. "We played together atop this mountain when we were kids. And you'll be standing there, instruments at the ready, if one night I get sliced open in turn?"

Isaiah nodded at him. "If I'm alive to see it, I'll lead the band."

Reginald raised his eyebrows. "And you'll sing the old songs every night until then to help *them* sleep?"

"We've all got our part in the bargains that've been made." Isaiah looked unperturbed by his role in this.

Reginald looked down at the corn knife, picked it up, tested its weight in his hand.

One of Isaiah's sisters lifted a fiddle to her shoulder and set her chin on it, bow at the ready. The others lifted instruments as well, eyes on Reginald, watching him like hawks.

Reginald stepped back once from the table, the knife in his hand. He looked up at the whorl of famished stars above them, the gaping hunger of eternity, and smiled. "You must be getting something out of this, whatever you are. Everyone talks about 'our whole lives,' about sacrifice, but those are human concepts. They don't say what that means, what part of that is *sustenance* for you. But some part of it must be, or why would you bother? But maybe I don't *need* to understand. I just know I've got something you want."

Owenby-Vince spoke in a sing-song unison, two voices coming from one mouth. "They want to taste this world, Reginald. That's all. They want one little life from it every now and then, and in return we all thrive. They want you to walk out the front door of that house every morning, every night, as you see fit, and take them with you so they can see a little bit of this insignificant place with your eyes, feel it with your flesh, taste it with your tongue. We are as strange to them as they to us. They remember when these mountains were bare. They witnessed the very first tree on this mountain grow up, get old, die. They understood that. It made sense to them. But now it is we who fascinate them, and we are totally alien to their experience of this place. They do not understand what it means to be a person, Reginald. But if we stay and let them taste the world through us, if we give that all to them at the end, their understanding can grow."

The dissonance of their voices—one Reginald had only ever heard in judgment, one he'd mostly only ever heard in lust—was also a kind of harmony. It occurred to Reginald Vince and Owenby didn't sound all that different from one another as they went on. "Have you never stared at the bee and wondered how the world looks through the glittering globes of its eyes? Have you never seen its fervor for the flower and thought it might be nice to lose oneself in pleasures like that? That is all they ask. That, and you must continue the line in some manner. Adoption is acceptable. There is a life they wish to understand, a promise to continue, and they require both: the life you will give them and the life they will take. They would allow you whatever pleasures you require as long as you satisfy that minor requirement. And when you die here, on this altar, under this sky, in *this* realm through the back door of *that* house, all that sensation will become theirs, and they reward you with a kind of eternity no other gods can deliver."

Reginald openly scoffed. "One wandering the wooded slopes of Moriah Bald forever, staring in at other people with yellow foglamp eyes? Eternity trapped as a shadow of myself, trying to fill back up on the experiences of others after mine have been taken away?" Reginald flipped Owenby-Vince off with the corn knife still in his hand, but he didn't look away from the sky. His voice shook slightly. "And if I say yes, you'll leave everyone else alone? Tomorrow just happens, like yesterday, and we all get to go back to our lives?"

"The price of having a life shouldn't be giving yours away." Lewis' voice was soft.

Reginald squeezed Lewis' hand and turned his face to him, studied his pleading brown eyes, the line of his perfect jaw, the staggering V of his collar bones even under an old tee shirt. "But what if it is? Hell, it already has been, once or twice. But you're right. I'm not about to give mine away. I'm about to take mine back."

Reginald took three quick steps and plunged the corn knife deep into the chest of Shadow-Owenby, then dragged the blade down to open a jagged wound.

Golden light spilled from the gash in Shadow-Owenby's midsection. Vince threw his head back and howled. Beside him, as though that golden glow were draining out of it from the inside, the light behind Owenby's shadow-form's eyes flickered and went dark. Its body emptied, collapsed, and pooled, dragging Vince down to his knees with it. The wrestler wound up on his back in the grass, eyes wide, mouth gaping, his chest barely lifting with panted, shallow breaths.

Reginald turned without hesitation and plunged the corn knife not into his mother but into her shadow standing three feet behind it. Even as he did so, he wondered, *am I getting revenge? Or am I setting her free?* The version of Dorothea that looked as she had in life burst into many thousands of blue-tinted fireflies, and the shadow form of her, like Owenby, emptied itself of animating essence and collapsed.

The sky above them silently howled. No sound bore down on them from above, but they all—Lewis, Reginald, Beck, Megan, and Ham—flinched and stepped backwards, squatted down, turned their faces, shielded themselves with upraised hands at the crushing impact of fury and indignation that blasted down on them from above. The silence was a scream they could *feel* as it hammered against them.

After two or three seconds in which Reginald and the others each experienced an eternity of psychic suffering, Reginald managed to turn his own wrist.

The blade now pointed at his own chest.

The drilling, bone-shattering mental and spiritual avalanche instantly ceased.

Around them, golden eyes bugged out and shadow hands reached forward.

"Don't fucking touch me," Reginald growled.

The shadows hesitated.

Reginald straightened himself, pressed the blade to his own chest just enough to indent his shirt and the flesh beneath it. "This is not a negotiation," he murmured at the swirling, uncertain sky. He cleared his throat and spoke with more confidence. "If you want to make a deal, we do it on *my* terms. Because I've given up my life before to have a life of my own and I can do it again in the blink of an eye."

All things, natural and unnatural, waited and listened.

"The first of my terms: all these shadow monsters go away."

Nothing changed around them.

Reginald pressed the blade to his own sunken chest a little harder. He felt the burn of its tip pierce his skin and he made a tiny, involuntary sound of suffering.

A not-voice whispered from a foreign sky, not in sound but in surety, *The ancestor forms must stay.*

"No." Reginald returned to the stone altar in the center of Moriah Bald, lifted the knife, and struck it hard against the stone. It did not break, but it rebounded and clattered, skittering across the surface of the stone, scarring it. The tip left a gouge much deeper than a thin steel corn knife should have made against stone.

Around them, the shadow forms did not fade, but they did step back once.

Reginald pressed a hand to the tiny wound in his chest, felt hot wetness there, and held up his bloodied fingertip. He lifted his eyebrows. "I need you to understand that I mean what I say. The second of my terms…" Reginald again lifted the knife and struck it against the stone.

This time, it broke. The blade, oiled and sharpened across generations, was still old, still a thing of this world and not of theirs. Metal shattered in a spray of jagged shards, some slicing across Reginald's hand, others shredding his shirt like blood spatter on a crime scene wall. He felt the skin of his thumb and wrist, the bony flesh of his chest, the featureless plain of his abdomen, pricked all over by the shower of silvery steel. He felt warm blood bead against his skin, cool in the autumn air of night, and saw it well up out of the wound he'd made across the table of stone.

Reginald, too old for this shit and somehow also too young for it, turned his bird-thin face again to the vault of unfamiliar stars woven into a strange and starving eternity and finished stating his demands. "No more sacrifice. That's the last blood you'll get out of me, and I'm the last Voth. *The end.* You think you can tempt me into staying by offering to let me try to defeat you? Fuck off." Reginald gestured casually with the jagged stub of corn knife, indicating Lewis, then Beck and Megan and Ham, and even Vince, despite him giving himself over to them already. "It isn't only that you *don't get to* take our lives. You *can't* take our lives and keep them. We know already how to make a new one. My great-great-dumbfuck-the-whatever might have feared you, might have had no other option, no backup plan, but I'm different. I don't have to defeat you. If you want to enforce some bargain, you're going to have to beat *me.*" He reached to take Lewis' hand. "You bargained with Voths to take one life at a time, but let's see what happens when you have to conquer *two.*"

Behind him, he heard Beck speak, her voice low and mean in the way he knew meant *danger.* "Make that *five.*"

Reginald grinned up at the vault of hostile, jealous, hungry stars and felt the heavens tremble.

CHAPTER TWENTY-TWO — BARELY THE BEGINNING OF ANYTHING

The indistinct shapes of people Reginald did not and would never know wandered at the edge of his field of vision. He could have gone over and said hello, could have tried to be sociable in some way, and he knew that would, in fact, be the smart thing to do. People go to estate sales to score a bargain, sure, with dreams of being the one to score that perfect find: a diamond ring priced like cut glass, or a tureen no one realizes is stamped with a maker's mark rare enough to add three zeroes to its price at auction. They mostly go, however, looking for stories. An estate sale is a very polite feast for scavengers, and often the way to sell a thing is to give the buyer a story about it for free.

Reginald also knew Lewis was, quite simply, way better at that stuff, and Lewis had been quietly but effectively working the crowd all morning.

It didn't hurt that they'd been in the news. Rowan's impromptu interview with Reginald must have been getting views, because it stayed on WSOL's front page for weeks. Reginald couldn't go to the gas station without having someone's gaze linger on him as they tried to work out where they'd seen him before. He could always tell when realization dawned: they'd abruptly look away. But while that made personal attention a real pain in the ass, it had made Dorothea's various knickknacks and other dustables an item of interest to a certain kind of vulture and Reginald, quite frankly, was happy to take their money.

He and Lewis had spent three weeks going through every square inch of the house, pricing things, trying to do research on how much some of them might be worth. In the end, Reginald got sick of it all and declared they would price it like a yard sale. *If somebody else scores big on the carcass of my mother's borderline hoarding, well, good the fuck for them.* After that, preparation got a lot faster, and Reginald could breathe easier. As the last of the leaves fell and the fall air began to carry that sharp, near-ozone tang that meant snow might be on its way to the high mountains a little early this year, Reginald started to relax. It seemed like things might get easier if he just held the course. He'd have to do all this again with his brother's house, eventually, and then with his trailer, too, and then he'd have to spend months or even years turning his mother's house into his own, but maybe that was okay. He didn't plan to sleep there much, anyway. They didn't technically live together, but Reginald spent all his time and every night with Lewis instead of in Dorothea's house. Reginald promised himself--and Lewis--he would never, ever live in Dorothea's house again, though he would still own it. Every time he walked out of it and locked the door behind him, he got the feeling the Powers Beyond the Mountain endured some minor discomfort. Reginald savored that notion.

And when the spicebush turned a richer yellow than ever, and the berries smelled extra good, he'd taken it as some small sign the Powers were signaling they'd uphold their end of the old bargain after all and hoped to charm Reginald into making a new one.

When Reginald finished emptying the last cabinet and Lewis cleared the last closet, the two of them fucked in the middle of Dorothea's kitchen to mark the end of her reign over the Voth ancestral home.

Sometimes Reginald wondered if those remaining of the shadow-stuff ancestors who'd come before him had watched through the kitchen window from the edge of the woods bearding Moriah Bald, and if there were enough left of who they had been for them to muster disapproval.

A part of him hoped so.

A part of him hoped not.

"Is the fiber working out?"

Reginald snapped out of his reverie with a little jump and nearly dropped the ancient alarm clock in his hands. It wasn't fancy, but it was entirely mechanical, complete with a key on the back to wind it every night, and he knew someone very young or very old would buy it out of odd nostalgia. He turned around and offered Kate a smile that might have passed muster at fifty paces but not here, not this close—and she was standing very close.

"It's great." Reginald tried not to show the distress that welled up inside him. He'd known moments like this would come: Moments when the ones the Powers had taken would test him, try to provoke him, take his measure as the new Voth in charge.

Reginald had imagined himself meeting their smug intrusions with a mix of commanding presence and iron-clad fearlessness. Instead, now that one had happened after weeks of dreadful anticipation, he spun the clock around and around in his hands as he cleared his throat and tried to recover. "Yeah, it's great." He drew a breath. "Thank you. It really lives up to your promises." Parts of Reginald started to recover their dignity, and he pressed on. "I mean, I guess. Honestly, past a certain speed I don't know that I notice a difference if I'm just streaming a movie."

Kate smiled more broadly, and Reginald *wanted* to grab her by the back of her $750 dollar ski jacket and march her off his mother's—*his* property, because *that* was the grin of whatever the Powers had done to make her *this*. "Well, if you ever think maybe you're not getting what you were promised, just let me know. I'll make sure they take care of you." She paused a moment. "The fiber people, I mean." Her smile grew another notch. Kate looked around for a moment, then back at Reginald. "Sale going well?"

"Very." Reginald cast his gaze around at what was left: mostly his mother's and his father's old clothes, some sheets worn thin with age, and the chipped cups and bent forks found at any such thing. On the front porch were a few larger pieces of furniture and a sign inviting people inside to make offers on anything else. "Some kids from that college in town bought most of the big furniture and some of the clothes and went to get a truck so they can come back and haul everything off at once. There isn't actually much left for sale."

Kate smiled in a way anyone else would have seen as friendly or at least polite, until her eyes fell on the painting of the stone altar atop Moriah Bald that had hung in the house's living room. It leaned against the bottom of the steps up to the Voth house. "You're selling your mother's art?"

"Oh, did she make that? Funny, I never knew she painted." Reginald felt the winds turn in his favor and he gestured flippantly with one hand, the clock in his other. "Explains why it's so crude. But I figure it's worth a dollar to someone who doesn't know better."

Kate's expression hardened. "I don't recommend being so thoughtless with your heritage."

Reginald let himself smile a little as he replied. "Kate, I've got the real thing any time I want to climb it. I don't need a version of Moriah Bald in acrylics on my living room wall, too. I'd offer to sell it to you, but those kids bought it already. By tonight it'll be hanging in some fraternity basement, and good riddance."

"I'll give you $100 right now. Cash. On the spot." Kate's lips formed a hard line she tried to tune up into a smile, but her nostrils flared. For just a moment, Reginald thought he smelled the ozone tang that follows a lightning flash close by.

"Sorry, but I wouldn't want to make people think I'm the sort to back out on a deal, would I?" Reginald gestured around at what else remained. "Let me know if anything else catches your eye. Hurry, though. I think Lewis and I need to start boxing up what's left so we can donate it. I plan to be rid of everything as soon as humanly possible." Reginald started to turn away, setting down the clock as he did so, letting it fall onto its back on a folding table covered in scattered PleasantMemories™ figurines and decades-old issues of *High Country Cooking*. He stopped himself, looked back at Kate, and gave her that same pleasant, plastic smile. "And have a great Thanksgiving."

"Any more visits from your mother?" Kate's tone had a jagged and bloody edge, and she snapped off the last word like a bite attack.

Reginald paused. Had he ever told Kate and Johnny about seeing his mother's ghost? He'd told Lewis, Beck, Megan, Ham… surely by then none of them would have told Kate or Johnny.

Reginald turned back to Kate, and her eyes glittered with satisfaction. "You know, it's funny," Reginald said. "My mother spent decades waiting for me to come home. She kept my room the same as when I left. I've spent my entire adult life haunting this place and I never even knew it. I've wondered, since she died, if she treated the last few Thanksgivings like a séance, waiting to hear me join her at the table. I'm glad she got to meet Lewis before she died. I finally get to say she met the guy who's fucking me. I'm sure she hated him, but it hardly matters now. She's the dead one, and I'm alive, and it turns out I'm not that afraid of ghosts after all."

"The Powers will have their way, sooner or later, Reginald Voth." Kate's face had turned hard as stone, a slim but visible grimace carved across it. "You may think you've won, with your new boyfriend and your haughty manner, but The Lords are patient. They were patient enough to await the arrival of a family willing to serve them once. They can wait again." Kate took a step closer. "Perhaps they can even hurry things along. Or maybe someone will tell that bitch from the sheriff's department that your mother's property was the last place anyone saw Owenby alive. They mention him a lot on the news, you know. Everybody feels sorry for the missing preacher."

Reginald shifted his weight to his left leg and propped his fist on his left hip. "Mincing around making threats won't work on me, Kate. Somebody got Owenby's car out of here before anyone could see it. I'm guessing you people do a pretty good job of cleaning up after yourselves. The Powers have plenty of practice keeping human sacrifice a secret. I doubt they're too interested in exposing it now. And I'm guessing you're pretty much a direct pipeline to the Powers at this point, so I hope they've got their ears on: I'm going to be the last Voth on this mountain, and when I die at a ripe old age from something tremendously boring I'll be pulling the plug on the whole works. If they want a Voth to go climb that mountain every full moon to listen to Isaiah and his family sing the old songs, or whatever little tune up this whole bullshit thing is supposed to get, then they'd better mind their p's and fucking q's and give me a reason to play along. Gods need followers, Kate, *not the other way around.*"

Kate's eyes narrowed, but Reginald put up his index finger in a *nuh-uh* gesture. "I mean it. I'll bulldoze this whole place flat and turn it into a gas station. Then they'll have to find a whole new *mountain*, I reckon, and those are starting to get scarce around here. So, if you'll excuse me, I've got tchotchkes to box."

Over the course of his adult life, Reginald had turned Thanksgiving into a day of respite. Once he'd given up going to his mother's for a tense meal with his immediate and extended family, he'd started his own tradition: a turkey breast in a crock pot, a pan of cornbread, roasted brussels sprouts, and a book. Some years whatever guy was fucking him would worm his way into the day, but most years it was solo, and that was how he preferred it.

This was his first Thanksgiving in sight of the house where he grew up, and the first where he was the one playing host. It had been Lewis' idea. They invited Beck, Megan, and Ham, and the five of them put together a pretty nice potluck at Lewis' table. Dorothea's house sat empty, locked up tight, electricity cut off and phone lines canceled. Reginald had kept only two things from his mother's home: the painting of Moriah Bald, which, in fact, he had *not* sold to frat boys, and his mother's sewing basket. He wasn't sentimental about them. He simply wanted to make sure he had something to remind himself of the stakes of choosing to live with Lewis. He had let his guard down with Lewis as love demanded, but once in a while he needed to remind himself to remain on guard against everything *else*.

Lewis cooked a turkey and was, of course, a gifted chef. Reginald made his cornbread and brussels sprouts, Beck brought an ice cream cake, and Megan made a squash casserole. Ham's contribution was to play DJ while Megan and Beck bragged on his knack for picking various songs with each person in mind. It turned out to be what commercials on television had always claimed Thanksgiving would be: a few people who liked each other quite a bit getting together and enjoying each other's company. It reminded Reginald of the times in college when he and a few of his friends went to the gay bar the Saturday after Thanksgiving for a potluck and penny drafts. That had been his first taste of found family, and now, while everyone waited to find out what it meant to go on living here, a place haunted by Reginald's relatives and with ancient forces glaring down at them from on high, Reginald realized how much he'd missed the kindness people could offer each other even in dire circumstances. For very likely the first time since that night atop Moriah Bald, he relaxed.

At some point, he laughed at someone's joke and realized it was the first time he'd felt like himself in five weeks.

Later, over bowls of melted ice cream and the bottles of wine Lewis broke out from his ridiculous stash, the conversation wound down. They'd talked enough about their jobs and their relatives and whether they did or did not like the coming holidays. They'd talked about what they might do for New Year's. They'd talked about when Reginald might sell Bobby's house.

They ran out of things to talk about that were *not* the deal Reginald had refused to renew with the Powers Beyond the Mountain, and now the topic squatted, invisible but obvious, in the middle of dinner's remains.

Beck kept her body language casual, but her eyes were deadly serious as she met Reginald's gaze. "Have you heard from the wrestler guy?"

Reginald's eyebrows bobbed up and down in a jerk. "No. He tried to text each of us, but we didn't respond."

Megan cleared her throat very softly. "Did he seem…"

"Normal?" Lewis flashed a small smile. "More or less, yes. But I don't know that I would ever trust him again. He sided with Them when push came to shove."

Reginald didn't look up from his plate. "It occurs to me from my family history that the Powers basically trafficked men and women into and out of the lives of each generation: someone to have a baby, or plant one, then get out of the picture. It's so awful. I've had plenty of men come and go, so to speak, but we always both were happy that way. I wonder if any of them were…" Reginald bounced his own fork in his hand and finally looked up. "Were they disappointed? Sad? Or did the Powers arrange their feelings so they'd go and stay gone? I think about them a lot: all the people who got caught up at the fringe, whose lives got turned upside down. The Patties who, I don't know, got drawn here to be followers? The parents who were lured in to make a kid and get out? They had a hole blown in the side of their lives, and for what?"

Megan spoke in her calm and gentle voice. "You can't fix that. But you can learn something from it, maybe. I don't know. That's a lame platitude, but what else have you got?"

Reginald tried to crack a joke. "Okay. Lesson learned: never hook up with a closet case." Nobody laughed.

Beck kept going. "And what do we do about the future?"

No one asked what she meant. Ham even paused the game on his phone and looked up with the disconcertingly serious expression unique to kids too smart for most of the adults around them.

"We make nice. For now." Reginald looked around at the others as well, then at Ham. "We keep you safe. And you tell your moms the second anybody else in the neighborhood tries to talk to you, corner you, threaten you, anything. If you go for a walk and catch them watching you, you go home and tell your moms."

Megan had no more skepticism to fall back on. "So, you think they'll try to do what they wanted to begin with, turn Ham into the next, I don't know, patriarch? The next generation of people tied to them?"

Lewis nodded. "Reginald and I have done a lot of talking about his family history. There were instances in the past when they might have tried to do similar things. Maybe. It's hard to know for sure."

Reginald shrugged with his hands. "They didn't exactly keep records, but we found some diaries in the top of my mother's closet that suggest maybe at various points the Powers thought they could, you know, switch branches of the family tree if things didn't work out. And there were a couple of times when first-born kids didn't make it to adulthood, and I'm guessing they switched up who was next. And we saw more shadows than the six ancestors who came before me. So if they can cope with that, they can probably cope with the fact I'm never having kids and that Bobby is dead and do whatever is necessary to make Ham—" he turned his attention to Ham again—"*you*, sorry, I don't mean to talk like you aren't here. At any rate, yeah, I think they'll bide their time and make a play to get what they originally wanted."

Beck nodded, then looked at Megan, at Ham, and back at Lewis and Reginald. "I won't lie. We've talked about moving."

Lewis smiled a little. "Just the other night, I told Reginald I'm surprised you haven't already."

"I kind of think you should." Reginald took Lewis' hand atop the table. "Y'all don't need this shit. Nobody does. I'm stuck with it, and Lewis seems to think that means he is, too, but y'all should clear out while you can."

"I don't want to." Ham spoke in the quiet tones of one unaccustomed to being listened to by adults. "I like my friends at school. I like our house. And if we try to move, what if they do something bad to stop us? What if they hurt my moms? Or me? I don't think we can just sneak off. They'd know. Something would happen."

Megan and Beck exchanged another glance, and Reginald knew this had been a conversation they'd chased in circles at their own table more times than Reginald would ever know.

"So, we're all sticking around," Reginald stated it as a fact, not as a question. "That means we need to watch each other's backs, not just Ham's. He's right. None of us is especially safe. They need some sort of transfer of the curse, the bargain, whatever you want to call it. If they think it's in their interests to play nice, they will. And if they decide the thing to do is to split us off and take us out one by one, they'll do that instead. They could cause a hell of a lot of heartache on their way to getting Ham and me to agree." Reginald sighed quietly. "I don't mean to be doom and gloom. But the longer I'm here, the more certain I become that I'm here for good. That means they can use hurting y'all to get to me. And if you try to get away, they might hurt you even worse. I'm sorry."

Lewis laughed suddenly, and the others' reactions fell on the spectrum between an arched eyebrow and openly startling.

"Christ, Reginald, you are such a fucking drama queen. You talk like you've made our choices for us. You're not the only one who's *choosing* to stay." Lewis squeezed Reginald's hand, and the laughter fell away. "But I get what you mean, and you're not wrong."

Beck, arms crossed across her stomach, shrugged her shoulders. "None of us is ever safe anyway. Might as well be unsafe in our own homes, with each other around."

Megan looked from Ham to Reginald and Lewis. "What we want more than anything is for Ham to get to grow up and live his own life, exercise his own agency. If we stay here to give him the chance to do that, it's not your fault. It's no one's fault, at least not the fault of anyone still alive. But I appreciate that you wish it were different."

"So, we're all agreed." Beck looked from Reginald to Lewis, from Lewis to Megan, from Megan to Ham, and back to Reginald. "We stay here and protect ourselves as best we can."

"Yeah." Reginald nodded.

Lewis smiled wryly. "And we're already the neighborhood watch."

"I like that." Megan flashed a small smile. "I like it a lot."

Beck looked at Reginald. "Why not just tear that place down? Or hire somebody to cut down all the trees, drive a bulldozer up the side of Moriah Bald, and shove that altar right off the top?"

"Because I don't know if it would work," Reginald smirked. "And because a part of me knows living well isn't just the *best* revenge, it's the *only* revenge. The only way to break the cycle is to do it myself and live my life free. So here I am."

They sat in thoughtful but not awkward silence for a few moments. Beck broke it by clearing her throat. "They'll be onto us. They've got to know we're talking about them, right? And they'll notice if we stay tight, keep an eye on each other, all the things we'll have to do: we'll need you to babysit Ham, and we'll have to, I don't know, feed your fish, everything. We're going to be taking in each other's mail when we're on vacation and watching for something strange and texting each other about every stranger and all the rest of it for as long as we're all here. We'll never be able to trust an outsider, not completely. We'll never know for sure whether somebody new is on our side or not."

Reginald stuck his spoon in what remained of his bowl of ice cream cake. He lifted it up but didn't take the bite, waited, set it back down. "Same as always."

"No," Lewis countered, "not the same. Now you have friends on this mountain. For the first time, you aren't alone."

Reginald let his face relax into a small smile. "You're right. We all have each other, and that's more than anyone else up here has ever been able to say."

THE END

ABOUT THE AUTHOR

Michael G. Williams writes queer-themed horror and science fiction celebrating the monstrous and the macabre. His books include the award-winning vampire series *The Withrow Chronicles* (Laine Cunningham Award); the thrilling urban fantasy time travel series *Servant Sovereign*; the sci-fi mystery *A Fall in Autumn* (Manly Wade Wellman Award); and a mess of short stories. Michael strives to present the humor and humanity at the heart of horror and sci-fi with stories of outcasts and loners finding their people and power. *Children of Solitude* is his thirteenth book.

Michael co-hosts *Arcane Carolinas* and *Data@Rest*, studied Performance Studies at UNC Chapel Hill and Appalachian Studies at Appalachian State University, and is a brother in St. Anthony Hall and Mu Beta Psi. He's a member of SFWA and HWA and serves as a Trustee of the NC Writers Network. He lives in North Carolina with his husband and a variety of animals.

ALSO AVAILABLE FROM MICHAEL G. WILLIAMS

Urban Fantasy

Servant Sovereign: The Complete Collection

Individual Volumes of *Servant Sovereign*:
Through the Doors of Oblivion
All the Pomp of Earthly Majesty
Shut the Gates of Mercy
The Last Scene of a Strange Career

Horror

The Withrow Chronicles (Falstaff Books)
Perishables
Tooth & Nail
Deal with the Devil
Attempted Immortality
Nobody Gets Out Alive

Science Fiction

Autumn (Falstaff Books)
A Fall in Autumn
New Life in Autumn

Anthologies featuring Michael's stories:
Wrapped in Red: 13 Tales of Vampiric Horror (Sekhmet Press)
Wrapped in White (Sekhmet Press)
Wrapped in Black (Sekhmet Press)
A Woman Unbecoming (Crone Girls Press)
Playing with a Full Deck (Amphibious Press)
Nevermore (Falstaff Books)
Southern-Fried Cthulhu (Mechanoid Press)

Nonfiction by Michael:
Arcane Carolinas, Volume 2

FOLLOW MICHAEL G. WILLIAMS

Michael's Semi-Monthly Newsletter

www.michaelgwilliamsbooks.com/newsletter/

Autographed Books & Michael's Blog

www.michaelgwilliamsbooks.com

Michael on BlueSky

@mcmanlypants.bsky.social

Michael on Facebook

www.facebook.com/MichaelGWilliamsAuthor

Arcane Carolinas

www.arcanecarolinas.com

Arcane Carolinas on Facebook

www.facebook.com/arcanecarolinas